M000306234

NECESSITIES

a novel by
BOYD TAYLOR

Necessities
Copyright © 2017 by Boyd Taylor

All Rights Reserved
No part of this book may be reproduced or utilized in any form or by any means, electronic or mechanical, including photocopying, recording or by any information storage and retrieval system, without permission in writing from the Publisher. Inquiries should be addressed to the Publisher

This is a work of fiction. All names, characters and incidents are the products of the author's imagination or are used fictitiously. Any resemblance to current or local events or to living persons is entirely coincidental.

Katherine Brown Press
Austin, TX
antelopecity@iCloud.com

Editor: Mindy Reed, The Authors' Assistant
Cover Designer: Douglas Brown, Album Artist
Interior Designer: Danielle H. Acee, The Authors' Assistant

First Printing 2017

ISBN: 978-0-9894707-3-5

PCN 2017957135

Printed in the United States of America

To Ray, a true Shakespearean

Acknowledgments

This book was a long time in gestation. Jack Rosshirt, himself a lawyer and a writer, listened patiently as the story took form in my mind and gave me helpful notes when he read the text. James Wilson, neighbor and accomplished lawyer, gave me numerous suggestions, but perhaps most important, guided me through the trial procedure. His advice when my legal logic failed me was invaluable. Susan Madden, proofer par excellence, read the first completed draft with her eagle eye and corrected me when I strayed from my narrative. Phyllis Schenkken, teacher and friend, made dozens of comments and as an Ohioan told me about sauerkraut balls. Max Sherman gave me the benefit of his professional insight. Margery Hauck saved me from some serious missteps. And of course, thanks to Mindy and Danielle at The Authors' Assistant for treating *Necessities* as if it were their own.

Despite all this help, the book and its flaws are mine.

Boyd Taylor
Austin, Texas
October, 2017

The art of our necessities is strange,
That can make vile things precious.
—William Shakespeare,
King Lear 3.2.70

PART ONE

JOURNAL

ONE

I had never been in the Ritz-Carlton before Cory took me there, the winter she came looking for me in Cleveland. Hotels were out of the question during my senior year in St. Louis at Washington University, when we had our one-night fling. I had an apartment off campus. She had signaled at the Journalism department Christmas party, but I was seeing someone else. She was good-looking, sure, but I was put off by her attitude and the aura of entitlement that followed her around. When we met up again, this time at a staff meeting for the college paper, she flirted shamelessly. I thought, *what the hell? Why not?* I ordered my long-suffering roommate out of the apartment, and we spent the night in my lumpy single bed. The next morning, she looked around but didn't say anything. She didn't need to. Her glance told me everything I needed to know. It was one night, over and done with. I wasn't looking for a permanent arrangement. Even if I had been; even if I'd known then how rich she was, it wouldn't have mattered because she was done with me after that night. When I saw her in class, she averted her eyes and turned to talk to her wide circle of hangers on. I was a middle-class boy from Texas, and she was an Ohio newspaper heiress, sent to Washington University to please her father by studying Journalism, but pleasing herself by studying Art History, or at least that's what I'd heard.

I'd forgotten about her, or thought I had, until one of the wars in Iraq—the one I was in. I found myself calling up the memory of that night many times when I couldn't sleep—wondering if I would ever get home.

Why her and not any of the others who'd shared that lumpy bed? I don't know. There was something special about Cordelia Lehrer.

So, after all those years, I never expected to look up from my desk in the newsroom of the *Cleveland Post* and see her, blonde, leggy and as beautiful as ever. In fact, her fresh and flowery scent, that light wistful perfume, preceded her.

That scent, which had lingered in my bed after she'd left it years before, alerted me to her presence. I had just filed my column on the Republican primary. I looked up from my computer screen and greeted her with a grin. "Well hello, Ms. Lehrer. You can't live without me, can you?"

"Caught me out, darling." She looked around the drab over-lit newsroom. She sat on the side of my desk, leaned down and kissed me on the cheek. "Do you have time for a drink?"

Of course I did.

When I got back from Iraq, I had been lucky enough to get on the staff of the *Cleveland Post*. I traded on my war wounds and my Distinguished Service Cross to shame the editor into hiring me. I was a good newshound, and I knew that my petty blackmail would soon be forgotten.

I was back in Cleveland, and Cordelia was an Akron girl from a newspaper chain family. I'd often thought about contacting her, but never did. I assumed she had married a rich boy and taken her place as a society belle in Akron, or wherever she had settled down.

I got my coat and led her out of the newsroom. I enjoyed the envious looks of the other reporters. "This is really good for my reputation, Cordelia."

She laughed. "Unless you've changed a lot, your reputation can stand polishing."

Her laugh was still a mixture of archness and randiness. Of course, she wasn't the same girl she was in college, but the years had been very kind to her. She had turned into a striking woman, her blonde hair straight and long. She had on a black sweater, a long black skirt and boots. Her brown cashmere coat was draped easily over one arm. When she turned to talk to me, her deep hazel eyes were clear. The little scar on her chin was still there. She had told me it was an honor badge from a skiing accident at Aspen. She still didn't wear much makeup. She didn't need it.

I took her to Barney's, near the paper. It was early, and we were the only customers. We sat across from each other in a booth by the front window. I looked out to see it was getting dark. People hurried past, their heads down against the cold winter wind blowing off the lake. When I looked back, she was staring at me. "Why didn't you ever call me, David?"

"I didn't imagine you'd want to hear from me. Where've you been all this time?"

She sighed and reached across the table for my hand. She stroked it gently. "Europe—Paris and London. Working at Sotheby's, like a good art historian."

"Tough duty."

She turned my hand loose and looked up at the waiter. "What wines do you have?" The waiter and I exchanged smiles. "Red or white. The usual for you, David?" I nodded and waited for her to choose.

"Anything. The white, I guess." She watched the waiter walk back to the bar. "Nice place."

I waited.

"Of course, I enjoyed Europe," she continued. "But I thought about you often. I always thought we might have had a future."

I sat silently, wondering if this were going where I hoped it was.

"Did you ever think about me?"

"Every day," I said. The waiter returned to the table with my vodka on the rocks and a large glass of white wine for her. She looked at it with distaste. "I thought about you every day," I repeated. That wasn't true exactly, but I certainly wasn't going to confess that fantasies of her got me through the war. And the hospital. And rehab at Brooke. That would have been too easy. If this was more than a catch up visit, she'd have to work a little harder. If not, so what? I had accepted long ago that she was out of my life forever. Yet, here she sat, making a face while she sipped her wine.

"You're a liar, but I'll choose to believe you." She tried another sip of the wine. "God, this is awful. Why do you come here?"

I raised the glass of vodka. "I don't drink the wine."

She straightened the sleeve of her sweater. "So, tell me. Is there some-one in your life?"

I took the plastic toothpick out of my drink, knifed one of the olives with it and popped the olive into my mouth. "No, not a soul." That was the truth. Jan Beck, the perky redhead weekend weather girl I had lived with for two years had decamped for an evening news assignment at WMAQ in Chicago. I had been alone for three months, rattling around in the apartment we'd rented together. Our few phone conversations made it clear that we had both decided to move on with no hard feelings. It was fun, but we had both known it wasn't forever.

I didn't do forever. Never had, never would. It had nothing to do with my missing parts. Jan had always acted as if my war wounds didn't matter. She didn't seem to notice when I unstrapped my prosthetic legs at night and heaved myself onto the bed. Not easy to do, but I had exercised enough that my upper body could handle it. If she watched when I strapped my legs back on in the morning, or when I chose to use my wheelchair instead, she said nothing. *Would Cordelia Lehrer be as indifferent?* I doubted it.

I missed Jan, and her happy-go-lucky weather girl personality, of course, but there wasn't the empty ache my drunken buddies described feeling when their girls left them. I occasionally had bouts of self-pity when I thought about my missing legs, blown away in an Iraqi street battle that sent part of me one way and my legs another. Whenever that began to eat at me, I reminded myself I had survived when my father left and again when my mother was killed. Those were the *real* aching losses, and I'd survived them. Compared to that, the loss of my legs was nothing, nothing at all. Strap on the Army-supplied prostheses and get on with it. Find a job, find a girl to lay and live the life I'd always planned on living. There were the nightmares, of course, but the Army doctor assured me that they would pass in time. "See a shrink and he'll give you some keen mind-altering meds." I'd ignored that advice. I didn't need meds, and I most certainly didn't need a shrink. *Fuck that. Fuck them all. If it hurts, swallow a couple of Vicodin.*

She stroked my hand again. "Are you alone because of your…injury?"

"You heard about that?"

"I've kept up with you, David. You're a genuine war hero—a brave man who risked his life to save his comrades."

4

I motioned to the waiter for another vodka. "Your family's in the newspaper business. You know you can't believe everything you read in the paper. Especially press releases from the Department of Defense."

"But is that why you're alone? The injury, I mean."

I let out an angry sigh. "Just spit it out. If you're asking if I can still function, the answer is yes. I lost both legs below the knee. My dick is intact."

"Now you're just being crude."

We sat silently for a few minutes. Finally, we both said, "Sorry" at the same time. We laughed. I speared the remaining olive and swished it in the icy vodka. "Enough about me. You never married? No English aristo or anyone like that?"

"God, no." She pushed the wine glass away. "Let's go someplace I can get a decent glass of wine."

I threw some bills on the table and stood up, making sure it looked as effortless and natural as I possibly could. I gulped the last of my drink and helped her with her coat. "Some place such as...?"

"Such as my hotel. Daddy keeps a suite there. God knows why, as much as he hates Cleveland."

It wasn't far by taxi to the Ritz-Carlton. She opened the door to the suite with a flourish, threw her coat on the antique chair by the entrance and turned to me, arms widespread. "Welcome to Chez Lehrer."

I looked around. It was actually an apartment with a kitchen, a separate dining room, a living room and a bedroom, each with a view of Lake Erie and large-screen televisions in every room. It was pitch dark outside, only the blinking lights of the city far below were visible. The windows vibrated a little with the howling wind. I couldn't see the lake, but I could imagine the whitecaps.

She opened the refrigerator and extracted a bottle of Montrachet. She handed it to me. "Open this."

I took it to the kitchen. After rummaging through a drawer for a corkscrew, I took the opened bottle and two heavy Baccarat glasses into the living room where she had settled on the sofa. The entire room was done in some luxurious shade. Mocha maybe? I poured two glasses of wine and handed her one.

She reached up to clink my glass. "To St. Louis."

"To Cleveland."

"Now show me your legs."

I shrugged. "Morbid curiosity?"

"Not morbid, no. But curious, yes. I need to see."

"Okay." I pulled my pants legs up around my knees. The extra-light titanium prostheses glowed in the dim light.

"Oh my," she said, leaning forward and touching the shiny metal. "How do they work?"

"Very well. I can do just about everything in them. For sports, like jogging or boxing or basketball, I have a pair with blades. They don't fit into shoes like these."

"Wait a minute. Did you say *boxing?*"

"Sure. I flit around the ring on my blades like a butterfly."

"And sting like a bee?"

"Yes, I do." I pulled her up off the couch and kissed her. "I usually take them off for sex."

"Then we should take them off. Show me how."

I led her into the bedroom and sat on the side of the bed. I pulled the strap loose on my left leg. "Like this."

She was a fast learner.

⟨⟨⟨⟨⟨

I woke to see her dressing. I wasn't surprised, but I was disappointed. "So soon...?"

"I'm afraid so, baby. I have this charity mess in Akron I need to get back for."

I pulled her down against my naked body. "One for the road?"

She laughed and pushed me away. "No time."

"What was this, a pity fuck? Or a good story you can tell your girl-friends—how you screwed an amputee in the company apartment?"

"I don't have any girlfriends. And if it was a pity fuck, why would I want to see you again? Be in Akron on Saturday. Try to get there by noon. There's a family lunch every Saturday with my father."

I sat on the edge of the bed, looking for my clothes. I pulled on my shorts. "I'm not sure I can get off work on Saturday."

She handed me my prostheses and kissed me lightly on the lips. "Sure you can. I put my address and number in your phone."

I need to put a password lock on my phone, I reminded myself.

"Remember, by noon," she insisted.

I strapped on my T22s and stood up. "Am I wrong, or was this some sort of audition?"

"You might call it that. If it is, you're getting a callback. Who knows? You may even get the part."

After Cordelia left, I sat on the edge of the bed and thought. At the *Post*, I had worked my way up from covering charity events and school board meetings to being a lead reporter for state and local politics. During the last campaign, I was assigned to the presidential press pool for the Ohio primary. It had been a hard slog, and I valued the job. *I probably shouldn't just run off to Akron whenever I please.* Of course, that was exactly what I was going to do. Why not? Despite my injury, I had learned to run, and even to box, again, bouncing lightly around the ring in my sports titanium and carbon fiber T22s—the latest artificial limbs the government could buy. I did everything the therapists demanded, everything and anything to prove to the world, with its maddening condescension, that I was not someone to be pitied. I was not a loser. I was a winner. *After all, I had just screwed Cordelia Lehrer, and by God, I'd screw her again.*

TWO

Cal Gentry sat across the newsroom from me staring intently at his computer screen. Cal and I were working on the latest scandal in Columbus, a state purchasing agent with his hand in the till, and an update had been penciled in for the Sunday paper. I pulled up my notes, read through them quickly and sent them to Cal. After a few minutes, I went over to his desk.

"What's up?" Cal asked.

"I just sent you my notes. Can you handle the update for Sunday?"

Cal turned away from his computer. "I guess. I ought to get the byline though." He smiled as he said it.

"Sure, you should." I leaned in close so we wouldn't be overheard. "The thing is, there's this girl in Akron…"

"The blonde?"

I grinned. "Well, …yes."

"Stop smirking, you son-of-a-bitch." Cal turned back to his computer. "Got it," he said, bringing up my notes. "Did you show her your medal?"

"Whatever it takes."

"Not your bionic legs? You went for the legs?"

"It was worth it, buddy."

"Okay. You go and play, and I'll take care of things here."

"I'll do the same for you some day."

"Sure. Like I'm ever going to meet a girl like that." As I left, I heard Cal mutter, "Lucky shit."

He was right.

The drive to Akron was only forty-five minutes. It was a bright winter day, warmer than usual, and calm; one of those days you get sometimes in the winter in Ohio. I let up on my accelerator driving rod and took my time, remembering the night at the hotel.

Akron is small and easy to navigate, especially with my GPS, which led me past the crumbling Rubber Bowl stadium, a reminder of Akron's glory days as the rubber capital of the world. A few minutes later, I reached the address she had put into my phone. It was a modern six-story building. I parked in a Visitor's Only parking space where my old Corolla was the runt of the litter. I pushed the driving rods to one side and extricated myself from the car, hoisting my body up onto the pavement. It wasn't easy, but I had done it thousands of times. I left my gear, my duffle, my lightweight chair, and my running blades in the car. There would be time enough to get them if she asked me to spend the night. I walked to the lobby door.

The doorman waved me through. "Mr. Lewis? Sixth Floor."

It's nice to be expected. When I got off the elevator, the apartment door was open, and a tanned young woman wearing jeans and a Cleveland Cavaliers jersey stood waiting.

She extended her hand. "David? Come in. Cory's so happy you could make it. She's getting ready. That could take a while, but you know Cory."

I shook her hand and looked at her. "I'm David Lewis." As I said it, I realized that she obviously knew who I was.

She laughed. "I'm Francoise Gaulle, Cory's personal assistant. Call me Francie. Would you like something to drink?"

Ah, a personal assistant. F. Scott Fitzgerald had it right. The rich are different from you and me. "No, thanks. I'm fine."

Francie was short, compact, and obviously very fit; good-looking with a no-nonsense air about her. She spoke with a noticeable French accent as she pointed out the view of Akron and the local landmarks from the wide living room windows. "Cory's been living in this building since we came from Europe. She took the three apartments on this floor and combined them. It worked out nicely, don't you think?"

It *had* worked out nicely. My apartment in Cleveland would fit easily into one half of the living room. "You two met in Europe?"

"Paris, actually. I was out of work at the time. We met at an art exhibition. She mentioned she was looking for someone to handle schedules and bookkeeping, all things she doesn't like to do. I said, 'How about me?' and here I am." She pointed out the window. "In Akron, Ohio."

"A change from Paris."

"I love it," she began, then turned to the door. "Here's the woman herself."

Cordelia swept into the room. She had on slacks and a thick wool sweater. "David." She took my head in her hands and kissed me. "We're late. Daddy doesn't like the family to be late for our weekly family ordeal."

Sounds like fun, I thought.

Francie handed Cordelia her coat. "David was here exactly on time. You're the one who's late."

She laughed. "I know, I know. I'm always late to everything." She stood back and looked at me with an appraising eye. "No tie?"

I was wearing a pair of chinos, my corduroy jacket, and a white starched dress shirt. It was pretty formal for me. "Does it matter?"

"It's the first time for you to meet Daddy. He needs a tie, don't you think, Francie?"

Francie winked at me. "Mr. Lehrer will expect a tie, I'm sure."

"Find him one, will you, while I show him the view?"

Find me one? Do they keep a supply of men's clothes? As soon as Francie left, I pulled Cordelia into my arms. "I've seen the view. It's you I want to see." I kissed her.

"Now I'll have to redo my lipstick," she said with a little pout. "Oh, what the hell, come here."

We were still hugging and laughing when Francie came back, waving a red tie. "Try this."

Cordelia laughed. "This girl is a marvel. She can do anything. Where did you get it?"

"From the doorman." She handed the tie to me. "Be sure and give it back to him when you two come home tonight."

When we come home tonight. I liked the way that sounded.

When we got downstairs, the doorman smiled and gave me a thumbs-up signal. A bright yellow Porsche Panamera Turbo waited in a No-Parking-Emergency-Vehicles-Only space outside the front door.

"Would you rather take your car?" She looked around the parking lot, full of Lexuses and Mercedes. "Let's see if I can pick yours out." She pointed at my car. "It's not the lime green one over there by any chance, is it?"

I grinned.

She turned to the doorman. "Pete, bring Mr. Lewis' car. You know which one it is."

The young man hesitated only a second. "Yes, ma'am."

I tossed the car keys to Pete. "It's not quite a Porsche," I said to Cordelia with a grin.

"I think the common touch might do quite nicely today," she answered.

Pete quickly returned with my car, jumped out and ran around to open the passenger door for Cordelia while I got settled behind the wheel. Pete had pushed my driving rods to one side, and I struggled to snap them back into position. Cordelia pointed at the rods. "What on earth are those things?"

"Driving rods. One for the brake pedal and one for the accelerator." I finally got the rods in place and started the engine. "I forgot to tip Pete."

"We don't tip. Francie takes care of all that. She's very generous, too. Now wave your magic wand and accelerate that rod out of here. We're late. How fast will this thing go?"

I waited until we hit the highway before pressing hard on the accelerator. The old Corolla hesitated, and then responded unwillingly.

"Impressive," Cordelia said. "Do they even still make these?"

"Yes, they still make Corollas."

"That's surprising." At the Heath Road exit, she said, "Exit here, then take the next left. The guardhouse will be around the next corner."

The guardhouse?

A uniformed guard stood outside a small stone enclosure. He hesitated, saw who my passenger was, and waved us through. We drove for a half-mile up a winding road. As we crested the hill, we came to the manor house, a red brick pile, complete with a stone tower and portico. Gables poked out from the slate roof. I nudged the Corolla into the circular gravel drive and parked between a Volvo wagon and a Mercedes coupe. On the south side of the house, I could just make out a large swimming pool, sparkling in the winter sunshine. Another stone building overlooked the pool. Beyond it were two grass tennis courts, neatly groomed.

"Welcome to The Heath."

"The Heath?"

"Yes, The Heath. Mother loved English literature."

"Oh."

"I see we're last. Oh well, what the hell? It's better for our grand entrance. I can't wait to see my sisters' expressions when they see you." She took my arm and led me into the house.

I looked around. "My God, how big is this place?"

"I've no idea." *One doesn't ask*, she seemed to say. "More than enough for a widower and a boatload of servants. Ask Daddy. He loves to talk about The Heath." She kissed me on the cheek. "Are you impressed by the splendor of it all?"

"Gee golly, yes," I said.

She nodded at the butler who opened the door. "Where are they, Dakila?"

"In the Conservatory, Miss Lehrer," the small man replied. He was Asian.

We walked into a large entrance hall, two stories tall. Sunlight streamed through clerestory stained glass windows. Directly ahead of us was the dining room where the long dining table had been set. On our right, the Great Room, maybe forty feet long and empty. At its far end, a stone fireplace reached to the ceiling. A gigantic elk's head hung above it, and immense logs were brightly burning.

She led me to the left into a wood-paneled room with a large glass conservatory at one end and a bar in its center. Two couples stood there, holding drinks and talking quietly. They looked at us and nodded when we entered, then resumed their conversation.

Away from the bar, nearer to the entrance of the room, a large florid man with a shock of white hair sat comfortably in a black leather Eames recliner, watching a sixty-inch flat screen TV. He looked up at us, muted the TV, and smiled at Cordelia. "Give your daddy a kiss."

Cordelia leaned down and kissed him on the cheek. "Sorry we're late, Daddy."

"No, you're not, or you wouldn't be late." They smiled at the shared joke. He looked up at me. "Is this he?"

She took my arm again. "Daddy, this is David Lewis."

I reached down and shook the man's oversized hand. "Mr. Lehrer."

"So, you're the hero. Get the man a drink, Cordelia." He pointed at the chair next to him. "Come sit by me and tell me about what's going on at the *Post*. Is it true they sacked Brennan?"

For the next fifteen minutes, Lehrer quizzed me about the *Cleveland Post*. He was well informed. "What got into Tom anyway, endorsing a Democrat? Did he forget who owns the paper?"

I answered uncomfortably. "I'd just been hired when that happened."

"Well, memories are long in this business, no matter how good you are. And now he's gone. What about the new man?"

"Bill Bristol? He's okay."

"Another left-winger?" Lehrer pulled himself out of his chair. "Don't bother to answer. All reporters are half-socialist, I understand." He turned off the TV. "That's enough shop talk for now, anyway. Come meet my other daughters…and their husbands." He winked when he said it, apparently letting me in on a joke that I didn't get. Lehrer was a large man, about my height, but a lot heavier. Even so, he moved like a younger and lighter man. In fact, he carried himself like a former athlete.

The group at the bar watched us approach. Cordelia sat at the side of the room, leafing through a fashion magazine. She looked up and smiled, but made no move to join us.

A tall, plain woman in a no-nonsense navy blue sweater stepped forward. She glanced sharply at Cordelia, who ignored her, and then at her father. Finally, in a tone that said, *well, if no one else will introduce you, I suppose I'll have to,* she extended her hand and said, "Hello. I'm Ginny McGentry."

"My eldest." Lehrer poured himself a glass of whiskey. "My eldest barren one." He raised the decanter in my direction with a questioning look. I shook my head. *No whiskey in this group.*

Ginny braved an insincere smile at her father and sniffed a little. "This is my husband, Douglas."

Douglas McGentry was also tall and heavy-set and appeared completely uninterested in me. It seemed to take some effort, but after a pause, he extended his hand. "How d'you do." His handshake was the smallest of formalities. He turned back to the other man at the bar to continue their conversation. The man he was talking to was wiry and nervous. He was tapping his hand on his wine glass, watching me. Finally, he decided it was all right to smile. "Hi. I'm Tom Pearson, and this is Reggie."

Reggie was a small blonde in a dark dress with a long strand of pearls and a toothy smile. "I'm the middle one."

Her father interrupted. "This daughter's also barren. Is it my genes or the men they chose?" He smiled malevolently at the couple, then turned toward the dining room. "Time to eat, children."

Reggie called after her father, "Still trying, Daddy. Aren't we, Tommy?"

Her husband cleared his throat nervously.

She turned back to me. "Daddy loves his little jokes." We followed her father in a slow, unwilling procession. She composed herself and said to me, "It's so good to meet one of Cordelia's young men for a change. She hardly ever brings them around." She glanced down at my legs. "A war hero. And in the newspaper business, too. How interesting. We must hear what you think about our newspapers."

Before I had to decide what to say, we were in the baronial dining room. I hoped the matter of my views on the Lehrer newspapers would be dropped. I had looked online for data about Lehrer and the KL Media Group before I left Cleveland. The Group owned fifty daily newspapers, most in small markets in the Midwest and Southwest, but also some on the West Coast. The Orange County, California newspaper had the largest circulation. According to Wikipedia, Kingston Lehrer started with the purchase of a paper in southern Ohio fifty-five years ago. After that purchase, he went on a buying spree, acquiring most of his newspapers over the next few years. According to an article I pulled up from the *Wall Street Journal*, Lehrer had a reputation for slashing costs and concentrating on local news, operating in localities where local advertising still brought a premium. Usually, they were conservative communities receptive to Lehrer's far-right political positions. The article quoted an unnamed executive at the Akron headquarters as saying the family-owned chain was doing so well, a public stock offering, or perhaps even a sale of the company was possible and that the founder and his heirs might cash out their interest in the company, which was now tied up in family trusts.

I also looked at the online version of a couple of the newspapers. If they were the norm, Lehrer's papers gave readers a good dose of libertarian, anti-government editorial content, along with second- or third-tier syndicated material and an abundance of local sports and social news. Lehrer sat at one end of a table, which could have seated thirty more, and the rest of us took our places around him. The family all attacked lunch with gusto, seeming to enjoy the watery vegetable soup and the white fish in thin tomato sauce. No one spoke until they had cleaned their plates. Lehrer looked at my half-finished serving. "Not hungry?"

The others watched silently while I hurriedly forced down the rest of the fish. Lehrer motioned to the butler who was hovering nearby. "Coffee for everyone, Dakila." The butler turned and clapped his hands. A young servant appeared with a silver coffee pot. I didn't want coffee, but I hadn't wanted my fish either. We all drank the weak coffee slowly, waiting for Lehrer to speak.

He shifted his big frame in his oversized, throne-like chair and stared at me. "I'd be interested in your opinion of the war. I never believed our country's vital interests required us to engage in a land war in the Middle East. You have paid a high price for that policy." He waited for me to reply.

"I'm just glad I didn't come back in a body bag."

"Indeed." He tapped his cup for more coffee. "So, you support an ill-advised war, despite your own injuries?"

"I don't know whether the war was ill-advised. I do suspect I was ill-advised for volunteering." I smiled. Only Cordelia returned my smile.

"Indeed, indeed. Perhaps we can discuss this further, privately. I would like to give you a selection of our editorials on the subject to see what you think."

I refused more of the weak coffee from the servant. "Sure. Anytime."

Lehrer shifted his bulk again. "We'll save the war for another day. I don't believe you answered Reggie's question. What do you think of our newspapers, Mr. Lewis?"

"I don't know much about them, certainly not enough to have an opinion."

Lehrer grunted. "My daughter says you're a good reporter. You would never have come over here without doing your research."

The two couples watched my discomfort with satisfied smiles. Cordelia whispered to me, "Good luck."

I hesitated. I didn't think telling Lehrer my true opinion was a good idea, since what I'd seen so far told me that the KL papers were third-rate at best. It probably wouldn't work to lie either. I was pretty sure the old man would be able to tell and I'd be worse off than if I'd told the truth.

Lehrer tapped on the table impatiently. "Come, come. We're just small-town newspaper people here. We'd value the opinion of the mainstream press." The way he said *mainstream press* left no doubt of his loathing of it.

I smiled. "If your objective is to be out of the mainstream, then I'd have to say you've made it, at least from what I've seen. Your papers are far right of center, aren't they?"

Lehrer seemed pleased he had gotten a little rise out of me. "We're for individual responsibility and individual freedom. Sometimes we're to the right of the mainstream, sometimes to the left. We believe in limited government at all levels. That also happens to be exactly where the communities we serve want us to be. That accounts for our remarkable profitability. Right, Tom?" He looked at his thin, nervous son-in-law.

Pearson nodded eagerly. "That's right, Chief. KL is the most profitable newspaper chain in the nation, and that's because your small and middle market strategy has been precisely on point."

I recognized the financial man's phrases from the *Wall Street Journal* article and I didn't have to guess who had planted the item about the chain being a good candidate for a stock offering or even a sale. I smiled at Pearson and thought I might have found a way to change the subject. I held out my coffee cup for more of the tepid coffee, then said to Lehrer, "Since the results are so good, I wonder why you are exploring a sale? At least according to the *Journal*."

Pearson choked on his coffee and erupted into a coughing spasm.

Lehrer's face clouded over. "Don't believe what you read in the *Wall Street Journal*. It's hardly ever accurate." He stared darkly at his son-in-law, who managed to stop coughing. "The family will always run this newspaper chain, isn't that right, Tom?"

Pearson swallowed nervously. "Of course, Chief. Of course."

"And you agree too, don't you, Douglas?"

The other son-in-law patted his mouth with his linen napkin and said, "I don't understand the financial mumbo jumbo, Chief. That's between you and Tom."

Lehrer nodded with satisfaction. He turned back to me as if to say, *See?* "I built this business up from nothing, just with these..." He clenched his big fists. "...and this." He pointed at his head. "Muscle and smarts. Street smarts is all I had. So, no one, and I mean no one..." he looked menacingly at Pearson, "is going to keep my family from owning and running these newspapers forever."

Forever's quite a while, I thought.

Lehrer seemed to understand what I was thinking. "All the voting stock is in trust, and I am the trustee," he explained. "When I'm dead, the new trustee will follow my wishes or he will be replaced. It's ironclad. End of discussion." He stood up. "Come with me. I'll show you around The Heath."

We left the rest of the family in the dining room. Cordelia picked up her magazine, resumed flipping through the pages and waved at me with an amused smile.

Douglas McGentry called out, "More coffee, Dakila. Ándale!"

A Spanish-speaking Asian. Probably Filipino.

Lehrer led the way back to the entrance hall. He pointed to a large painting of a young woman who looked a lot like Cordelia. "My wife, Maude.

It's been twenty-seven years since she died, and I think about her every day."
He paused. "Her memorial service was in the Great Room. There were flowers everywhere." He wiped a tear from his eyes. "What a crowd! There was a string quartet in the music room, and it filled the whole house with some of her favorite music. Not anything I could name. Bach, maybe? Yes, I'm sure it was Bach." He shook his head and coughed slightly, then pointed to a stone stairway that led downstairs. "Let me show you the cellar." He went down the wide stairway with quick steps, not asking if I could navigate them. I went down easily enough. *Coming back might be harder.*

The large cellar had a flagstone floor and rock walls. Round wooden tables and chairs were placed throughout. "Originally this was a theater with thick tapestries on all the walls—for sound control, I suppose. I ripped them all out and there were these perfectly formed rock walls. They really knew how to build a house back then."

"So, you didn't build it?"

Lehrer laughed. "I'm surprised Cordelia didn't tell you. She loves to reveal our family skeletons. No, I bought it from the United States government at auction. It was the home of Nose Comeri."

"That name sounds familiar."

Lehrer unlocked a large wooden door. Inside were racks upon racks of wine bottles. "It should. Nose was the *consigliere* to Bob-Bob Volici. Bob-Bob ran the rackets out of Cleveland after World War II. Nose was Bob-Bob's nephew and Bob-Bob gave him the Akron gambling and prostitution business." He snorted. "Nepotism!" He glanced upward, in the direction of his sons-in-law and the dining room. "This house has always been filled with it. Do you know the trouble with nepotism? It's inefficient. It rewards mediocrity."

Lehrer took out a dusty bottle of wine; he proudly turned the label to me. "Do you know wine?"

"No."

"Too bad. I suppose it's an acquired taste. This is a bottle of Château Lafite Rothschild, 1959 that I'm saving for my wake. It may turn by then. I hope so. That would be a great joke on my family." He put the bottle back in the rack, handling it very carefully. "Maybe I'll open it if I am ever given an heir."

He locked the door to the wine room. "The Pittsburgh mob coveted the Akron territory. They were always after Nose. They torched his first house. Nose's wife and daughter died in the fire." He led me out of the cellar and shut the door. "After the fire, Nose built this place. It's all rock. He wasn't going to have another fire. He built guardhouses and an electrified fence around the entire three thousand acres. It must have cost a fortune. Everything was completely secure, or so he thought. None of it saved Nose, though. They ambushed him on the main road, just short of the guardhouse where you came in. Poor Nose. Well, the government seized the house for back taxes and I bought the entire thing for a song." He winked. "Now, that's the kind of big government I can support. Take from the mobsters and give to the deserving rich! Now we only man one guardhouse. My enemies aren't as violent as Nose's were." He laughed again. "At least I hope not."

Without acknowledging the possibility that I might have difficulty climbing the steps, he said, "Those steps are a trial for an old man. Let's take the elevator."

When we got back upstairs, Reggie and Ginny were still sitting at the table, sipping coffee and looking bored. Cordelia was gazing out the window, and Tom Pearson was busy on his cell phone. Douglas McGentry was gone. Lehrer opened one of the glass doors onto a stone terrace that stretched the length of the house. A blast of cold air blew through the room, scattering newspapers and rousing the family from its *ennui*.

"For God's sake, Daddy, please close the door," Ginny shouted.

Lehrer ignored her and marched to the edge of the terrace. I followed him, closing the door behind me as I went.

"Look at that view," Lehrer said. The wind blew his abundant hair.

Nose had built his fortress on the highest hill of the densely wooded property. The winter sunlight reflected off the evergreen trees and several ponds shimmered in the distance. A riding trail cut through the trees. Rooftops were barely visible on two smaller hills below.

Lehrer took in a deep breath. "The Cuyahoga Valley. Beautiful, isn't it?"

"It is."

"That's Ginny's house, to the north. Reggie's is there, on the hill to the west."

Where you can keep an eye on them. "So, it's a family compound. Like Hyannis Port?"

Lehrer gave me a sharp look. "Trying to rile me up, young man? It's much bigger than Joe Kennedy's place. Actually, I liked Joe well enough. He wanted a president in the family and he got one. I can understand that. All fathers have dreams for their children. Joe got what he dreamt, but at such a terrible price." He stood silent for a minute. Finally, he roused himself. "Over there, that hill? That is Maude's Hill." He pointed to the north. "I named it after my late wife. I think it's the prime spot. That's where Cordelia's house will be when she settles down."

He stared at me, sizing me up. I figured he was probably wondering if I was the one who could settle her down. I tried to imagine what kind of house she might build on that hill. *What would it be like to live over there, under the watchful eye of this unforgiving old man?* "She seems very happy in town."

"Oh yes, in her very expensive condo. That's well enough for now. But when she marries and has children, she will be here with us." He turned and checked one of the terrace bird feeders. "The staff never fills them. Never."

He smiled mischievously. "Well, come on, let's stir things up a little. I make them stay all afternoon every Saturday. I feed them gruel and watch them pretend to enjoy it. I tell them they can't leave until I'm tired of them. Sometimes, I'm tired of them after the first ten minutes, but I make them stay anyway. It's good for them. After they leave, I sit down in the family dining room with the week's newspapers and have sautéed walleye and coleslaw." His eyes twinkled. "Maybe some sauerkraut balls. Did you ever have sauerkraut balls, young man?"

I smiled. "Yes, sir. At Dot's in Cleveland."

He looked at my legs. "Cordelia says you can box…on your prostheses. Is that true?"

"It is. I'm light on my feet, so to speak." I had spent months learning—first to walk, then to exercise, then to run, and then greatest test of all, to climb into the ring again. "I had some matches staged by the National Amputee Boxing Association."

"Did you win?"

"I did."

"Good man." He opened the door and shouted, "Bird feeders, Dakila! The rest of you, to the barn!" To me he said, "Come with me. I want to show you something."

I followed him down the hill to the big stone barn where he pulled open the door. It was dark inside, save for the lights hanging over a boxing ring in the center. I could hear the sounds of a man working a punching bag. As my eyes adjusted to the dim light, I saw Douglas McGentry in trunks and a sleeveless shirt, attacking the bag while a lanky Filipino man held it for him. Douglas looked stronger than I would have thought, well over six feet and two hundred pounds, I guessed. He had only a little flab around his mid-section, which betrayed his age and the hours he spent in an office. Douglas looked up at me for a second, and then returned to his routine, grunting with each hard jab.

Lehrer said, "This was where Nose staged fights back in the day. The place can hold about 200 people, and he filled it up regularly. He made a lot of money handling the book and probably fixing the outcomes, too." He called to Douglas. "Douglas, David is a boxer also. Would you like a sparring partner?"

I shook my head. "No, Mr. Lehrer."

Douglas joined in. "I'm willing, Chief. But if he doesn't want to, well…"

Lehrer ignored my protest. "Of course he wants to. Just go easy on him. You outweigh him by thirty pounds, and he is our guest."

"Chief," Douglas said, "it's probably not a good idea. I mean…" he hesitated and then motioned with a gloved hand at my legs, "he's…"

"A cripple?" I asked. *I'll show you a cripple, you son-of-a-bitch.* I turned to Lehrer, who was smiling broadly.

"My gear's in my car."

"I'll have someone fetch it." He turned to the Filipino. "Pedro, get Mr. Lewis' equipment for him." The young man left in a trot.

Lehrer rubbed his hands together. "I'm really looking forward to this."

ᴄᴄᴄᴄᴄ

I supposed the match was to be a test of some sort, for Douglas, me or maybe for both of us. Perhaps it was just an old man showing his power, throwing a double amputee in the ring against his son-in-law. Maybe all I had to do was not embarrass myself in the ring. I decided to do much more than that.

Pedro returned with my gear, and I was ushered to a dressing room to change. I had a choice of sweatpants or shorts. I decided on the shorts. I wanted Douglas to see my running blades. I hoped I could find an opening while he was watching me glide around the ring. I took off my daily-use legs and carefully put on my running prostheses. Carbon fiber running feet combined with a special knee makes a real difference in agility. I knew Douglas would be surprised at my mobility. I had never boxed a civilian before, and I was counting on the T22s to give me an edge.

The family gathered to watch. I climbed easily up into the ring and through the ropes. Pedro handed me a helmet and laced up my gloves. Cordelia gave me a wry smile and toasted me with her wine glass, presumably filled with Montrachet. Douglas shadowboxed in the opposite corner of the ring. Ginny and Reggie sat in chairs below Douglas' corner. Tom Pearson had ignored Lehrer's order and had not come down to watch.

Pedro motioned us to the center of the ring. We touched gloves and he threw up his hands, signaling for us to start. We sparred around a little, neither landing a punch. Douglas might have been pompous and slightly overweight, but he was also a skilled boxer. He stepped inside and deftly tapped the side of my head. I shook it off, but he followed it up with sharp jabs to my arms. I danced away, protecting my head. He closed in, trying to punish me. I slipped his punch and landed two heavy shots to his midsection. He grunted and tried to tie me up, but I was under his guard, landing four hard jabs to his rib cage. I bounced away, just out of his reach. He tried to close in, but I danced away from him. He followed me, grunting and breathing heavily. I dropped my gloves and dared him to catch me, leading him around the ring like a matador taunting a tiring bull. He stopped in the center of the ring, breathing heavily. I stepped in quickly, taking his shots on my gloves as I pounded his stomach and caught his hipbone twice. He staggered back.

"Low…low blow," he said, looking at Pedro who ignored him. He tried to turn away but I spun him around and hit him low and hard, left, right, left, right. He dropped his hands and sagged against the ropes; red blotches were visible on his torso where I had punished his body. I knew I could finish him off. Instead, I backed away and motioned to Pedro, "I think he's had enough."

The Filipino stepped between us and signaled that the match was over. I trotted over, offering my gloves. "Thanks for the workout."

He stared at me, and then muttered, "I suppose a man wearing those things has to resort to fouls."

I laughed. *Of course they were fouls.* I knew it. Pedro knew but he didn't try to stop me. Douglas McGentry now knew who I was and that I would do whatever I had to do to win. So did Kingston Lehrer.

Lehrer handed me a Gatorade. "Great fun."

I finished off the Gatorade, climbed out of the ring, and looked back at Douglas. He was still sitting on a stool in his corner where Pedro was toweling him off. I took a glass of Montrachet from Cordelia. *This feels almost as good as having sex with her.* She put her arm around my waist and kissed me on the cheek. *Almost as good.* I turned back to Lehrer.

He said, "I can always guess where a man learned to box. I would say The Golden Gloves. Is that right?"

"Regionals in Dallas and a fight club in Cleburne, Texas."

"And when did you start boxing? In high school?"

I nodded.

"Douglas, on the other hand, had his first boxing lesson when he was fifteen, growing up in Cleveland Heights. He boxed all through prep school. He was number one middleweight on the Brown varsity team. Of course, he's a little past his prime. He needs to lose a few pounds."

About twenty.

"I always had my doubts about those Ivy League boxers," Lehrer said. "Next time, maybe we can see you and Douglas have a real fight, to a conclusion."

I nodded. "Sure." *Douglas will never get into the ring with me again.*

THREE

Cordelia, or Cory (she laughed and said that I had earned the right to call her that), waved at the security man who hopped to attention and did everything but salute as I drove past him and on to the perimeter road.

She laughed. "So, what do you think of my family?"

I tightened my seat belt and tried to push the speedometer past seventy. "I heard the word 'barren' in a conversation for the first time in my life, not once, but twice."

"If my sisters weren't such cows, I'd feel sorry for them, the way Daddy treats them."

I slowed down as we entered Akron proper. "Could he feel the same way about you some day?"

"You mean if I don't produce an heir?"

"That's what *barren* means, I believe. What if you turn out to be, well, that way, too? It could be some family genetic thing."

I pulled into the condo drive and cut off the engine.

"No way," she said. "I'm fully functional."

"You're sure?"

"That's what the fertility clinic tells me."

I shrugged. "Not my business."

"Don't look so surprised. I needed to know. It's a fight to the finish in this family."

To a conclusion, as her Daddy referred to it. I folded the doorman's tie. "What shall I do with this?"

24

"Leave it at the desk."

"How big a tip?"

"I told you. We don't tip."

We don't tip. I like the sound of that we. But I would give him a twenty when I left the next day.

That night, we lay in bed together, trying to catch our breath. I poured us a glass of wine from the chilled bottle that had been waiting for us along with a note from Francie that read: *Have fun. See you in the morning.*

Our bodies pressed lightly against each other. She drained her glass and held it out for more. "Daddy liked you, I could tell."

"I did my best."

"The look on the others' faces when you destroyed poor Douglas."

"I made an enemy."

"No. You already had an enemy. You just put it in physical terms. Daddy respects toughness."

I moved my arm and shifted closer to her. "Imagine building a chain of fifty newspapers from scratch, with just these and this." I made a fist and pointed to my head in imitation of the old man.

She laughed. "Don't believe all that 'poor boy makes good' nonsense. He's repeated it so many times he believes it himself. Do you know how my father got his start?"

"How?"

She got out of bed, stretching like a drowsy cat. "Just a sec."

She crossed the room and crouched naked in front of a bookshelf. Her body caught the light in the half-dark room. "Here it is," she said. She brought a large volume back to the bed and handed it to me. It was old, bound in buckram with a red spine. The cover was engraved: *Forest Hill, September 26, 1905.* I opened it carefully. On the frontispiece was a stern-looking man, with John D. Rockefeller's autograph beneath it. The title page read: *A Visit to Mr. John D. Rockefeller by Neighbors and Friends at Forest Hill, Cleveland, Ohio.*

"Look at the third signature."

"Barkley?"

"Amos Barkley. He was my mother's grandfather. He was a business partner of Rockefeller's. He had one son and the son had one daughter, Maude, my mother. So, when Mother married Kingston Lehrer, she brought her oil fortune with her."

"That's where the money came from to build the KL chain?"

"Yes, from my mother. That's where it all came from."

❮❮❮❮❮

I woke to bright sunlight. I removed my arm from around Cory, careful not to disturb her, and sat on the edge of the bed while I strapped on my everyday T22s and got up. Standing at the window, I could make out The Heath in the distance. It was another perfect winter day—no snow or fog, cold enough, but not freezing—a Sunday you ought not waste. I pulled on some pants and a sweater and made my way as quietly as I could toward the smell of freshly brewed coffee. Francie stood before a Rube Goldberg coffee maker. When she saw me, she pressed buttons and the machine began to crank up like a gardener's leaf blower. In half a minute, steaming black coffee poured into a waiting china cup. Francie handed me the coffee. "You look like you could use this."

I inhaled the charcoal aroma. There was a thick layer of *crema* on the surface of the coffee. I inhaled again and then took a large gulp. It was very hot. "That's the best coffee I've ever tasted."

"It's Italian. The machine brews a cup at a time, a lot like you get from a Roman barista. I told Cory I wasn't coming to Ohio if I couldn't have decent coffee."

I finished the cup and handed it to her for a refill. The machine did its noisy magic again.

"Want to get some fresh air? Cory tells me you're quite the athlete. The bionic man."

"That's me. The bionic man."

"We could go for a run, then maybe shoot some hoops?"

I was sore where Douglas had landed punches. A stretch and a run would help. I looked back toward the bedroom.

Francie laughed. "She won't be up for two or three hours, if then."

"Well, sure, then. My running blades are somewhere around here."

"I believe I saw them in the hall. I'll go get them."

Francie took my cup and started the machine again. "Meanwhile, finish your coffee, read your paper." She handed me the Sunday *Post*. "You've got a byline on the front page."

I sat down at the kitchen table with the paper. Cal had done a good job with our story, although there were some things I would have changed. For one, I would have made sure my name was first in the byline.

Francie came back with my running blades. "I should warn you, I'm pretty good."

She moved like an athlete, I could see that. "How good?"

"I played for Aix-en-Provence in the LFB."

"What's that?"

"The LFB? It's the *Ligue Feminine de Basketball*, the French national league. I was the league's leading scorer my second year. If I had been tall enough, I'd probably still be playing. Instead, I moved to Paris and got on the staff at *Paris Match*. You've heard of it, *non?*"

"The mag? Sure."

"My uncle was a fashion editor there." She smiled. "*Oui, népotisme* there, too. But when poor Uncle Pepi was shown *la porte*, I was out of work."

I took my blades into the bedroom to change. *That's great. It's Let's Dump on David Weekend. First, Douglas McGentry, now a French Amazon.*

⟨⟨⟨⟨⟨

When we returned from our run, Cory was doing yoga exercises in the living room. We watched for a moment as she raised her arms. I couldn't take my eyes off of her. A small, quiet girl with an armload of dirty linens smiled shyly as she scooted by us.

"Hello, Bituin," Francie said.

The girl blushed and turned away.

Francis explained. "She's very shy. You met Dakila, the man who runs things up at The Heath? Bituin is one of Dakila's many nieces. He has an endless supply. However many household workers Cory's father needs, Dakila can supply them. She hasn't been in this country very long."

"They're father's spies," Cory said, coming out of her *asana*. They are everywhere and there's simply no use arguing about it. It's how Daddy keeps tabs on his family." She breathed deeply.

"God, you're beautiful," I said.

She smiled and slid easily into the lotus pose. "I am, aren't I?"

Somebody had retrieved my lightweight chair from the Corolla so I was able to shower and change. When I finished, I rejoined Cory in the studio. She was alone. She stretched her long legs. "I love lazy Sundays."

I rubbed her shoulders. "Your personal assistant is a hell of a basketball player."

She sighed. "That feels good." She turned and kissed me. "Francie plays pick-up games with the Akron College varsity."

"The Zips? Can't you do something about that name?"

"I wouldn't think of it."

We leaned back against the studio wall quietly. After a while, she turned to me and said, "So, David, baby, are we going to do this thing or not?"

"What thing exactly?"

She stroked my arm, then turned my hand palm up and intertwined her fingers with mine. "Get married, have a son, inherit the Lehrer empire and live happily ever after."

How could I not want to be with her? Beautiful, smart, funny, rich... not to mention, rich. Ah, very rich. I asked her the question that had been bothering me. "Why me, Cory? Cordelia Lehrer can have any man she wants. Why choose a middle-class double-amputee reporter?"

She thought for a minute. "Baby, don't underestimate yourself. I want to marry someone I like who knows the newspaper business, someone that my father will respect and accept."

"That last part may be hard. I am a working member of the left-wing reporter class."

She laughed dismissively. "Oh, that. Would that keep you from running our papers?"

I thought about it. "I wouldn't say it to your father, but political philosophy doesn't interest me. Most pols are either crooked, insincere, stupid or all three."

"Well there you go, then. Daddy likes you. We'll have to suffer through a few more Saturdays…"

I interrupted. "No more boxing matches! Or do I have to knock poor Tom out?"

"I doubt it. We'll let Daddy get to know you better; you can spout some Libertarian jargon and then we'll ask for his blessing."

"You want me to lie to my future father-in-law?"

"If you would, please."

One thing she didn't ask. She didn't ask if I loved her. She certainly didn't say that she loved me. If she had asked me, of course I would have said whatever she wanted to hear. I'm not sure what love even is. But she didn't ask. She sought me out when we hadn't seen each other for seven years. We're sleeping together. The sex is great. She's incredibly rich. She just asked me to marry her. What more could I possibly want?

"So, I got the part then?"

"There is one more thing."

There's always a catch.

"I need you to go to the Fertility Medical Center at the Cleveland Clinic and get tested."

"A fertility test?"

"Don't worry, baby. I'm sure your little soldiers are healthy and numerous. But I have to be sure. Francie has made an appointment for you on Wednesday afternoon. She'll come to Cleveland and take you to the Clinic. They will send the results directly to her."

"You don't trust me?"

"I trust you, baby, but I don't want to tempt you. And I need the results before next weekend."

"If I fail?"

"Then don't bother coming on Saturday."

I kissed her on the forehead. *So much for love.*

FOUR

I passed the fertility test with flying colors. Francie called me with the good news. "By the way," she said, "I'm sending you KL Media's latest financials. Look them over before Saturday and we can go over them after."

I raided the *Times'* archives for copies of the fifty KL newspapers. I tried to find them online, but what I found was amateurish and outdated.

‹‹‹‹‹

Our lives fell into a routine of sorts, dedicated to winning Lehrer's approval. Francie had an economics degree from the Sorbonne, and the night before Cory and I drove out for Saturday lunch, Francie walked me through the tortured corporate organization of Lehrer's empire. When we returned from lunch, she answered the questions I had after quizzing Tom Pearson and enduring his droning replies. He did seem to know his stuff, though.

One Saturday night, Cory had gone to bed and Francie and I sat at a table going over my notes. I looked up at her and asked, "What in the world are you doing here, Francie? You know all this stuff so well. A personal assistant?"

She cocked her head and gave me a Gallic shrug. "I came because Cory promised me a management job with the newspapers."

"You could do something like that in your sleep. You're that good. What happened?"

"I think she underestimated the male chauvinism that permeates her family and the family business. Three daughters with no influence, really."

"Cory can usually get her way with her father."

"Not when she wants to bring a French woman into the publisher's office. She tells me to be patient; that it will all work out."

Maybe when the old man dies, I thought.

I kept at it, learning the business. I read all the KL papers, skimming the local sports and weddings and obits, reading the editorials' railing at big government—or in some cases any government at all—so I could talk about those subjects with Lehrer. Cory recounted the family history for me.

I began looking forward to Saturdays with the family…almost. I was able to talk newspapers and business with Lehrer, gain a better understanding of the financials from Tom, and, after a while, even got the meaning of family jokes and signals without the others knowing I knew.

The lunches were still deadly affairs, but my in-laws-to-be watched grumpily as Lehrer and I chatted about world affairs, politics, economic theory and sports. I adopted a political stance just far enough left of Lehrer's to be believable, but not so far as to be unacceptable to him. After lunch, if it was a warm afternoon, there was tennis on the estate's grass courts. I could play well enough that Douglas claimed tennis elbow and wouldn't play, even mixed doubles. Boxing was never mentioned again; not even by Lehrer.

I played golf with Lehrer on the three-hole course behind the barn. Tom and Douglas joined us once, but soon tired of the constant newspaper talk. Lehrer watched the sons-in-law leave and shook his head. "Sometimes I wish divorce wasn't a mortal sin. But the girls chose those two and they will have to live with their mistakes for the rest of their lives." He turned to me sternly. "There will never be a divorce in this family. Divorce for any reason, and I mean any reason, and they're cut off completely and cast out of my sight forever. That prohibition survives me. It's in their trusts." He shook his head vigorously and looked at me. "Cordelia's trust, too."

Jesus.

Later, Lehrer stopped the cart and turned to me. "Cordelia gave me the results of your fertility tests, yours and hers."

"She did? She didn't mention that."

"Yes, well. It's settled then. What would you like to do at the newspapers?

31

I'd like you both close at hand when my grandson is born. But none of that left-wing garbage, do you understand?"

I hesitated. I didn't want to be too critical, but I didn't want to seem too toady either. "I think there are overdue improvements to the online versions of the papers. I could work on that."

"Why would I want to spend money on that? My readers want a paper they can hold in their hands."

"Things change, sir." I tried a different tack. "I notice there's a lot of variation in the papers' editorial policies. I think we could tighten it up, feature your editorials more. Not shortchange local news of course, but have a consistent editorial policy throughout the chain."

"Now that makes sense. You and I are on the same page there. But not all that online nonsense."

I hurried on, trying to find ways to resonate with Lehrer. I didn't give a crap about the editorial policy, but I did need the papers to succeed and for me to be seen by the family as the reason for the success. Above all, I needed to make sure Lehrer got the credit. "The local papers buy their own syndicated features, columnists and comics. If we centralize that in Akron, I believe we can have better quality at less expense and make your message a lot more consistent."

"You've done your homework, haven't you?"

"I like the newspaper business, sir. And I like what you have here. I'll do whatever you want, wherever you think I can learn."

"I think you'll start by working with Martin Scowcraft, my executive editor. Let's see how the two of you hit it off and we'll go from there. He will help you get your feet on the ground. Martin and I go back a long way, to the first paper I bought."

Perfect. Cory will be very happy. "Thank you, sir. I won't let you down."

If Lehrer worried about what his other sons-in-law would think about me joining the business, he didn't show it. He was getting what he wanted, a good chance at an heir, a newspaperman in the family and a happy favorite daughter. He shifted heavily in the golf cart, which creaked ominously from his weight. "How much compensation do you have in mind?"

I gave him my rehearsed reply. "That's up to you, sir."

He grunted. "Indeed? I never trust a man who doesn't know what he wants."

"I do know what I want. I want to marry your daughter and learn the business from you. Anything else is gravy."

"Hmm. Not like Douglas. He brought down a room full of lawyers and spent days negotiating the prenuptial agreement and an employment contract. I tell you what. I'll pay you what I'm paying him, plus a dollar. With Cordelia's trust income, you should be able to support her. Although, you have probably noticed that she has expensive tastes."

I grinned. "I have noticed."

"The family lawyer will get you the prenuptial agreement. Have your lawyer look it over if you want, but it's not negotiable."

"I don't have a lawyer and I don't have money to waste on one."

Truth be told, Francie and I had already negotiated the prenup and my high-priced lawyer back in Dallas had signed off on it. I reviewed it in my head: *A ten million-dollar life insurance policy on Cory's life, payable to me. Cory's trusts will pay our living expenses and she will own all of our real estate, including the new house on Maude's Hill. I get a new Maserati roadster modified for all-hand operation as a wedding gift and one million dollars every year for ten years, beginning on the birth date of our first-born son. I run the papers. Cory makes all parental decisions. All that for bringing my sperm to the party, screwing the best-looking woman I ever met and landing a dream job. Hell, I should be paying her.*

"Divorce?" I had asked Francie.

"Then you get nothing, David, because her Daddy will disinherit her if there's a divorce for any reason," she replied.

I extended my hand. Lehrer shook it in his big paw. "Thank you, sir," I said.

"Don't let us down, me or her, or you'll find out I can be a vengeful man."

He wasn't smiling. "You can count on me." *I hope my little soldiers are listening.*

He motioned for me to start the cart. "Let's play that last hole again. And get this wedding over with so you and Cordelia can start making me a grandson."

《《《《《

Later, at the condo, Francie poured a glass of frigid Montrachet for herself and Cory and scotch on the rocks for me.

"To a marriage made in Akron, I mean, Heaven," Francie said, raising her glass. "No, I say, especially to you my dear Cory, *Bénissez-vous les deux et l'enfant qui sera bientôt avec nous.*"

Cory smiled in return and said, "*À l'enfant,* who will soon be with us."

I had no doubt what Job One was.

I switched to wine, Francie and Cory to Cristal champagne. "How are your sisters going to take the news?"

Cory smiled. "They can't be too surprised. The four of them are probably trying to decide what it means."

"What it means?"

"What it means to them. All they think about, all day, every day, is when will Daddy die? Are they really condemned to live in Akron the rest of their lives, or can they break the family trusts, split the money and divorce each other? Believe me, if I had their lives, I'd be thinking the same way."

"Your father says the trusts are unbreakable."

Francie spoke up, "Of course that's what his lawyers tell him. They drafted the trusts. But if all the heirs agree, no trust is unbreakable. And that is why the others need to get along with your future bride."

"They need her to agree."

Cory yawned and stretched, arching her back.

God! So sexy!

"We play along with them, then when Daddy dies, we buy them out for a song and you and I will own everything."

I took her hand and pulled her to her feet. "You're a beautiful conniving little bitch, aren't you? Let's go to bed."

She put my arm round her waist. "That's the nicest invitation I ever got. But now that we're engaged, we need to wait until we're married."

I didn't believe what I was hearing. "Why?"

"Because, I don't want anyone counting months on us. Our child will definitely not be conceived out of wedlock. No sex until we're married."

"You'll never last that long," I said, patting her on the head.

"*Got along without you before I met you, gonna get along without you now,*" she sang. "I'm serious. It's important that my child be the only legitimate grandson of Kingston Lehrer."

Her child? "My God, Cory, it's not the throne of England."

"As soon as you can get out of your job at the *Post* you can start work here. The sooner the better. Francie has found you an apartment at the Quaker Square Inn. It's not far from the office. You can stay there until we're married."

I absorbed all the news. "I'm not used to being told what to do, Cory. Don't think it's always going to be this way."

She kissed me. "Don't be silly. You're going to run the papers. No one will tell you what to do at the office."

"Except your father. And what about Douglas and Tom?"

"Oh, them. They're parasites. Neither one's ever worked a day in his life. Douglas is the last of a wealthy Cleveland family, or at least it was wealthy before his grandfather and father spent all the money. And Tommy, don't even get me started on Tommy. He's got that Wharton MBA and so he thinks he's some kind of business genius. But all they really want is to stick around until Daddy dies so they can sell the papers. They've already sent Ginny and Reggie to cozy up to me and feel me out." She mimicked them perfectly. "'What do we want with newspapers? Will you try to block us from breaking the trust?'"

"What have you told them?"

"Nothing. I let them think that all I want is a good-looking man to take to bed and that I don't care about the papers. We'll keep them thinking that, won't we, baby? Until it's too late."

I gathered up my stuff; *I might as well head back to Cleveland for the night.* I had one last question before I left. "If your father despises Douglas and Tom, why is he so set against the girls divorcing them?"

"His Catholic upbringing, I suppose. He's a secret Catholic, you know."

"What does that mean? Who cares anymore?"

"Mother's family certainly cared. He became an Episcopalian because the Barkleys would never have allowed my mother to marry a Catholic, especially a sewing machine salesman."

"So, he converted, but his fingers were crossed?"

"Something like that. He brings Father Joe to The Heath every Sunday afternoon to conduct Mass and hear confession. Everyone in Dakila's family is Catholic. Daddy always attends, and afterward, he and Father Joe hole up in his study. I suspect he hears Daddy's confession then."

"That's weird. Why doesn't he just go public with it?"

"I've often wondered. This town? The papers? A promise to my mother? I don't know. We're not allowed to mention it. Can you believe he had Father Joe come out to consecrate my sisters' wedding vows? 'For the benefit of the staff,' he said. But really, it was to be sure they were married in the eyes of God."

"Whew. Will we have to do that too?"

"Probably." She cocked her head, "What 's your religion?"

"I don't have any. Not really."

"Your parents never had you baptized or christened? Anything like that?"

"Well, I know Mom and Dad were Catholic. I remember going to mass when I was little. After my dad ran off with his secretary, my mother stopped going, and my brother and I did, too."

She thought a minute. "Oh, this is perfect. Listen to me. You need to visit Father Joe. Tell him your life story and tell him you worry about getting married outside The Church. Ask him for his advice."

"Where's this heading?"

"You're going to be the brave Catholic my father never was. I'll tell Daddy that you're insisting that we get married in the Catholic Church. He'll respect you all the more for it. Tell Father Joe I want an Episcopal service and you want a Catholic service. Tell him you've convinced me to raise our children as Catholics. Ask him if he might get us a dispensation from the Bishop for a joint wedding. It will be perfect!" She giggled. "Daddy can say, 'I'm proud of my new son-in-law. He's a war hero, you know, and a Catholic. If he wants a Catholic priest at their wedding, I'm certainly not going to be the one to say no.' Go see Father Joe right away and I'll tell Daddy." She gave me a goodbye kiss. She was obviously pleased with herself. "What a wonderful idea. Don't you agree, Francie?"

ꞔꞔꞔꞔꞔ

Father Joe's church was in an undistinguished section of the city. A tired-looking housekeeper met me at the entrance to the Rectory and showed me into the priest's study. He was typing hesitantly on his keyboard. He looked up. "Come in, young man. Sit down, please. I'm working on my homily. Just let me finish this thought."

I sat across from him and waited for him to finish his slow typing. He was a small man with dark sunken eyes. He looked less like an Italian priest than some Don's *consigliere*.

"And, save," he said, shutting the laptop and looking at me. "So, you're Cordelia Lehrer's young man. What brings you here?"

"A favor, Father."

He listened carefully as I explained Cordelia's request.

"Unusual, certainly. But the entire Lehrer family is unusual. You are Catholic, you say?"

"Since birth, Father."

"Have you been attending Mass in Cleveland, making your confession?"

"I'm afraid not, Father. Not for many years."

"Why is that, do you think?" He paused when the housekeeper brought in a tray of coffee and cookies. "Please," he said, "help yourself."

"I'm fine, thanks." *I wasn't expecting to have to give the priest my life story.* The housekeeper left and shut the door. He waited for my answer.

"I don't know why, Father. It just happened."

He eyed me skeptically. "Your unhappy experience in the war perhaps? Maybe you felt the Church failed you?"

I shook my head. "No, Father. It was long before that."

"What was?" He poured us both coffee. "You say you're a cradle Catholic and you want a Catholic marriage and a Catholic home, and yet you are estranged from the Mother Church. I simply asked you why."

What the hell? Maybe I need to tell someone. "I can speak to you in confidence?"

He smiled. "You have been away from the Church for a long time. I am a priest. Tell me whatever you need to."

I sighed. *I don't want to talk about it. I don't want to have to remember.* I sighed. "My mother was killed in an automobile accident. It was my fault."

"Were you driving?"

"No, nothing like that. It was my older brother's wedding night. My mother and a neighbor wanted to go home after the reception, but I wanted to stay and party. On the way home…they were hit by a train. The car was dragged three hundred yards down the track and they were both killed, instantly."

"You believe they wouldn't have been killed if…"

"If I had driven them home. Mom was a terrible driver. It was late. She didn't ordinarily drink, but she'd had some champagne. I know I would have seen the train and stopped in time." I paused before going on. "The priest came to the house. He said it was God's will. I cursed him and shoved him out the front door. I never went back to church after that."

"Is that it?"

"No. There's more." *It feels good to say it out loud.* I continued, "I fell apart. I had finished up college and should have been out looking for work but I couldn't. I got into some scrapes with the law. That was when my older brother stepped in. He's a problem solver. There's nothing so bad he doesn't have an answer for. That's why he did so well at the Air Force Academy and why he's made general. Of course, he had a solution for me: 'March down to the recruiting office and enlist. It'll give you purpose and challenges and when your tour is over, you'll no longer think you killed our Mother. Because you didn't.' If my brother makes a suggestion, it's really an order. I followed orders and enlisted. The first year of my tour I lost my legs." I looked up at the priest. "I killed my mother and I hate my brother. Is that screwed up enough for you?"

Father Joe heard my confession, blessed and forgave me and suggested we talk again after Sunday afternoon Mass at The Heath. Meanwhile, he would look into some sort of joint wedding.

At first, I felt better, having spilled my guts to the priest. But in my heart, I knew that I had killed my mother and that my brother had betrayed me. No amount of holy water mumbo jumbo would ever change that.

FIVE

It wasn't hard to resign from the *Post*. "Grab your stuff and go," the managing editor said. He shook my hand. "God help you with the old man. Real reporters don't last long working for him. Of course, being married to the boss's daughter will probably help."

Have I detected a hint of jealousy?

⟨⟨⟨⟨⟨

I settled into my temporary home, a suite in the old Quaker Oats factory, which had been repurposed as a hotel. *Oh well, it won't be for long,* I told myself.

"I always wanted to sleep in a silo," I said to Francie when she handed me the key. I looked around. A new wheelchair was in the corner.

"The new lightweight Model 400X, just like you specified. There's another one at the office and one at the condo. Also, Pedro has been assigned to you. You do remember Pedro? He was the referee at your famous boxing match with Douglas."

"I liked his style. He let us box."

"Pedro will drive you, run errands, whatever you need."

"Very thoughtful."

"Cory just wants you to have everything you need."

Except her bed. "Thank her for me."

"Thank her yourself tonight at dinner." She took my hand. "It's all going to be fine after the wedding. Once that's over, everything will be fine."

⟨⟨⟨⟨⟨

I showed up for work at the KL offices in my reporter's uniform, chinos and dress shirt, to which, as a precaution, I had added one of the power ties Cory gave me as an engagement gift. The offices were in a four-story building in an office park a few blocks from my hotel. I was underdressed. All the men wore suits and ties. The few women I saw wore conservative dresses and heels. *Was there a funeral I didn't know about?* I could see that this was not a working newspaper office. There were no cubicles, no cluttered desks with blinking computer screens, no noisy phone calls. Everyone seemed to have a private office. Most of the doors were shut, and there was no newsroom buzz. It could have been an insurance company or a trust company.

I had asked Lehrer why the headquarters was in Akron, where he didn't own the local paper.

"Two reasons," Lehrer had replied. "First of all, my wife and I settled in Akron before there even was a newspaper chain. There was no reason to move. Second, it's better to live where you don't own the paper. People here don't bother me. They don't care what I do with my newspapers because it doesn't affect them. The last thing I want is disgruntled readers, or worse still, advertisers camping on my doorstep. That's why I have editors."

A receptionist smiled and directed me down a wide hall to glazed glass doors with, Offices of the Publisher printed on them. A middle-aged woman in a dark dress and pearls greeted me. "Good morning, Mr. Lewis. I'm Amy Batson, Mr. Lehrer's secretary. He and Mr. Pearson won't be back from New York until tomorrow. He instructed me to get you settled in."

The area where we stood was the home of Amy and another somewhat younger woman who nodded to me but didn't speak. At one side of the room were a sofa, three chairs and a handsome silver coffee service which graced a mahogany sideboard. Amy pointed to her left. "Mr. Lehrer's office is there."

I glimpsed a large desk and a leather chair.

"Mr. Pearson's is there." She motioned to a closed door across from Lehrer's office. "Next to it is Mr. McGentry's office. He's expected in this morning."

Apparently, Douglas McGentry didn't keep very strict business hours.

"And you will be here," Amy said, pointing at an office next to Pearson's. "May I offer my congratulations? Cordelia Lehrer is a lovely young woman."

"Thanks very much," I said, looking around.

"I think you'll find everything you need. Your driver brought your... ah...things."

She looked at my wheelchair and running blades which Pedro had placed against the wall. *You're in for a culture shock, Amy.*

"Would you like coffee?"

"Absolutely. I'll be working with Martin Scowcraft. Is he in?" *Nobody else is,* I thought.

Amy frowned. "Mr. Scowcraft makes it a point to be the first person in and the last to leave. His office is just down the hall, on the other side of Mr. Lehrer's." She pointed out the double doors.

"Then hold that coffee while I go check in with him."

As I moved toward the door, it opened and Douglas McGentry appeared. "You're here, are you?" he said, coming toward me. "Hard at work already?"

I managed a tight smile. "Just trying to learn my way around."

McGentry yawned and looked into my assigned space. "Lo these many years that office has been reserved for Cordelia's husband. And now here you are." He raised his eyebrows at my blades and the wheelchair. "Where's the Chief?"

"Amy said he and Tom are still in New York."

McGentry stretched. "Poor Tom."

I waited for the explanation. After a pause, McGentry decided he would favor me with one. "Traveling with Kingston Lehrer is unimaginably boring. You have to sit there and listen to him tell some Jew investment banker about the business. It's unbearable, at least for me. Tom thrives on it." He turned away. "Amy! Call the club and tell them I'm on my way. I'm late for my tee time." And then he was gone.

I walked a few steps down the quiet hall to an office with the door ajar. I tapped on the door. A skinny man with a bow tie and rolled up sleeves was barely visible behind a stack of newspapers. He peered at me through thick-lensed glasses. "You need something?"

"My name is David Lewis. The new boy. Are you Martin Scowcraft?"

Scowcraft shook his head ruefully as he got to his feet. "Just what we need is another relative to support." He came around his desk and extended his hand. "I'm Martin. Welcome aboard. I hear we're getting a newspaperman this time?"

"That's what I call myself," I said as we shook hands. *"Cleveland Post."*

"Sit down. What were you doing over there?"

"Seven years as a reporter. I was working on the state desk when I left."

Martin asked about some mutual friends, then leaned back in his chair and eyed me closely. "Congratulations. For what it's worth, I'd say Cordelia is the pick of the litter."

I nodded in agreement.

"She's pretty like her mother, and, I imagine, hard-headed like her father."

"You knew her mother?"

"Maude. Yes, I knew Maude."

"How long have you been with Lehrer?"

"From the beginning." He pointed at the stack of newspapers on his desk. "Before there were any of these." He snorted. "Fifty papers to go through every day." He shoved the pile toward me. "Help yourself. I know what you're thinking, and you're right. Crap is still crap. God, I haven't talked to a real newspaperman in years. Where are you officing? In the Publisher's Suite with the rest of the family?"

"I was hoping there was a place for me out here. I'm supposed to be your assistant, or so I'm told."

He smiled. "Yeah, the Chief wants me to find out how good you are."

"That's what he told me, too."

Martin laughed. "Subtlety's not his strong suit. But he and I understand each other." He pointed behind him to a closed door. "The back door to his office. He and I are in and out of each other's office all day. I'm the only one who doesn't have to make an appointment."

I must have smiled because he went on, "Don't get me wrong. That's not all good. I have to listen to bullshit that has nothing to do with running these newspapers. But I can still say *no* to him, and I may be the only one who can. There is an office next to mine, where my last assistant sat."

"What happened to him?"

"We shipped him out to Nebraska to make room for you. He's a good boy, but of course, he's not family."

"I hope he's happy out there."

"He'll be miserable."

There was an awkward moment. I said, "I'll take the office. Let me go tell Amy."

"She won't like it."

"Why not?"

"It'll be harder for her to keep tabs on you. Besides, I'm a bad influence."

"How so?"

"I guess I speak truth to power. That can get uncomfortable around here."

As he'd predicted, Amy thought it was a bad idea. "Mr. Lehrer said…"

"It will be fine, Amy. Please have Pedro move my things."

When I returned, Martin pointed at the stack of papers. "Take these. Skim them. Red question mark for *bad*, red check for *good*, double questions marks for *take action*."

"What about double checks for *very good*?"

"If you find one of those bring it to me because I want to see that son-of-a-bitch with my own eyes. Most important, look for editorials that stray from the party line."

"Party line?"

"What the Chief would have written."

"How will I know that?"

"You'll know."

"Isn't this micromanaging?"

Martin exhaled and reached for a stack of correspondence. "Not really. I never tell a local editor to fire somebody."

I took the newspapers and headed for my new office. I turned and said, "What do you tell him?"

"Well, sometimes I tell him that certain fellows might need to find a new profession."

SIX

The months passed quicker than I expected. Cory kept to her abstinence vow as if she were a Carmelite novice. She was obsessed with wedding plans and the design of the house on Maude's Hill. Francie's brother, Claude, showed up from Paris to design the wedding dress. An architect arrived from Chicago to design the house.

We were all standing on the outcrop at the end of Maude's Hill. I had to admit it was a good view. Nothing blocked the view from where our living room was planned. It would be a great place to watch winter storms and summer sunsets. The architect pointed out the location of the rooms, the nursery, and the studio. Claude put his arm around Cory and kissed her on the cheek. He glanced over at me and whispered in her ear. They giggled and she shook her head, no.

Francie took my arm as we walked back to the Range Rover. "Don't pay attention to my brother. He's playing games."

"Did they have a thing in Paris?"

She laughed. "Claude and Cory? Of course not."

I didn't believe her, of course. They kept flirting. I could barely hold my temper. I confronted Cory angrily when we were finally alone.

"You've slept alone too long, baby. Claude wasn't flirting with me. He was flirting with you."

"With me? He's gay?"

She kissed me. "What a wonderful reporter. You couldn't tell? He asked my permission."

"I hope you didn't give it."

She kissed me. "Oh, baby, I told him there wasn't a straighter piece of timber in the state of Ohio than you."

"If this abstinence crap goes on much longer, I might be tempted." But when Claude eventually did approach me, I laughed and pretended he was joking.

I spent as little time as possible at the Silo and immersed myself in small town news from fifty small towns. I jogged to the office most mornings. Pedro met me at the health club downstairs. He brought my clothes and my everyday T22s, packed everything away, helped me in and out of the shower, helped me dress, gave me my schedule for the evening, and waited for instructions. Soon I couldn't remember what it was like before I had my own personal aide.

Martin taught me the work and shared family stories. He had devoted his life to this business and he was happy to have a family member, or at least a future family member, with an interest in it.

One Friday afternoon, when all the crises had been dealt with and the Chief was sent home happy, Martin took me for a late lunch. He opened the glass doors and blew a kiss to Amy. I told Pedro to go home and followed the skinny executive editor. He headed downtown. "Italian?" He didn't wait for an answer. He walked fast, almost trotted, through a red light, across Market Street. My everyday T22s weren't made for the pace and my legs ached, but I kept up. He stopped at a small storefront restaurant.

"*Angelino's,*" he said, which agreed with the sign on the door. A table with a red check tablecloth was waiting for us. A gray-haired man with a plump face smiled. "The usual?"

"Double. Pete, this is David Lewis. He will soon be Mr. Lehrer's son-in-law. Unless the bride comes to her senses. David, meet Pietro Angelino, the perpetrator of this sorry excuse for Italian food."

We shook hands. Pete smiled and waved us to the waiting table. "He must like the food," the owner said. "I know he doesn't come here to flirt with the waitresses."

"Because there aren't any. You drink scotch?"

"A beer. Dortmunder, if you've got it," I said.

"I got it." Pete turned away, shouting our order to his bartender.

Martin rested his elbows on the table and stared. "So, what do you think so far?" I waited for the waiter to put down our drinks.

"Small town papers aren't that different. Cover the council race and play up the sports. Be a booster. Reflect what your readers believe. It's like papers used to be," I said.

"Before the Internet."

"Even before that. It's just a matter of time before our papers feel the squeeze. Readers leaving, advertisers, too."

"Our online editions stink," he confirmed.

"Yes. We should be moving the papers online, right now. Before it's too late."

Martin took a long drink of his scotch. "What do you think I've been trying to do? The Chief doesn't believe in digital, so now we're twenty years behind. Half our papers don't even *have* an online edition. The computer programs are pitiful. Several of the presses need replacing, and every time I ask for money to upgrade something, that little prick Pearson vetoes it."

"Why does the Chief let him?"

"Because all the Chief knows about running a newspaper is whether it's making money. The reason these papers are so screwed up is they're making so much money. Why mess with success?"

The waiter brought a basket of warm bread and olive oil. I broke off a piece of bread and dipped it in the oil. "This is good." I finished my beer and shook my head when the waiter brought Martin another double scotch. "I don't understand."

Martin pushed his empty glass away and picked up his fresh scotch. "Kingston Lehrer is a financial genius, or at least he was in his prime."

The food arrived and we turned to it eagerly. The lasagna was good and we finished it without talking. Martin stared at the remains of his scotch. "Coffee?"

"Sure." I wanted to hear whatever the Executive Editor of KL Media would tell me.

Martin motioned to the waiter. *"Due caffè corretto se vi piace."* He finished his scotch. "The grappa here is not bad. Where was I?"

"You said that Kingston Lehrer was a financial genius."

Martin smiled. "Those were great days. Just me and Tony…"

"Tony?"

"He was *Tony* in those days. Hell, it wasn't until we signed the sales contract on the first deal that I knew his name was Kingston. Tony Lehrer, that's what he was in high school. He must have used his full name when he married Maude, but I was so excited to be in that wedding, I didn't notice."

The waiter set small white coffee cups in front of us. The coffee was steaming and the grappa made my eyes water. I sipped the coffee slowly, letting the coffee and brandy settle the big lunch a little.

"Maude's family didn't think much of Tony. Maude was an heiress. The Standard Oil Trust. You knew that?"

"Cory mentioned it."

"Tony's old man was a small-town hustler, always trying to get rich, not ever getting there. But Tony was a very persuasive young man and I guess Maude loved him. So, finally, there was a big wedding at Forest Hill. You know it, the old Rockefeller summer home?"

"Sure. Everyone in Cleveland knows Forest Hill."

"After the wedding, Tony brought his bride here and went to work for a bank. His new in-laws arranged it. He could have had a good life living off his wife's trust fund, but he was determined to be somebody, not just a rich woman's husband." He looked at me and shook his head. "I'm sorry. I wasn't thinking about you."

"That's okay. It comes with the territory."

"Anyway," he went on, "that's all he talked about, being somebody." Martin took off his wire-rimmed glasses and wiped them with the big white napkin. "It was the Linotype machine that made him rich."

"The Linotype machine?"

"Well, really, it was the death of the Linotype. I was a reporter for the local paper. Tony and I hit the bars together sometimes. One day, I mentioned that a new invention was changing a lot of things at the paper."

"That would be the Photon?"

"Bingo!" He waved at the waiter. "*Due più dello stesso.*"

We were the only customers left in the restaurant. Pete was busy at the cash register and the waiters didn't seem impatient for us to leave.

Martin waited until the new espressos appeared before going on. "You wouldn't remember, but up until the Photon, nearly all the newspapers in the whole country were set on Linotype machines. It was a big old contraption invented by a German watchmaker in the 1880s. It set type in molten lead. The thing was very precise, but also very complicated, over ten thousand moving parts. It took an apprentice four years to learn to operate it. Printers who qualified as Linotype operators were proud of their craft and they had a very powerful union. Those guys were nearly irreplaceable, and the publishers knew it.

"But after World War II, along comes this French inventor with a new machine, the Photon, that set characters on film instead of in lead. The system was called photocomposition. He demonstrated it in Boston. It was amazing. It set type six times faster than the Linotype. Prescott Low in Quincy, Mass. bought the first one and worked out the bugs. When he got it running, his production costs went down like a rock. Low didn't need a bunch of highly trained printers. A few guys hired off the street with a few days training could operate the Photon. Before long, newspapers all over the country started using it instead of Linotype. Those papers realized immense labor savings once a Photon was installed."

I looked at my watch. It was already four. "Mind if I call Pedro and tell him where I am? I want to hear the rest of this."

"Don't bother. He's right outside waiting for you."

I looked out the window. Pedro was leaning against the fender of my car. I called to the owner. "Pete, could you send my driver out there a beer and some rolls?"

Martin looked at me and said, "No doubt you're asking yourself what the Photon had to do with Kingston Lehrer building a newspaper chain?"

I nodded.

Martin smiled broadly. "I love this story. Want a cigar?"

"We can smoke in here?"

"As long as the Pussy Patrol doesn't catch us." He waved at the owner. "Pete, bring us a couple of Havanas."

The owner nodded and Martin waited until he showed up with a box of cigars, and a sign that he placed on the table. It said, "Smoking Area." We each selected a cigar and the burly Italian cut it for us. I inhaled deeply. Pete left and came back with a bottle of grappa. "Gentlemen," he said and returned to his work at the register.

Martin poured us each a healthy shot. "This is the best part. You know how much the Chief hates the United States government?"

"I may have read something about that."

"Well, next to the invention of the Photon, Kingston Lehrer owes his success to the United States government, and in particular, the Internal Revenue Service."

"I need a drink on that," I said. The bitter grappa burned on the way down and then left me with a fuzzy warm feeling. I poured myself a big glass of cold water and pushed the grappa out of arm's reach.

Martin went on, "In the 1960s, the IRS did a study of family-owned newspapers and how they ought to be taxed when the owners died. Back then, the top rate was seventy percent, so it was a big deal. To make matters worse, the IRS started appraising these businesses at what someone would pay for them, and not what the owners had invested in them. Say a man had spent his life building up his newspaper. When he died, these new rules meant his family would have to sell out, just to pay the tax. I'll tell you, the tax planners and lawyers were very busy thinking up ways to escape the estate tax." He raised his glass. "To lawyers."

I tipped my water glass in answer. My head was just starting to clear from all the alcohol.

"That's where Kingston Lehrer saw his chance. Over the next ten years, he began traveling the country, courting publishers. He told them, 'I'll buy your newspaper and you get the money instead of the government.' The lawyers structured the deals so that there wasn't any tax. He looked for papers in small markets, where the paper had a monopoly. It turned out those were usually very conservative communities, and the more of those publishers he went after, the more conservative his own politics became. Tony Lehrer didn't give a rat's ass about politics, but as time passed, Kingston Lehrer certainly did. I guess he finally convinced himself. He told those publishers he would continue their traditions, and by and large, he's kept his promise. Of course, other people were out there buying up papers, too, but the Chief knew from the beginning the kind of papers he wanted. At one time back then, we were buying a paper every month. I quit my job and went along, helping him appraise the papers, figuring out how much we could increase earnings by getting rid of their Linotypes."

"How did he pay?"

"He used Maude's inheritance."

"Then you put in the Photon and made a fortune?"

Martin laughed. "Something like that. But first he had to make a deal with the printers' union." He stood up. "Excuse me. I need to piss."

While he was gone, I checked my phone. No message from Cory, but five from local editors.

Martin slid into the booth and sighed heavily. "Damn prostate. It's hardly worth it, getting old. Now, where was I?"

"The printer's union."

"Ah, yes. The printer's union. Did you ever hear of the ITU?"

I shook my head. "I can't say I ever did. 'Fame is fleeting but obscurity is forever.' Napoleon, I think."

Martin ignored me. "The International Typographical Union was one of the most important unions in the country. In 1963, it was able to shut down every Manhattan newspaper for four months. It was the nation's oldest union. By 1982, it ceased to exist. 'How did that happen?' you're about to ask in amazement."

"My words exactly."

"I'll tell you how. When we bought our first newspaper downstate, it was a shock to discover that we couldn't put in the Photon after all. The union wouldn't permit it. The international headquarters had directed every local to strike if a publisher tried to install a Photon machine. We took a strike.

Needless to say, the Chief was nervous. It was Maude's money. Not only that, we had two other deals on the table. That's when the Chief learned how to work the unions."

"What did he do?"

"He found a labor lawyer who had been through this very thing with other publishers. He told the Chief to offer the local a deal. He told them, 'Decertify, that is, quit the ITU and allow me to install the Photon. In return, I will give your members a very generous pension and benefit package.'"

"And the local union bought that? Really?"

Martin nodded. "A few years earlier, it would have been unthinkable. But Photons were popping up everywhere. The demand for skilled printers was falling, and fewer new members were joining the ITU. As their numbers declined, so did their pension funds. The printers' pensions were getting more iffy every day. Our local finally agreed to decertify and let us install the Photon. The skilled printer became as outdated as the buggy whip maker, but printers could afford to retire, which they did. We made the same deal at paper after paper. Other papers all over the country did the same thing. Pretty soon, the ITU was gone and the Photon was everywhere."

"Amazing." I looked at my watch. "Jesus. Cory's taking me to some party tonight. I need to go." I stood up. "You coming, Martin?"

"You go on. I think I'll stay a while longer."

My back was stiff from sitting so long and my legs ached. I could still feel the effects of the alcohol when I stepped out onto the sidewalk. Pedro was waiting patiently at the curb. "Hey, man," I said, "Let's go home. I need a shower. My beloved is dragging me off to some dinner somewhere."

Pedro helped me into the car. "Miss Lehrer says she wants to show you off."

"Love conquers all," I said, and I fell asleep for the rest of the short journey to the Silo.

SEVEN

That Saturday morning, I was the only one in the office. I was halfway through the previous days' papers, making notes as I went, when I heard the Chief. "Where is everyone?" he barked.

"In here, Chief," I yelled. Shortly, the owner of all the newspapers stacked on my desk appeared in the doorway. He looked around. "How does this compare to your office at the *Post*?"

I stood up and smiled. "It compares pretty well, considering I never had an office there." I poured some coffee from my thermos and offered it to Lehrer.

He ignored me. He stalked around the room, examining my mementos and looking down at my desk, reading my notes.

"Actually," I said, "I'm a little self-conscious about all of this—a real office with real windows."

Lehrer grunted. "You'll get used to it pretty quickly. McGentry and Pearson certainly did." He plopped into a chair. "Did I ever tell you how I came by my name?"

"I don't believe you did, Chief."

"I am Kingston Anthony Lehrer III."

"The Third?"

"My grandfather was quite a famous actor. Kingston Lehrer I. He traveled all over the country performing Shakespeare. No doubt you have heard of him."

"Of course." *Lie.*

"Then you will know that he was renowned for his performance of Lear in Shakespeare's *King Lear*. His real name was Kenneth O'Leary. One day, for commercial *and* artistic reasons, he changed his name to Kingston Lehrer. 'Kingston Lehrer is King Lear,' the posters read. Brilliant, don't you think? As actors do, he had affairs with stage-struck young women all over the country, but he always came home to my mother. Their child, my father, was Kingston Anthony Lehrer II. He was a failure. I confess that. He melted under the heat of his famous father's success. I determined early on, watching my father with his pitiful ventures, that I would not be like him. I have been determined to become a man my grandfather would have been proud of."

He got up and then decided to sit down again. "You may have sensed that Cordelia is my favorite. Ah, that beauty, even as an infant. You and I must watch over her, keep her close, keep her safe. I intend to die a happy king, attended to by my loving Cordelia, my kingdom intact for the next generation. Do you promise me you will keep her safe, my boy?"

"Of course, Chief. I promise." Without another word, he stalked out of the office. I heard him yelling for his driver.

That's one conversation I'll never tell Cory about. And I never did.

❝❝❝❝❝

Somehow, I got through the weeks before the wedding. The weekends were the worst. The Saturday excursions to The Heath were bad enough, but after Cory told her father that I was Catholic, he insisted I return on Sunday afternoons and attend Mass in the Barkley Chapel with the staff. The first Sunday I was ordered to appear, Pedro woke me and made sure I got dressed and was there on time. The entire Filipino staff filled the small ornate chapel. Father Joe stood at one side near Cory's mother's crypt. He was talking to Dakila. When he saw me, the priest motioned for me to take a seat in the back where my wheelchair was waiting for me. I got settled and heard the Chief come quietly into the room. He patted me on the shoulder and sat down in an overstuffed chair next to me.

We watched the Filipino servants take communion. When they were finished, Father Joe brought the wafers back to Lehrer and me. I flipped back the footrests on my chair and stood up to receive communion.

After the services ended, the Chief said to me, "You go ahead. I need to talk privately with the father."

Maybe Father Joe is going to hear his confession. Who knows?

A quarter hour later, the portly man bounced out of the chapel, his arm around the priest's narrow shoulders. He seemed rejuvenated. "Shall we have a little something for the road, Father?" he asked.

The priest nodded with a smile and Lehrer led the way down the stairway to the cellar. He poured us each a glass of "a very good Petrus."

The old man teased Akron gossip out of Father Joe. The topic turned to politics and he surprised me by listening patiently to Father Joe's social views. He was deferential even when he disagreed. Of course, they did agree on doctrinal matters—divorce, women in the clergy, abortion, gays, especially gay priests. As Father Joe left, Lehrer handed him a thick envelope, which I assumed was stuffed with cash.

"For your ministries."

The priest made the sign of the cross. "Bless you, my son," he said. "Your gifts are so important to the parish."

We repeated the same ritual every Sunday. But one Sunday after the priest left, the Chief said, "Stay a moment, David. Have some more wine." I sat back down. All I really wanted was to go back to the Silo and watch some golf. And nap. I really needed to recharge for the week, but I stayed.

He leaned over the stone table and stared at me. "So, what do you think?"

"About Father Joe?"

"No, not Father Joe," he said impatiently. "The papers. Take for example, the *Texas Valley Sentinel*. It was one of the first papers outside of Ohio that I bought. An old ranching family had owned it forever. They didn't really want to be in the newspaper business, but they didn't want to sell to a Yankee, either. So, for three months, I was the best Southern gentleman they ever met. I hired a local attorney to represent me. His firm still works for us. All in all, a very good deal for both sides."

"How long before you got the Photon in there?"

Lehrer frowned. "You've been talking to Martin?"

"Of course. You told me to learn all I could from him."

"I suppose he's been telling you the family secrets. Martin is a good man, but when he drinks he has a tendency to talk too much. After the wedding, when you are ready, we'll have to put Martin out to pasture." I must have looked surprised because he went on, "Martin thinks he built this business, but in fact it was these," he clenched his fists, "and this." He pointed at his head.

And your wife's money.

He settled back down. "Where were we? Yes, the *Sentinel.* You are right. The Photon made it possible to save the *Sentinel* deal. Even the unions saw that. Eventually. After the strike." He looked up at me through his bushy eyebrows. "Well, what do you think of it? The *Sentinel,* I mean."

As it happened, I had just critiqued an edition of the *Sentinel* for Martin. "I'd rather not say yet. Can I think about it and talk with you tomorrow?"

The Chief leaned in. "Young man, I don't need you to tell me everything's wonderful. I have others to do that. Goddammit, tell me what you think."

Cory, Francie and I had talked about what I should do when this moment came. "Be strong. He needs to know you'll stand up to him," Francie had advised. Cory added, "We want Daddy to respect you. Be courteous, but firm. Don't back down."

I met the old man's eyes. He stared at me, almost daring me. I took a deep breath and plunged ahead. "If I had to grade it, I'd say the news writing is a C minus, the editorials are a D, the layout is a C, the features are a D minus and the advertising gets a B."

Lehrer stood up. "What the fuck do you know?" He stormed to the stairway. "Dakila," he shouted, "bring me my jacket. I'm going for a walk. And help Mr. Lewis upstairs. He's a cripple, you know. He has no legs, but he thinks he knows more about my papers than I do."

I went home furious, and glad not to have to relive the moment with Cory. When she called, I didn't pick up.

Pedro came in. I was in front of the TV. "Miss Lehrer said she couldn't reach you. Shall I call her for you?"

"Tell her that her father is a prince. A real fucking prince."

❴❴❴❴❴

Monday morning, I braced myself for another assault, but the old man was back in my office as if nothing had happened. "Tell me, my boy. What makes a good reporter? And how can I get more of them?"

You're an amazing dipshit, old man, or you have short-term memory loss.

EIGHT

Father Joe outdid himself. He not only secured the Bishop of Cleveland's consent to a joint Catholic-Episcopal wedding, he also arranged for the Bishop himself to officiate. Not to be outdone, Father Livingston, or Father Willie as he preferred his Anglican parishioners call him, had convinced a retired Episcopal Bishop of Ohio to join in the ceremony.

The outdoor service took place on the promontory at the top of Maude's Hill. The contractor had outlined the rooms of our future house with tape and small flags. The wedding planner had arranged for an altar in what would be the Great Room. The other rooms were marked, especially the nursery. Away from the main house was a studio with a gym and office for me, and quarters for Francie and our household staff were nearly complete.

"When we get back from our honeymoon, we'll live in the condo until the house is finished," Cory told me. "Just you and me."

"What about Francie?"

"We'll need our privacy. Francie can live in the studio until the house is finished. She'll look after things and keep the contractors honest."

Three hundred of Akron's finest, joined by important business acquaintances of Lehrer, descended on the site, transported in luxury busses from the manor house up to Maude's Hill.

It was midway through the ceremony before my headache subsided. I had enjoyed myself too much at my bachelor party. Cal Gentry had reserved the VIP Champagne Suite at The Cabaret, on the west bank of the Flats in Cleveland. The suite came equipped with a fireplace, plasma screen TVs and plenty of girls. Limos ferried the Akron contingent to Cleveland and back to the country club where Francie had reserved all the villas for the wedding party. By the time we got to The Cabaret, I'd already had three drinks. The party was well underway.

"Somehow, I never pictured Cleveland like this," a friend from college said, taking a scotch from one of the scantily-clad waitresses.

"I've always enjoyed it," I answered. *Actually, I was banned from this very club for fighting when I took offense to a remark by some suit and decked him.*

Classmates from college and buddies from my old outfit had made the trip. Former colleagues from the *Post* filled the room. Booze, dirty jokes, ribald toasts, lap dances for me by several of the half-naked girls, more booze, slurred responses by me, more booze and then, at last, the ride home, which I didn't remember.

I jerked awake. *I'd better pay attention.*

I repeated after one of the bishops:

*In the name of God, I, David take you
Cordelia, to be my wife, to have and to hold
from this day forward, for better or for worse,
for richer for poorer, in sickness and in health,
to love and to cherish, until we are parted by death.
This is my solemn vow.*

I turned to my brother, Tim, for our mother's wedding ring. Tim smiled benevolently, tall and handsome in his dress uniform, his brigadier's star reflecting in the late afternoon sunlight.

I hate that smile.

The tent for the dinner and dance was lavishly decorated. The tables were draped with white linen tablecloths, and a single white orchid in a crystal vase had been carefully placed on each table. The band was warming up, food was being served and the toasts began. Most of them followed Father Willie's example. He combined fulsome praise for Cory's sainted mother, Maude, with admiration for Cory's business genius father.

In his best man's toast, Tim declared nothing but pride in his younger brother and praise for the bride's beauty. He didn't call me a war hero, which, coming from him, would have sickened me.

The Chief, however, couldn't resist. He toasted Cory and me. "My new son-in-law, a war hero who sacrificed himself for his country. Recipient of the Purple Heart and the Distinguished Service Cross, and if it had been up to me it would have been the Medal of Honor. A man who has overcome the disability he brought back from Iraq and is now an accomplished athlete. He is a formidable boxer, as my son-in-law, Douglas, can attest." The boxing story had made the rounds of Akron society. The crowd laughed and Douglas offered up a tight smile. Lehrer went on, "To Cordelia and David. Happiness and fertility."

"Happiness and fertility," the cries rang out with laughter.

I kissed Cory and she whispered, "The pressure's on, baby."

After our first dance, the portly old man guided Cory gracefully around the dance floor. I had obligatory dances with Cory's sisters and watched her pretend to enjoy dancing with Tom and Douglas.

Later, Tim found me alone looking out over the countryside. There was no moon, and the lights in the tent glowed like a million fireflies. Tim tried to make conversation. "It's hard to believe, but I like the old man. I never expected to."

"You two have a lot in common. And, of course, he admires your star, seeing that he never served."

"You sound bitter." He sighed. "It's your wedding night. Aren't you happy?" He paused. "You don't still blame me, do you?"

"Blame you for what?"

"For your injuries. Do you blame me?"

I swallowed the entire glass of champagne and looked around for a waiter. "My *injuries*? Why would I blame you? Just because you convinced me to enlist, then advised me to volunteer for combat, where I had my legs blown off and now I have to spend the rest of my life on these..." I pulled up my trouser legs, exposing the shiny artificial limbs. "Why would I blame you?"

"After Mom died, you were lost, confused, in trouble. I hoped the Army would make a man out of you."

"You were partly right. It made half a man out of me."

"If you feel that way, why did you ask me to be best man at your wedding?"

"Father Joe said I should be *reconciled* with you."

"Father who?"

"The skinny priest standing over there watching us. He's my priest. He says I need to forgive you."

"Hold on. You've gone back to the Church? I've heard you curse it a hundred times."

"It pleases the Chief. Father Joe said I need to talk things through with you."

My brother was three inches taller than me, near the maximum height for an Air Force pilot. "Davie, I'd like my brother back. I don't believe what I did was wrong; I only wanted the best for you. If I wronged you, I'm sorry. Forgive me."

I looked at him and spat out the words. "If you don't believe what you did was wrong then you can go straight to hell, *General.*"

Before he could answer, the Chief approached us. "You never told me your brother was an Air Force general, David." He took Tim by the arm and led him away. I heard him say something about "This administration's crazy military policy."

Cory came up behind me and put her arms around me. "Time for the big reveal. Do you want to know what I've planned for our honeymoon?"

I relaxed when she touched me. *To hell with Tim. To hell with Father Joe.* I turned around and embraced her. "Okay. Where are we going? Bali? The Arctic Circle? Remember I have to be back in the office in a couple of weeks."

She kissed me on the cheek. "No, you don't."

"Now wait, Cory. You promised."

"I told Daddy that what you would like best for a honeymoon would never to be away from the business. So he is giving his favorite daughter and his favorite son-in-law a ninety-day tour of every KL Media newspaper."

"What?" I had hardly had time to think about a honeymoon. I had left it all up to Cory, but I had never expected this. "Every paper? In ninety days?"

Cory put a finger to my lips. I could smell her scent. "Francie has arranged everything. You can spend face time with every editor; learn what makes them all tick. And best of all, Daddy's letting us use the Gulfstream."

What'll poor Douglas do? Have to go in the Lear?

I kissed her. "This is really what you want for a honeymoon? A ninety-day business trip? Really?"

"Of course. And I promise that we'll have plenty of time to ourselves."

Us alone in the back compartment of the Gulfstream. "Count me in." I pulled her closer. *God, it's been too long.* The Filipino girl Pedro brought to the Silo for me was diverting, but Cory was…well she was Cory. I took some more champagne from a passing waiter. "When do we leave?"

"Tonight. They're expecting us in Orange County the day after tomorrow." She smiled at my surprised look. "Pedro packed for you. Everything's taken care of. The plane's waiting. As soon as we're done here, we can go."

Tonight!

NINE

The Gulfstream 450 was waiting at Akron Fulton. Francie welcomed us on board with a flourish. "I'll be your flight attendant for tonight's flight to John Wayne Orange County Airport. Our flying time will be approximately four hours and thirty minutes. We will be flying at an altitude of 41,000 feet. The weather en route is clear, although we may encounter some turbulence when we near the Rocky Mountains. So, I suggest you keep yourself tightly fastened." She smiled and pointed to the rear of the cabin.

The jet was originally configured to carry up to a dozen passengers, but the KL jet had been modified. A partition separated the small front cabin, with its three seats, a lavatory and a fold-down bench, from the larger rear cabin. There, a sofa folded out to make an almost full-sized bed, large enough to accommodate Kingston Lehrer's large frame on his winter trips to Hawaii or the south of France. The compartment had its own lavatory, with a small shower and a hanging rack for garment bags. My running T22s were strapped in place. A special wheelchair on rollers was attached to the wall within reach of the bed.

Francie closed the door behind her, saying, "Remember to stay tightly fastened, my darlings."

On the table by the bed was an ice bucket with a bottle of Cristal champagne and a basket of fruit and sandwiches. Cory latched the door. She shrugged off her blouse and said, "Let's get those things off and make a baby."

《《《《《

A tap on the door woke me. Through the blur, I heard Francie's voice. "Welcome to Cali, my darlings. When you feel like it, pull on something. There's a car waiting to take you to La Jolla. You have a suite at the La Valencia Hotel with a balcony and a great view of the ocean, all that stuff you won't be interested in. It's still dark here. Rest up today and tonight, enjoy yourselves. I'll pick you up to go to the paper tomorrow morning."

Cory snuggled close to me. I felt her naked body against mine. I asked, "A quickie now, or do you want to wait until we get to the hotel?"

"Why not both?"

《《《《《

The sun was bright and reflecting off the Pacific when I cracked the drapes and looked out. I had lifted myself on my wheelchair to go to the bathroom and pee. I didn't need to ask how the chair got there. Fantastic Francie. From the bed, Cory said sleepily, "Come back to bed, baby."

"This view is fantastic."

"It's better over here."

《《《《《

The next morning, we were on the road up the Pacific Coast Highway to Murtainville, the home of KL Media's Orange County newspaper. I watched the surf crashing on the rocks and the surfers paddling out to meet the waves.

"Did you ever surf, baby?" Cory asked, patting my thigh.

I turned away from the view. "I used to. But no more. Even T22s can't handle that."

Don Parsons, the local editor, met us at our hotel. He was a tanned fit fifty-year-old. He and his plump wife seemed awed in Cory's presence. She said, "I'll wait for you in the lobby, Mrs. Lewis. When you're ready, I'll show you around town. I've asked some friends to join us after for lunch."

"The name is Lehrer-Lewis, but please, call me Cordelia."

"Do you golf, David?" Parsons asked. "I thought I might set up a game this afternoon with a couple of our advertisers."

"I'd really like to see the office, meet the people, then sit down with you and hear how things are going."

He glanced down at my legs. "Oh, sorry."

Pitying bastard. "I do golf, actually. Maybe before dinner you and I can hit the practice range."

He brightened. "Of course, of course." He turned to the scrawny young man who was standing behind him. "Now, let's gets some pictures. This is a front-page story, the Chief's daughter and her war hero husband in town."

ɔɔɔɔɔ

The pattern repeated itself day after day as Cory and I flew across the country. The luncheon for Cory at the country club, the meeting with the editor, the pep talk with the staff, a game of golf or tennis or a jog or a workout at the YMCA, photo ops highlighting the amputee's athletic skills.

"Your thighs look so impressive in those little shorts," Cory said, showing me the pictures in one paper.

"They do, don't they?" I skipped over the war hero story. The Akron office had spit it out to every paper and they all ran it verbatim, with the same pictures, one of me getting my medal from some general and one of me wearing my T22s in the ring at the San Antonio fight club.

Together, we ranked the editors, one to fifty. We had trouble finding a number one. The editors all regurgitated the Chief's libertarian agitprop. Those who were sincere were usually low on the list. Some embraced it but tried to read my reaction to see if I was a true believer or like them, an employee with a job to do. Only a couple admitted to not swallowing the party line. One, a hefty guy in the Texas Panhandle said, "Personally, I think it's nonsense, but he's the boss."

I left them all guessing where I stood. I said to Cory and Francie in the plane one morning, "The last thing we want is some local editor complaining to the Chief that his son-in-law is a communist or worse yet, a Democrat."

On one leg of the trip, as we settled into the Gulfstream after a rating session, Cory asked, "What are your politics really, baby?"

I smiled. "Left wing, right wing, big government, little government, frankly my dear, I don't give a damn."

"That's my boy." She picked up the phone and spoke over the intercom to Francie, who closed the compartment door. Cory smiled. "My hero. Come here. We still have an hour before we land."

When I looked at pictures of us before and after we married, the difference was obvious. Before I had a pugnacious half-smile, almost daring the viewer to challenge me; in pictures from the honeymoon trip I had the self-satisfied look of a man with a beautiful girl on his arm who was getting all the sex he wanted whenever and however he wanted it.

And then we got to Austin.

TEN

Austin was the end of our tour. We had visited the papers on the West Coast, in the Mountain States and the Midwest. We had been wined and dined in the Texas Panhandle and the Rio Grande Valley. We had been to Alabama and Mississippi. Now we could relax. That was why we were in Austin. To relax.

I finished my jog around the river that separated north and south Austin. The locals insisted it was a lake. I drew hardly a glance at my T22s from cyclists, moms pushing baby carriages, puffing geezers and brothers in skin-tight cut-offs. I hardly noticed the really good looking girls; I was so sexually content. I bounced into the lobby of the restored downtown hotel.

A bellboy met me with a towel and a bottle of Evian. "Your wife is in your suite, Mr. Lewis. She said to tell you to come right up, she has some news."

The lobby was a smorgasbord of Victorian fussiness, over-the-top 1950ish Texas excess, and California mid-century modern. I gulped down the water while I waited for the elevator finally to deliver me to the twelfth floor where our only neighbors were a family of Columbians of all ages. They occupied the *Price Daniel Suite*. We had the *Allen Shivers Suite*, which Francie had been assured was the best in the hotel.

I rang the bell to the suite just to hear it play UT's fight song, *The Eyes of Texas*. I preferred TCU myself, but it wasn't important because when we left Texas, I had no plans ever to return.

Cory and Francie were sprawled on the overstuffed chairs, smiling happily. I settled on the sofa across from them, unstrapped my T22s, and threw them onto the sofa. I rubbed my aching thighs. "So?"

"We need a drink to celebrate," Francie said. She went to the kitchen and returned with a bottle of Cristal and three glasses. She popped the cork and poured herself and me glasses of the bubbling Champagne. Cory held out her glass. "No, none for you, little mother." She produced a pitcher of orange juice. They looked at me.

It dawned on me. "Little mother? Is she serious? Are you...?"

"Pregnant? I am, you virile war hero. Only eight more months and you'll start drawing your million a year stud fee."

I joined the laughter. "You're one month pregnant? Are you sure?"

She got up and came over to me and kissed me. "I was referred by Dr. Gildstone to the finest ob-gyn in Austin, who confirmed it." She held up her orange juice. "A toast, to Kingston Anthony Lehrer-Lewis. To Baby Tony."

Francie and I joined in. "To Baby Tony." I was having trouble digesting the news. *Something's wrong. Oh.* "What if it's a girl?"

Cory sniffed. "Don't rain on my parade. If it should be a girl, I'll just abort the little bitch."

We laughed. "That's a joke..." Long pause. "Isn't it?"

"Of course." She lay down on her yoga mat and began stretching. She was so incredibly fit that I had a hard time picturing her with a baby bump. She paused in the butterfly pose and said, "No more pressure trying to get pregnant. Won't that be a relief?"

I grabbed the bottle and poured myself another glass of Champagne. "Oh, hell yes. A real relief!"

When I woke from an out-of-the-ordinary mid-afternoon nap, hung over from too much bubbly, the women were gone. Francie had left a note:

Cory wants to see Austin. We're going to shop South Congress and then hit the bars on Sixth Street and listen to the music. (I promise no alcohol for the expectant mother). Meet us at the Upside Down seven-ish.

Won't that be a relief? she had said. The words rankled and didn't help my aching head. The last thing I wanted was a long night of bar-hopping with the two of them. *Let them listen to the starter bands trying to make it; it's all just noise to me. I can't tell the good ones from the bad ones, if there's even a difference.* I knew that it was mostly an excuse to have another beer. Cory would be the best-looking girl in the room, and I would be on the lookout for some would-be cowboy trying to make a move on her. I yearned for a fight, to prove to her that I was as much a man as she was a woman. However, things had changed between us.

All at once. She was pregnant. *I ought to be glad. I'm going to be a father. And a rich man.* But the honeymoon was over, and I dreaded learning what that meant.

As it turns out, I did leave the Upside Down Bar early—after a squabble with a tourist who got too familiar with Cory. I returned to the hotel, angry at the two women for putting me in that bar, angry at the tourist but most of all angry at myself for not controlling my nasty temper. When they returned, I was on my third scotch, munching on a twenty-five-dollar hamburger from room service, working on the report of our trip.

Cory shook my shoulder the next morning. "Wake up, Papa. We're going to meet someone. Get your legs on. Let's go!"

I turned over and mumbled, "Go away."

She was insistent. "Hurry. I don't want to be late."

That was a first.

A few minutes later, I staggered out of the bathroom, nearly dressed. I had strapped on my walking T22s and pulled on my jeans and a wrinkled brewery T-shirt. I grabbed the coffee Francie offered me and gulped it gratefully.

"You look terrible, David," Cory said. She and Francie exchanged glances. Cory retrieved a jacket from our bedroom. "At least put this on."

"It doesn't matter, does it?" I asked.

Francie took the coffee cup from me and handed me a piece of toast.

"What's this all about?" I asked, munching on my toast as I followed them to the elevator.

"We have an appointment with the publisher of this wonderful Texas magazine."

I stopped walking. "You woke me up for that?"

"No, no, you don't understand," Cory said. "He's amazing. He's a friend of Francie's brother." The elevator chimed *Home on the Range* and Cory pulled me inside.

"So, he's a 'friend' of your brother?" I said to Francie, making air quotes.

"Could be, I don't know."

The elevator doors opened, and we stepped out into the crowded lobby. "He's dying to meet you. We met his aide at the Upside Down last night and I told him about you. He called the publisher, his name is Drayton Philby, and he invited us to his office this morning."

"What's the name of the mag?"

"It's *This Texas*. You were looking at a copy yesterday."

"That liberal rag?"

"Play nice," Cory said, stepping into the waiting limo and smiling her best smile for the driver who nearly fainted.

It was a short ride to the *This Texas* offices. A well-groomed young man, wearing a tie and dark blazer, waited for us in the lobby. He air-kissed the two women and shook my hand. "Drayton is so looking forward to meeting you. Right this way." He led us down the hall. The parquet was covered with large rugs decorated with black and white squares. Large oil paintings with Texas motifs lined the walls. He opened a door and said in a clear voice with a distinct Southern accent, "Drayton, your visitors are here."

The office was all glass and contemporary furniture, with Oriental rugs covering the wood floor. A shrunken figure sat next to an uncluttered desk. Drayton Philby wore a blue blazer much like his aide's, with an open-collar dress shirt and a cashmere scarf wrapped loosely around his throat not quite hiding the wrinkled skin of an old man.

He looked in our direction with unfocused eyes and I realized Drayton Philby was blind. "Did you know?" I whispered to Cory. She didn't answer.

She briskly approached the man. "Mr. Philby, I'm so happy to meet you."

"Ms. Lehrer-Lewis, Drayton," the aide said. Philby turned toward her and shook her hand. "Drayton, call me Drayton."

"Of course. And I am Cordelia, Drayton. This is my assistant, Ms. Gaulle." Another handshake. "And this is David Lewis, my husband."

"Ah," Philby said, brightening. "The war hero." He took my hand and patted it warmly. "Sit, please, all of you. And you, sir, I'd be honored if you would sit here, next to me."

We took our places and the aide brought us coffee. "You're staying in that monstrous old pile downtown, I hear. Is it comfortable?"

"Yes, it is," Cory said. "We're staying in the *Allan Shivers Suite*, but I have to confess I don't know who that is."

"You are forgiven. A forgettable Texas politician."

Cory smiled and said, "It's very convenient to Sixth Street."

"I suppose it is. I hate that part of town. They should rename it D&D."

"Dungeons & Dragons?" Francie asked.

"No." He turned his head with a wolfish grin. "Drunk and Disorderly." We all laughed politely.

"It's a matter of taste, I suppose." He leaned toward me. "How do you find it, David?"

"Sophomoric. Pointless. A waste of time."

He nodded in agreement. Up close I could see how sunken his cheeks were, how unhealthy his pallor. He had difficulty breathing and he talked with a rasp. "When a person suffers a tragedy, it makes him less tolerant of other people's superficiality. Don't you agree?"

I grunted. "I was intolerant before I suffered my...tragedy."

"Well I confess, so was I. But I believe it does accentuate it. Even now, as ill as I am, I have no tolerance for indolence. Isn't that true, Paul?"

"Not at all," the aide said, laughing. "He's in this office at his desk every day, all day."

"Not for much longer, I'm afraid." He waved off our protests. "It's the truth." He leaned toward me again. "Tell me, David, how can you justify working for the most reactionary newspaper chain in America?" He smiled in Cory's direction. "No offense, Cordelia."

"None taken, Drayton. I'm interested in hearing the answer myself."

Philby motioned to the aide who handed him a folder. "My staff has compiled a *dossier* on you. What enticed a promising reporter from the *Cleveland Post* to Lehrer's employ? Other than marrying Mr. Lehrer's daughter, of course?"

"Isn't that enough?"

"She seems exceptionally lovely. You are a lucky young man. But still. How do you stomach all of that bullshit her father puts out?"

I don't tell the truth, how else? Who cares? I looked over at Cory. She was enjoying this. "What you call 'bullshit' is the voice of a true libertarian. Where you see right-wing, I see consistency. Not Ronald Reagan. Not George Bush. Unflinching, never wavering support for liberty against government intervention in any part of our lives."

"Such as the post office and the fire department? Privatize them?"

"Why not?"

"Isolationism?"

"A strong military to protect the homeland. No meddling overseas. No nation building. No U.N."

"Do you believe all that yourself?"

"Yes, with a few softer touches around the edges. Not quite so doctrinaire, I suppose."

"And do you expect to change the Lehrer newspapers with your moderating influence?"

I laughed. "The Chief doesn't take to moderating influences."

"So I've heard. You may be surprised, but I don't disagree with many of your father's positions, Cordelia. I know *This Texas* is a left-of-center publication, but my main job is to attract readers and advertisers. We all have to adjust to the market we serve, wouldn't you agree, David? In my experience, people who use their newspapers or magazines to try to convert people usually fail."

I nodded. "I certainly agree with that."

After a pause, Cory started to get up. "We've taken too much of your time…"

"No, please. There are two matters I want to discuss with you." He turned back to me. "David, *This Texas* wants to do a profile on you, possibly a cover story. May I send my best staff writer to visit with you?"

Before I could answer, Cory interrupted. "He'd be delighted, Drayton. Have your office call Ms. Gaulle and she'll make the arrangements." She stared at me, warning me to stay quiet.

"That's wonderful. Thank you so much, David." He patted me on the arm again as if I had actually answered. "Now, the second thing. Paul, hand me that prospectus." The aide handed him a thick legal document. "As you can see," Philby said, passing the prospectus on to me, "I am not well. I won't be around much longer. I have no heirs. I am going to sell the magazine and use the proceeds for charities I care for. Would you consider making me an offer for the business?"

"Why us?" I said. "It's hardly a natural fit." I resisted opening the prospectus.

"David, I believe you and I have something in common. A view of the world arising from personal misfortune."

I doubt if we have anything at all in common. "We appreciate the opportunity, but I really doubt if Mr. Lehrer would be interested in a Texas magazine, especially one based in Austin."

"Read the prospectus," Philby said. "You may be surprised how well we do at *This Texas*."

❮❮❮❮❮

Later, we had barely settled into the Gulfstream heading to Akron, the three of us, no bed in sight, when Cory said, "I want to buy it."

"Be serious, Cory. Your daddy will never buy a liberal magazine in liberal Austin, Texas."

She smiled. "I thought you knew me better than that by now. I'm the favorite daughter. I get what I want. I got you, didn't I? And now I'm carrying the heir. If I want *This Texas* you can bet your new Maserati that I will have it. So, get busy and figure out how much it's worth and how best to approach Daddy." With that she lay back dramatically on the sofa and said, "And Francie will be the perfect person to run it. Somebody, please get me an orange juice. I need an orange juice."

I opened the prospectus half-heartedly and made some notes. I was seeing a new side of Cory and I didn't like it very much. The honeymoon was definitely over.

"The ratios look good, wouldn't you say, David?" I looked at Francie, who sat beside me, reading over my shoulder. "I've run some numbers. Here, let me send them to you."

"Well, sure, if you'd like." I could understand Francie wanting it, but it was such a long shot.

From her languid pose on the sofa, Cory spoke up, "Pay attention to her, David. Francie studied economics at the Sorbonne. The *Maison des Sciences Économiques*—right, Francie?"

"Mais oui, mon amie."

"And she spent several years as an associate editor at *Paris Match*. You have heard of *Paris Match*?"

"I'm continually amazed by you, Francie." I looked at the French girl. "So you're not just a basketball player."

"Hmm," she said. "Look at page 154. I thought that was interesting."

"And Francie will make a wonderful editor-in-chief for *This Texas*. The Austinites will eat her up. French, beautiful, smart. She'll bring a bit of French sensibility to the magazine, n'est-ce pas, Francois?"

"Comme tu le dis, ma chérie." She tossed her head haughtily and threw her silk scarf over her shoulder.

As Francie had predicted, I did find page 154 interesting. There I read a description of *This Texas'* online business. It not only had developed its own digital magazine and special online features, but its product was good enough to market to other publications. The online business was very profitable. I put the heavy prospectus down and went on my laptop to the *This Texas* website. "Look at this," I said to Francie. "Look what they're doing." *It's all there, all the nuts and bolts to bring the Lehrer newspapers into the twenty-first century.*

ELEVEN

Kingston Lehrer scowled at my fifty-page proposal. Martin had retired, unwillingly, and blamed me. I was ready to see the last of him. But it did mean facing the Chief on my own now, making my *This Texas* pitch. Tom Pearson sat to one side, thumbing through his copy of my proposal. Lehrer shoved the binder across the desk. I caught it before it fell to the floor.

"Don't make me read this," Lehrer said with a scowl. "Tell me what it says."

Of course, he already knew. Cory had spent two hours with him at the house the day before. Tom looked ready to pounce.

"Chief," I began, "this is a recommendation that we make an offer to buy *This Texas*. It's a very profitable Texas magazine. It has a stable of good writers, an outstanding advertiser list, and most importantly, a profitable online division that can transfer its online products seamlessly to other newspapers and magazines."

Tom broke in. "With all due respect to David and his romance with the digital age, I don't give that part much value." He opened the binder and pretended to look at some numbers. "We don't need it. Our papers that can profit from online editions already have them. Why should we take on new debt, to buy a leftist magazine in Austin?"

Lehrer raised his bushy eyebrows. "Why should we, David?"

"We can change the politics, Chief." I slid the proposal back across the desk toward Lehrer. "It's all in here. Our online editions are homemade. No two are alike. Look at the table on page 10. I've compared the features in our editions to our competitors in each market. It's inescapable. We're a generation behind our competitors. We have to protect our markets. Readers are moving more and more to paperless editions." I looked at Tom, not trying to hide my anger. "We do need this. Anybody who knows anything about our papers knows that."

Lehrer looked up and gave me a sharp look. "I don't know that. Are you saying I don't know anything about my papers?"

I sighed. "No, of course not, Chief. Please, just read the proposal. It's a moneymaker."

Lehrer stood up and handed the report back to me. "I know that my daughter is very persuasive, especially to a bridegroom she has enthralled. But you tell her for me that Tom doesn't believe we can afford it. That is right, isn't it, Tom?"

"Absolutely, Chief."

"All right, David. You tell her that. And never bring me a fifty-page report again. I didn't build this enterprise by reading fifty-page reports. I built it with this," he pointed to his head, "and this." He made a fist. "Don't let your love for my daughter cloud your judgment."

❮❮❮❮❮

The next morning, Francie and I stood at the wall of windows in the fitness studio and staff quarters next to our new house, which was still under construction. I could see the outlines of the beech trees shimmering in the morning light. "What's our move-in date?" I asked. Cory had been griping about the delays, demanding the house be finished before the baby came, as if it was somehow my fault.

"Oh, another two months. Well, before little Tony comes."

The sex of my son was definite now. His grandfather was happy. His mother was happy. Only I was unhappy. "Is there something about the house I needed to drive out here for? Because I'm making no decisions about this house. You and Cory work all that out."

She smiled. "No, David. I don't need your opinion on the colors for the nursery. Are you still enjoying the Maserati?"

I'm in no mood to discuss what I enjoy with you. "It's fine."

"Are the hand controls okay? Much better than those detachable rods, I would imagine."

"No, you cannot imagine."

She gave a faint smile. She pulled up two chairs and we sat side by side, staring at the changing shadows in the changing daylight. She broke the silence. "How was your *This Texas* meeting?"

I sniffed. "Not well. I went in there believing Cory had everything greased. She didn't." I smiled ruefully at Francie. "And that was that. Shot down in flames." Fog was rolling over the hills. I could no longer make out the beech trees.

"Cory was afraid of that. She has a plan she wants me to go over with you."

"A plan? With you? She could tell me her plan herself. We sleep in the same bed." That was a lie. In fact, I had moved to the guest room.

"I need my rest for little Tony," Cory had said, "and you toss and turn all night and when you get up early, you wake me up getting into your chair and your leg devices and all that. I can never go back to sleep." She had stroked my cheek. "You do understand, don't you? It won't interfere with our sex life, really, it won't." But, of course, it had. From once or twice or even three times a day on the honeymoon tour, to once every three days when we got back to Akron, to once a week, to who remembers the last time? *Actually, I remember the last time. It was eight days ago at ten fifteen P.M.*

"It's for little Tony," she said, as she watched Pedro move my things into the guest bedroom.

The fog was so heavy now it almost seemed to invade the room. Francie said, "They're weak, David."

"Who's weak? Who do you mean?"

"Tom and Douglas. The only thing they care about is what they'll get for the papers when Mr. Lehrer dies."

"But the trusts won't let them sell the papers."

"Trusts are made to be broken. We've talked about that. Now Douglas and Tom have been visiting with lawyers. We know that."

How do you know? But I knew better; if Francie said she knew then she did.

"We've seen the letter from the law firm they hired in Cleveland. The trusts can be broken, but all the daughters have to agree. That means they have to have Cory's agreement."

"And she'll never agree, right?"

"That's right. She never will."

"So, they can't break the trusts."

"Yes, but they don't know for sure. They hope she will agree. They hope they can convince her. And you're the wild card. What do you want and how much influence do you have over Cory?"

Not much, I thought bitterly. "So, what's the plan?"

She leaned in close and said softly. "Suppose you wanted to sell. Suppose Cory was so in love with you that she would do whatever you wanted? But you wanted something in return."

"To buy *This Texas.*"

"Exactly. You want to modernize the papers. They'll sell for more that way. There will be more money for everyone. Maybe your price for convincing Cory is that you get the online division for yourself."

I thought for a minute. *It might work.* "If only they knew how little influence I have over Cory."

Francie smiled knowingly. "Cory will play her part."

In fact, she was already doing that, whispering to me during Saturday luncheons, speaking admiringly of me to the others, snuggling close to me when we said our goodbyes. All like a girl very much in love, but the act ended as soon as we got in the car and headed back to our separate lives. I had supposed it was to irritate her sisters and deceive her father, but as Francie talked, I understood what Cory had been doing. This had been her plan all along.

"Won't they see through it? They know how stubborn Cory is."

"Oh, Tom and Douglas will buy it. They believe any strong man can bring any woman to submission. And you are a strong man. The fact that Cory has always been so willful will make them enjoy seeing her dominated by you even more. They want to see it so much, they will convince themselves."

I thought about it. "There's no telling how long the old man will live. I'm not sure I can keep up the pretense."

Francis stretched. Her taut muscles rippled under her form-fitting workout suit. "You already are pretending. All you have to do is keep on pretending you are in love with a beautiful woman."

"But..."

"You never were in love with her, were you? Honestly. Were you? You were in love with the idea that legless David Lewis, from Cleburne, Texas, could have one of the most desirable women in the country. That's what you've been in love with, isn't it?"

"No, no. We had something together. I mean we have something. Once the baby comes, we'll have it again."

She patted me on the arm. "No. You won't. Cory wants me to tell you, that part of your relationship is over."

I was stunned. "Over? 'That part' is over and she sent you to tell me?"

"You know how Cory dislikes confrontation. She doesn't want to have to discuss it with you. Not now, not ever. You will have a very happy marriage. Just without sex."

"So, what was I, just a sperm donor?"

"Much more than that. You're a talented newspaperman. It's a business deal, David. One you were very happy to enter into. When little Tony comes, you will be a rich man."

"This was never part of the deal."

"You never discussed it. What are you going to do about it now? Divorce Cory and throw everything away? Think of it this way: Cory and you are partners. Together you'll build a media empire for your son to inherit."

"Maybe so. But to be in a loveless marriage...for the rest of my life?"

"Cory doesn't expect you to abstain from sex, just that you be discreet. That TV weather girl, the one you were living with? My sources say she hasn't found anyone. Why don't you spend some time in Chicago?"

"You know about Jan?"

"*Oh, ma naïve,* I have a thick *dossier* on you, all the way back to high school—your father deserting his family, your mother's death, your affairs in college, your scrapes in the military, every byline you had at the *Post,* your bar fights in Cleveland. I've got a copy of your concealed handgun application. I know your medical history and that of three generations of your family. All that and much more. You don't think Cordelia Lehrer would select you without knowing everything about you? So, yes, I know about Pam. My detective says she lives alone, sees no one. Look her up. It will do you good." She handed me a coffee for the trip into town. "But before you do that, take Douglas and Tom to lunch. A nice long lunch."

I walked to the door. "What kind of family have I gotten mixed up with?"

"A very rich one."

❦❦❦❦❦

I tried to talk to Cory about what she called, "our new arrangement," but she refused to discuss it with me. "Get over all that and get on with the plan," was all she would say.

I stepped into Douglas' office. "Let's have lunch. You and Tom and me. We need to talk."

He looked up with a sour expression on his face. "Talk? What about?"

"The Cavs, of course." I went on in a low voice. "The future. We need to talk about the future."

He looked at his phone. "I'm booked up this week…"

"I talked to Amy. You can squeeze this in and still make your tee time. She's already set it up at the club."

"Damned presumptuous," he muttered. "What about Tom?"

"Tom's on board."

"This better not make me late."

I smiled. "I won't let it."

At noon, Douglas led the way to the elevator. No one spoke. Downstairs, one of Dakila's many nephews sat behind the wheel of a black Mercedes S600. Doug and Tom got in the backseat.

"I'll meet you out there," I said.

Pedro waited for me in the Maserati. I slipped into the leather passenger seat beside him and swung my legs into the tight cabin. Pedro grinned with anticipation. "Ready?" He loved to drive the *Quattroporte.*

"Leave 'em in the dust, Pedro."

He down shifted and the Maserati leapt forward with a roar, leaving the Mercedes far behind.

"Tom's driver seems cautious."

"Oh, he is. He almost got fired when *Señor* Douglas found a scratch on the rear bumper."

"Did he do it?"

"Who knows? The *jefe* thought so and that's what matters."

"Is he another one of Dakila's nephews?"

"*Sí.*"

"So, he's your cousin?"

Pedro swung up onto the interstate and accelerated sharply around a car waiting for oncoming traffic. It was like riding on a bullet in flight. "Sidney? I never met him before he arrived here. Dakila's nephews are more like *ahijados*. Godchildren. But only while they are in this country, in this place, working for this family. When they return home, they are no longer *ahijados*. No, Sidney is not my cousin."

"Sidney doesn't sound Filipino."

"It isn't. It's the name *Señor* Douglas gives all his drivers. He says it is easier to pronounce."

He pulled up to the front entrance of the club and asked, "Shall I wait?"

"No need for that. I'll drive myself home. Can you catch a ride with Sidney?"

Pedro grinned. "Of course. We're family." He handed the key to an eager valet attendant.

I crawled out of the car and waited for the Mercedes. When it finally arrived, Sidney hopped out and opened the back door for Douglas.

"Be back here at six, Sidney," Douglas ordered brusquely. "On the dot."

We walked into the anteroom. The club was not as expensive-looking as you might expect for the shrine to American golf. I had been here a few times when Cory's friends had invited us so they could meet her war hero husband.

The headwaiter showed us to a table in a secluded corner of the grill. Douglas ordered a gin martini up and I had a beer. Tom asked for a cup of hot tea with lemon. While we waited for our drinks, Tom spoke up, his mouth pursed as if he could already taste the lemon. "How is Cordelia handling pregnancy?"

"Like a pro. She's handling it like a pro."

"Hmm. That's good. I wondered because she's always been a bit of a dilettante. Running off to St. Louis to go to school when she could have been at Wellesley or Bryn Mawr." He licked his thin lips. "Of course, she met you down there, so I guess that's the silver lining, isn't it?"

I didn't say anything, but Douglas grunted, "Silver lining. Indeed."

Tom continued, "Then all that time in Paris, doing God knows what. Now she's back here with you, a real newspaperman."

"Knocked up with a grandchild for the old man.," Douglas said sourly. He paused for the waiter to set down our drinks. The waiter sloshed a bit of hot water onto the tablecloth. He apologized and mopped it up hastily. Douglas watched with amused detachment. He turned to me and raised his glass in a mock salute. "To the expectant mother and her proud husband." He turned to Tom, who was nervously pouring hot water over his teabag. "David got the only fertile Lehrer daughter. How lucky is that?" He looked me in the eye. "Tell me, why we are here? I'd like to know."

"I think it's time we talked about the future of KL Media."

Douglas finished his drink and motioned to the waiter. Douglas waved off the menu and said, "The blackened pork chop for me."

The waiter turned to Tom. "Mr. Pearson?"

Tom answered, "A chicken sandwich, plain bread, no mayo, no chips, and a cup of fruit."

The waiter looked at me. "Of those two, I believe I'll take the pork chop."

"You eat pork?" Douglas asked. He lathered butter on a dinner roll. "Does your religion permit that?"

"I'm Catholic. You were at my wedding, remember?"

"Well, Lewis is one of those ambiguous names. It's often changed from Levi or something like that. There was a Lewis at school. Kept kosher, poor little bastard. I thought maybe you were just giving the old man his Catholic wedding. We all had to do it."

"I'm a cradle Catholic."

"I suppose that's better than Jewish, but I'm not sure."

"You're a saint, Douglas." *I'm going to kick your ass if you keep this up.*

We started on the lunch. The blackened pork chop was crisp and savory. Douglas ate his quickly and pushed his plate away. "Is this about that Texas magazine you want us to buy? Because if it is, I agree completely with Tom. It's not for us."

Tom ate half of his sandwich and motioned for the waiter to take the rest away. I leaned forward and spoke confidentially to the two men. "We have to make plans."

"We do?"

"Yes. We three. The men in this family."

Douglas looked attentive for the first time. "Plans about what?" He looked down at his watch. "It's almost two."

"We have to make plans for the day when the Chief is no longer with us. I haven't been here long, but I've seen enough to know that the business should have been sold long ago. Ten years ago, it would have brought twice what it will now. What's done is done, but it's not too late to add value to the papers so that when the day does come, we'll get the highest price possible. That's why *This Texas* is such an opportunity."

Tom spoke up. "You know the old man has set up trusts so KL Media can never be sold."

"The trusts? I've had my lawyer looking into it. It can be undone…" I paused for effect, "…if all three daughters agree."

Douglas and Tom exchanged a look. *So David has a lawyer too,* I guessed they were thinking.

I went on, "If the two of you can deliver your wives' consent, then I can deliver Cory."

Douglas laughed. "We are talking about the same Cordelia, aren't we?"

I let myself smirk. "The lady is in love with me. She's pregnant by me. Her father respects me as a newspaperman. I'm the family expert. I can convince her to sell. That's a fact. No ifs, ands, or buts." I sat back and let them digest that. *I would have been a convincing lawyer.* I fiddled with my napkin as if trying to decide what to say next. "But why would I want to do that?"

"A sale would make Cordelia even wealthier," Tom offered.

"That would be hers. What's in it for me?" I asked.

Tom glanced at Douglas who said, "What do you have in mind?"

I lowered my voice and they leaned in to hear me. "I want the *This Texas* online business."

Douglas sat back with a sniff. "I have no idea what you are talking about."

Tom spoke up, mimicking my whisper, "David wants us to buy *This Texas* and when KL Media is sold, he gets the magazine's online business. Sort of a broker's commission. Is that it?"

"Bingo!" *Tom's smarter than I thought.* "And I want a free hand running the newspapers in the meantime. No games. No sniping. I run them like a business and you back me up with the Chief." I sat back in my chair. "I don't give a fuck about *This Texas.* That's Cory's new toy. She wants to play with it for a while. It'll keep her out of trouble. But it is very profitable." I could almost see the wheels turning in Tom's MBA/CPA brain. "It'll add a lot more to the value of KL Media than what we pay for it. Giving me the online business will be the best investment you ever made."

Tom nodded. "I see where you're going. It might just make sense." He frowned. "It's a shame, but I've pretty well committed myself to the Chief that buying is a bad idea."

"How about this? I'll send you some information you didn't have before. Advertising data. Maybe there's enough there to change your mind." It was a dozen pages of SEC gobbledygook only a CPA could understand.

Tom brightened. He saw the path I was offering. "That's good. I'll study the new information." He smiled and turned to Douglas. "I'd say this might work. What do you think?"

He snorted. "None of that shit matters. What matters is whether David can deliver Cordelia's consent. If you can convince me of that, then we have a deal."

"Would my wife's voice convince you?" I touched audio/play on my phone and handed it to Douglas. As he listened, he broke into a wide grin. He was listening to us reading from Francie's script:

Me: "Cory, you trust me, don't you?"

Cory: "You know I do, baby."

Me: "There's going to come a time pretty soon when your daddy won't be here anymore."

Cory: (Sorrowfully) "I know, I know."

Me: "When that happens, and baby, I hope it's years off, but when it does happen, we'll have to decide what to do with the business."

Cory: "You don't mean sell the papers?"

Me: "Maybe. Maybe it'll be best for you, and for our baby. I promise you I'll figure out what's best. I promise you that."

Cory: "I know you will, baby. I trust you. I'll do whatever you say is best. I love you so much."

Me: "Good girl. Now give us a kiss."

Douglas handed Tom the phone. "Listen to that. It sounds as if Cordelia has met her master at last." He raised his glass. "Congratulations, David. I never would have thought it possible. How did you do it?"

Cory's a good actress. I almost believed her myself. But then I remembered our "new arrangement." *Bullshit.* I choked down my anger and smiled at my fat-ass brother-in-law. "The love of a good man," I said.

Douglas laughed. "Is that what they call it?" He scribbled his signature on the check. "This one's on me."

❮❮❮❮❮

The good feelings all 'round were evident at the next Saturday lunch at The Heath. Cory's sisters gushed and generally acted as if we were all the closest of friends. The other couples listened attentively to the Chief and me as we discussed the business world and its impact on the papers. Douglas even roused himself enough to ask a question or two.

After lunch, Cory's sisters cornered her. "Can we see the new house this afternoon?" Ginny asked.

"And tell us about the baby. When is he due? It is a boy, I hear," Reggie said.

Cory let herself be dragged off to Maude's Hill to give them a tour. As they left, she blew me a kiss. "Won't be long, darling," she said.

The four men went outside. Douglas practiced golf shots and Tom stood near him fiddling with his phone.

Lehrer and I sat at the other end of the terrace. The old man said with amusement, "You're all ganging up on me. What is it?"

"Tom's changed his mind about the magazine. The magazine down in Texas."

"Ah, 'Cordelia's Folly.' How did you convince him?"

"I gave him some new data. It can be big for us."

Lehrer sighed, not unhappily, but with resignation. "I have never been able to deny Cordelia anything. She's my favorite, you know. And now with little Tony on the way..." He patted me on the arm. "I like you, David. You know that. Also, I trust you. You remember your promise? You promised that you would watch over my little girl for me?"

"Of course, Chief. Always."

⸨⸨⸨⸨⸨

Driving back to town, Cory said, "The tour of Maude's Hill went very well."

"Tell me."

"They think you're wonderful. You're so wise. You understand everything about the newspaper business. You're a financial genius, too, according to Tom. I am very lucky to have you. The family is very lucky to have you. And whatever business decisions I make, I should always listen to your advice before I do anything."

I laughed derisively. "If they only knew." I looked over at her. She was pregnant and glowing. "And what did you say?"

"You would have been proud of me. I batted my eyes and said I understood completely, and that I could never, ever go against your advice."

"I advise we have sex tonight."

She pouted. "Don't talk like that."

⸨⸨⸨⸨⸨

Awaiting her delivery date, Cory took up residence in the company suite in Cleveland, the same suite where we had spent the night when she came looking for me at *The Post*. She had been in Cleveland only a week when she went into labor. She was rushed to her VIP suite at Fairview Hospital Birthing Center where her doctors waited in attendance. Francie called me in Chicago from the hospital.

"You need to be here when the family arrives. Give Jan a kiss and get your ass back here."

TWELVE

Two years later, the Chief burst into my office, glaring and red-faced. "David!" he yelled.

When I took over Martin's office and title, I kept his retro furniture. *Poor Martin. For some reason, he hadn't seen it coming.* I also inherited the privileged back entrance to the Chief's office, which he used a lot.

"Good morning, Chief," I said. "Would you like to see new photos of Tony?" I brought up yesterday's snaps of Kingston Lehrer's two-year-old grandson. I refreshed pictures of the heir daily on my computer. It never failed to calm the old man.

Lehrer leaned over my shoulder and directed, "Go back. That's a good one. That one, with Buster." Buster was the pony he had bought little Tony on his first birthday. "Tony's the image of his mother, isn't he?"

I agreed. *He is good-looking. He has her dark eyes and fair complexion. Unfortunately, he has my hair and chin.*

"Where is Cordelia?"

"In Austin, calling on advertisers."

"She should be here."

"She's learning the business. She and Francoise have gotten their ad metrics up. *This Texas* is more profitable than ever. That's good, isn't it?"

"I suppose. But I worry about Tony, both his parents gone so much."

I smiled. "He's not hurting for family, not with you in charge." Tony spent more time at the big house than he did at home. Lehrer had converted a room next to his study into a playroom for Tony and the child's nanny brought him to see his grandfather every day. The Chief had taken to going home for lunch with Tony, and often he didn't make it back to the office in the afternoon.

"Did you need something, Chief?"

He looked blank, then looked down at the copy of the *Velda Sun* in his hands. "Yes, yes, I remember. There was a man in the office when I came in this morning. His name is Bert something or the other, but he is from Velda, Texas. Look at this." He opened the paper to the center section. There was a large double page ad for a discount store. "He says he is our largest advertiser, or he used to be. And he says he's pulling his advertising and we won't get it back as long as we have a gay editor."

"Charlton Denning? He's complaining that Charlton Denning is gay?"

"Yes. Is he? Have you allowed a queer to be editor of one of my papers?"

I thought for a minute. *Everyone in Velda has always known Denning is gay.* "Beats me, Chief. Maybe he is. He's also got one of the best profit margins of any of our papers."

"I don't care about that! My position and my newspapers' position on homosexuality is very clear. It's a regrettable, but curable, condition. Homos are to be pitied and helped. They should not serve in the military. They should not be given security clearance, since they are so easily blackmailed." He paused for breath. "And most of all, a faggot should never work for one of my newspapers, much less be the editor of one."

Oh, God, he believes all that.

"This fellow is threatening to organize a boycott. Can you imagine the field day our competitors will have with that?"

Yes, I could imagine it. The mainstream press would enjoy a laugh at Kingston Lehrer's expense. I could see the headline: Conservative Newspaper Chain Boycotted for Being Too Gay-Friendly.

"Chief, let me talk to him. Maybe he's just blowing off steam. Is he in your office?"

Lehrer threw the newspaper down on my desk. "No! He left. I thanked him and told him that had I known about it, I would never have allowed a homosexual to be one of my editors." He glared at me. "This is your fault. You should never have let this happen. Go down there and get rid of that vermin. That's an order!"

There was no point in arguing. Nor trying to explain to Kingston Lehrer that Charlton Denning had been in Velda long before my time and that you can't fire a man for being gay these days. I'd have to find a way to do it as quietly as possible.

❮❮❮❮❮

"It didn't go well," I said to Cory. "His lawyer's threatening to sue." We had met in the general aviation lobby at the Austin airport. I was in Austin for a few days and she was on her way to Akron. We tried to time our travels so that one of us could be home with little Tony. The trip to Velda had been an exception.

"You'll work it out. You always do." She watched one of the KL pilots with her luggage. "Careful with that. There are jars of peach jam from Fburg in there."

"Yes, ma'am." He smiled. Cory always got a smile from any man.

"What the fuck is Fburg?" I asked.

"Fredricksburg, you Yankee. In the Hill Country. It's the source of the best peaches, better than Georgia's."

"Yippee."

She pretended not to have heard me. "How's little Tony?"

"Your father is leaving the office at noon so he can spend the afternoons with him."

"Really? I imagine you welcome that."

"Oh, he's still working. Except now he saves everything up and dumps it on me in the morning. Before coffee."

"You always have been useless until you've had your three cups of morning coffee." She turned to leave, looked around, saw people staring at us, and kissed me on the cheek. She whispered, "I hope you're getting everything you need."

I shook my head. "You're a piece of work, Cory."

"I'm just thinking of you, dear. We need our number one newspaper-man in top form."

"Very thoughtful of you." I saw the pilot signal he was ready to leave. "Off you go. Do you ever think about our honeymoon airplane rides?"

"That was so long ago, it seems like another life."

"You look good, Cory. Austin agrees with you."

She stopped for a moment and stared at the Lear, already on her journey home. "I love it. I love the magazine. We're making a big hit of it, aren't we?"

"You'd better. The Chief still hasn't accepted that he owns a liberal magazine in Austin. He'd dump it in a second if it weren't for you."

"Well, that will never happen, will it?" And then, she was on her way.

ᘓᘓᘓᘓᘓ

The Lexus she and I shared in Austin was parked at the curb. I popped the trunk and retrieved my driving rods. I stowed my carry-on in the backseat and set about attaching the control rods to the pedals. For some reason, the Lexus brake pedal was slightly out of my reach and I was always cursing by the time I got it in place. *I need a car with hand controls in Austin! No, no I don't. Do I?* And then the rod slipped into place and I forgot about it until next time, the same way I forgot about Cory when she wasn't there. Then when I saw her again, like today, my anger at how casually she had rejected me enveloped me and it was all I could do to keep the bile down.

I drove to *This Texas*. I wanted to check on the online division's relocation to the new offices. *Not much will have happened if it's like everything else I'd experienced so far in Austin.*

The old offices were bare and drab, furnished with KL leftovers Francie had found in some company warehouse. Tom had bargained so hard that a furious Philby stripped the offices of everything, not just the carpet and furniture, but the wall coverings, light fixtures and the statue of a young nude boy that had presided over the koi pond in the shaded patio outside his office. He also took the koi.

Anna Kaye Nordstrom met me at the entrance. Anna was a public relations expert who knew the people one needed to know to do business in Austin. She tried once to explain the labyrinth of Austin politics to me. I just threw up my hands. "I don't want to know!"

Francie had met Anna somewhere and hired her to introduce Cory to the Austin political and society scene. She must have done an excellent job because Cory was on the A-list for just about every social or charitable event that came along. "That wasn't too hard, lover," the athletic blonde had told me. "Austin is very egalitarian when it comes to money. If you have it, they love you; if you're willing to part with some, like your wife is, they adore you."

I kissed Anna on the cheek. The young intern at the desk was watching us closely. "This all looks the same as the last time I was here," I said.

"Your wife has finally approved the interior designs. Things will look different the next time you're down." I followed her into the bare expanse that had been Philby's office. She took my hand. "Sit down. You look terrible."

Francie had found an old partners' desk, which she placed next to the windows that opened to the koi-less koi pond. There was a chair for Cory and for Francie, each on opposite sides of the desk. I collapsed into Cory's chair. *Is that the scent of her perfume or am I imagining it?* "My legs are killing me. Get me some water, will you?" *These days, just meeting with Cory is exhausting.* I found the bottle of Vikes in my satchel and took out four.

Anna brought me the water and snatched two of the pills out of my hand. "Two's enough, lover, however bad you feel. What's wrong?"

I gulped the Vikes. "Oh, just the usual. I've been in a one-horse town, firing an editor."

"What did he do?"

"A hanging offense, in the Chief's eyes. He's gay. You can't have a gay editor, especially in Velda, Texas. Then the editor gets himself a lawyer who says he's going to sue. I gave the lawyer a lift to Austin. I thought it might help, but it didn't. I had to listen to him all the way down here."

"A lawyer? Velda? Is his name Cuinn?"

I rubbed my eyes. "Something like that. Why? Do you know him?" She stood behind me and rubbed my neck. Her strong fingers found the strained muscles. "Hmmmm, second career for you, Anna."

"I do know the lawyer. His name is Don Cuinn. In fact, I'm meeting him for coffee later."

"Is he a good lawyer?"

"Yes. Very good. Don't underestimate him."

"If he's any good, what's he doing in Velda?"

"It's a long story. He's had a tough time."

"Is he an old boyfriend?"

She smiled enigmatically.

I stretched my neck. "Talk to him, will you? I want to settle this thing."

"Sure, lover. That's what I'm here for."

Among other things, I thought, leaning back. I don't know what she said or did, but by that weekend, Cuinn and I had a deal. Velda's outcast would move to Austin and do freelance work for *This Texas,* starting with a local scandal that Francie put him to work investigating.

I freed myself from Anna's hands. "Where's my editor?" I asked.

"Francie's at a seminar at the LBJ School. She's one of the presenters."

I didn't ask what the topic was. I didn't care. "How's she doing?"

"Austin is in love with her. That French accent, that athlete's body. She's got a group of ex-athletes, women basketball players mostly, that she runs with. And of course, she's so smart."

"Whatever. As long as she makes her budget." I looked around the room. "What did Philby do with all the stuff he took out of here?"

She sat on the edge of the desk, showing me some leg. "He sold it all to the Ransom Center at the University."

I waited for the Vikes' warm flush. The years since Iraq had taught me something about how to manage pain. "What do they want with Philby's junk?"

"Oh, lover, they'll buy anything. Someday, they'll do an exhibit on *This Texas* as it was in its golden years."

"Before Kingston Lehrer got his hands on it."

"Precisely." She took my water glass. "Everything in Austin has a golden past somebody's trying to recreate."

"Why bother? As far as I can tell, Austin's still a provincial backwater that happens to be hot right now."

She laughed. "You sound like that Aggie governor we used to have." She sat in my lap and held my head against her body. I closed my eyes.

"You have an appointment with Hayden in the morning. Will you feel like doing that? I could put him off."

"Oh, hell, I'll be fine. As soon as Dr. Vike does his work. How's Hayden coming on the movie rights?"

"He's got some offers. That's why he wants a meeting with you."

My profile in *This Texas* had gone viral. My phone rang for a month with requests for interviews, TV appearances and talk shows. Everyone wanted a piece of the war hero who boxed and ran marathons and had snagged one of the most beautiful women in America. I needed help. Francie found Hayden Freund. He was my agent, and a good one. He had guided me through the first maelstrom. That led to a best-selling book, which Cal Gentry at *The Post* ghostwrote for me. Now Hayden was reviewing movie deals based on the book. I was thinking about forming a company to create content for the cable network I was about to buy. *By the time I'm through, KL Media will be so big, the papers won't even matter.*

Anna helped me up from the chair. "Do you want to go see the boys' new offices? They love them."

"They'd better, as much as you spent."

After we bought *This Texas*, one of my first decisions was to relocate the online business to its own offices. The techies liked the idea and it would give me more flexibility. If Cory and Francie failed, or the Chief lost patience with the magazine, or, even more likely, if Cory just got bored with it, I could sell the magazine but keep the online business.

Anna managed the move of *KL Online* to a popular location downtown near start-ups and tech businesses. When we entered the new offices, I waved at the crew and shook hands with Peter Hays, the online manager. The boys swarmed around Anna, laughing at her jokes in geek fashion. Anna was in her thirties, tall and movie star gorgeous. She was my techies' housemother. She had gotten them the open office layout they wanted, the break room with billiard and ping pong tables and three sixty-five-inch television sets locked into sports channels. It was all working. Profits at *KL Online* were rocketing.

I went over the numbers with Peter in the conference room, the only private room in the place. He critiqued his employees; I asked a few questions and agreed he should fire a couple of underachievers, hire some new guy, and go after a large Houston account—the usual stuff.

When we finally left, Anna looked at me and said, "You look exhausted, lover. Do you want to go home and take a nap?"

"Yeah," I said wearily. "Let's do that." *I'm too tired for sex, but we'll get around to that.* We usually did. I didn't doubt that Francie saw Anna's physical attraction as a side benefit; she knew me pretty well by now. She expected Anna and me to hit it off. She was right. Anna and I did hit it off. We ran a 10-K together. We talked sports. She was easygoing, quiet when I didn't want to talk and a no-nonsense sex partner. My stumps didn't put her off. She joked about them in a way even Cory hadn't done. *Here I am. Let's have some fun,* she seemed to say. *No obligations at all.* It should have been perfect, but of course it wasn't. She wasn't Cory.

Cory bought a penthouse on the top floor of a new downtown high rise a block off the lake. "I know it's expensive," Cory told me, "but it's marvelous—good size, fantastic views. I've already been offered five percent more than I paid."

"Sell it," I said.

Francie had bought a studio apartment twenty floors below. "It's all I need," she said. "And I have a great view of the alley and some homeless people living out of the dumpster. When I feel closed in or want company, I can go up to the pool."

The penthouse featured views from every room. The living room had a panoramic view to the south and west. The master bedroom, Cory's bedroom, on the east side, had its own balcony and an unblocked sunrise view. The guest bedroom, my bedroom, on the west side had a window wall facing south. My office adjoined my bedroom. The expansive living room was separated from the gourmet kitchen by a long granite counter. The kitchen had two deep sinks and a chef's prep area. A walk-in wine closet was on one side of the kitchen. The living room was flanked by a stone fireplace on the east wall and an oversized wall-mounted television on the west. Floor-to-ceiling windows and sliding glass doors led from the living room to a balcony that spanned its length.

I dropped my duffle in my bedroom and looked out. The Catholic college's Victorian tower sat proudly on a hill in the distance. Beyond that, the flat landscape was filling up with rooftops as far as the eye could see. I collapsed on the bed and unharnessed my T22s. I tossed them on the floor and lay back.

Anna was rustling about in the kitchen. She returned a few minutes later with two glasses of white wine. "I hope you want Montrachet. Would it kill you rich people to keep some red wine in that monster wine closet?"

I rose and took the glass. "According to my wife, it's the best French Burgundy you can get. I've gotten used to it." I washed down two more Vikes with the wine and sighed. The pain was going away and I knew I'd sleep soundly and maybe wake up refreshed. *Ready for another day totin' that barge.*

Anna covered me with a blanket and lay down beside me. She massaged my legs through the blanket. "Sleep, lover. Anna's here."

THIRTEEN

I stood on the terrace of manor house at The Heath and looked over the expanse of lawn between the main house and the stone barn. The lawn had been converted into a fantasy play land for Tony's fourth birthday party. Little boys ran from one attraction to another as a stilt-walker, clowns and jugglers performed for them. A carousel turned to the sound of a calliope. Its vividly painted horses bobbed up and down in cadence with the music that echoed across the lawn to where I stood. Buster, Tony's pony, waited patiently for the boy. The groom had brought in a half-dozen other ponies and some boys were riding in the training circle, carefully attended to by college students hired for the day.

Douglas stood next to me. He motioned at the scene. "There won't be anything to sell if the old fool lives through many more of your son's birthdays." At the other end of the terrace, Dakila had supervised the placement of Lehrer's big dining chair where the patriarch sat smiling. He moved slower these days, the once athletic body finally giving in to old age. Cory sat beside him, pointing at a boy screeching with pleasure held high in the air by the stilt-walker. Cory and her father laughed.

A Filipino waiter came by with a tray of champagne. I took a glass. "It keeps him out of our hair, doesn't it? He hardly comes into the office."

"Well, that is good," Douglas admitted. "He does love his grandson."

In fact, Tony was at his grandfather's every day, brought down from Maude's Hill by his governess. Betha Casey was a widow in her fifties, recruited by Father Joe. Tony ate lunch with his grandfather and they spent the afternoon playing games or reading or talking. He spoiled Tony, but Mrs. Casey was there, unafraid of Lehrer where the boy was concerned. "He's had enough cake, Mr. Lehrer," she would say, or, "It's time for his lessons. No pony ride today." Then they would troop off to the playroom where a young teacher from St. Theresa's Elementary School instructed the boy. He was reading at four. One afternoon a week, Father Joe came to instruct Tony in the Catechism. He sat through Mass, in his grandfather's lap at first, but later in a little chair of his own, kneeling and bowing and making the sign of the cross and saying the Our Father."

"Cordelia looks good," Douglas said. He yawned. "It must be difficult."

"How so?"

"Her being in Texas so much. Keeping the magic and so on."

I clasped him on the shoulder. "Don't worry yourself. The magic is still there." What I didn't say: *Cory's leaving for Austin as soon as Tony opens his presents.*

Food carts appeared. The boys squealed and ran around them. The smell of grilling burgers and hot dogs drifted up to where we stood.

"Still, every time I ask, she's in Austin."

I replied, "It's amazing what she and Francie have done with the magazine. Have you read it?"

Douglas shook his head. "I make it a strict policy not to read any KL publications."

"You'd be surprised. *This Texas* is good. And profitable."

"Yes. Tom gets almost giddy with pleasure when he tells me how well it's doing. And the online business as well. You like that, don't you? Your commission?"

I grunted noncommittally.

He put down his empty glass on the stone ledge that bordered the terrace. "You were right. Tom says our value has gone up by fifty percent. Congratulations," he said insincerely.

"Thank you," I replied in the same tone.

He spoke softly. "The Chief doesn't look well, does he? His departure can't be far off. All the more reason for you to be careful."

"Careful? In what way?"

"Your trips to Chicago. I understand, of course. When the cat's away and all that. But I would hate for some indiscretion on your part to bring, uh, discord, into your marriage. That would be unfortunate for everyone, including you and your precious online business."

"You're a thoughtful brother-in-law Douglas." I took his coat by the lapels, pulling him even closer. "What I do in Chicago is my business. But just so you know, nothing has changed between Cory and me." I straightened his lapels, brushed them off and stood back. "There. Better?"

He stumbled a little and grimaced. "At least you didn't hit me with a low blow this time."

Cory waved at me and I waved back. "My wife needs me. It's time to cut the birthday cake. But any time you want to put on the gloves again, say the word."

As I walked away he called after me, "We're depending on you, David."

《《《《《

A few days after the birthday party, there was a soft rap at my bedroom door. I sat up in bed and checked the time on my phone. I had been late getting back into Akron and had overslept.

"What is it?"

The door cracked open and a voice said, "It's me. Mrs. Casey."

I pulled the covers over my stumps. "Yes?"

"Mr. Lewis, Tony is up and watching television. He tried to make himself breakfast. Where is Tala, do you know? She doesn't seem to be here. Which is odd because she's always here when I arrive. She always has Tony up and dressed and his breakfast ready, but I can't find her."

"Call over and ask Pedro. Maybe she's sick." My driver Pedro and his Filipino wife, Tala, had moved into the staff quarters next to our house on Maude's Hill. Tala was our maid and cook.

"I called Pedro, Mr. Lewis. There's no answer."

"Pedro didn't answer his cell?"

"No, sir. I left a message."

Now that's odd. "Take care of Tony, will you? I'll get dressed and find out what's going on."

I was putting on my T22s when my phone rang. The caller ID read *King Lear*. "Yes, Chief? I don't want to cut you short, but I've got a little problem up here. I can't seem to reach Pedro."

"I know, David. That's why I'm calling."

"You know? What's going on?"

"Get down here as quickly as you can. Bring Tony. I don't want him alone."

"He's not alone. Mrs. Casey is here."

"Well bring her, too."

"What? Tell me…"

He interrupted impatiently. "Here. Come down right away." The phone went dead.

A half hour later, the three of us made the short drive down the winding road to the main house. Watching me nervously Mrs. Casey said, "Did I tell you about the guard?"

"No? What about the guard?"

"There were new men at the gate this morning. They wore badges. Not the usual Asian people. They wouldn't let me in until they called Mr. Lehrer. I suppose he told them it was all right to let me in because they did. They had the gate locked, Mr. Lewis, which I thought was unusual."

"Everything this morning is unusual, Mrs. Casey. But we'll get to the bottom of it."

The Chief was waiting for us in the drive. *Another first.* "Take Tony inside," I said to the nanny.

"Yes, yes, do that," the Chief said. He turned to me and said, "You and I have to talk. Come with me."

I followed the old man, newly energized by whatever had happened, into his study—a windowless room, deep inside the house, with soundproof walls. It had been the gangster Nose's safe room, built to withstand machine gun fire.

Lehrer closed the door and motioned to a leather chair. He sat beside me, not behind his desk. His eyes fluttered wildly. "It's awful."

"What happened, Chief?"

He looked nervously at the door. "Dakila came to my study yesterday. He threatened me."

"Threatened you? Dakila? Threatened you? How?"

"Last week he asked for an increase in what I pay him. You may not know, but I pay Dakila a lump sum to provide all the household services here—butlers, maids, gardeners, drivers, all of that. He brings in his people, who he says are his relatives. They're not, of course. Most are undocumented. It's been clear from the beginning that he was to take care of any immigration problems and withholding for taxes. Tom signed off on it. It's all perfectly proper." He sighed and fell back into his chair. His aging face was sown with wrinkles. But as he talked, his nervousness and fear were replaced by fury.

"He wanted more money?"

"Wanted? Demanded! He said everything was more expensive. Relatives were harder to get. There were greater risks with the new president. I had to double what he was being paid, or there would be trouble."

"What kind of trouble?"

"I thought he meant government trouble, which would be bad enough, but then I realized he was threatening us—my family, my girls, little Tony."

"What did you do?"

"What could I do? I agreed. Then I called the sheriff and told him what had happened. By now the Dakila family is on its way home. The sheriff gave them a choice. Be on the next flight out of the country or go to jail while immigration decided what to do with them."

"So they're all gone?"

"One hopes. But Dakila has connections. There's a Filipino Mafia, did you know? Criminals who may try to take revenge on this family."

"That explains the deputies at the gate."

"Yes. My main concern at the moment is my family—my daughters and Tony." He pulled himself out of the chair and stood behind his desk. "And my daughters' husbands of course. I want all of you here in this house, with me, where we will all be safe until this danger has passed."

Instinctively, I stood up. "Cordelia is in Texas."

"Go get her. Bring her home. As quickly as you can."

CCCCC

I waved at the concierge at the Austin condo and took the penthouse elevator to the top floor. The Lear had made a fast flight. The apartment was quiet. I decided to rest before telling Cory the news. I was pretty sure she'd resist going back to Akron. I took off my T22s and closed my eyes. I don't know how long I was asleep.

A noise from the other end of the apartment woke me. I could hear Cory's voice. *Somehow the Filipinos found her already? There's no time to put on my T22s!* I hoisted myself onto my chair. I reached my bedroom door then remembered my gun. I took the handgun out of my nightstand and put it in my lap. I wheeled across the living room toward the voices coming from Cory's bedroom. Moonlight streamed through the tall glass windows. The door to Cory's bedroom was closed. I rolled as close as I could. I picked up my gun and rammed the door with my chair. It flew open.

A figure leaped at me out of the darkness. I was back in Iraq. Everything went black. I don't know how long I blacked out, a few seconds maybe, but when I came to I had my gun in my hand. A lifeless figure lay on the floor in front of me. The moonlight lit the figure. It was Francie.

I had killed Francoise Gaulle.

PART TWO
TRIAL

FOURTEEN

Donnie Cuinn sat in a wooden lawn chair on the back porch watching the sunrise cut long shadows off the pump jacks on the other side of the fence. The chair needed painting and so did the pump jacks. He would remind the oil company it needed to take better care of their equipment on Elmer Thorpe's lease when one of Elmer's leases came up for renewal. He rubbed his hand over the smooth worn finish of the wooden chair. *That can wait another year.*

Mornings were the best time in the Texas Panhandle, better even than dusk in the summer when the winds died down and desert-like coolness spread over the prairie and even in August you needed a sweater. No, mornings were the best, before he made the journey from Antelope City to his office, a few miles away in Velda, and began the daily task of practicing law.

He liked it here. He had converted the old Thorpe store, part of a fee given to him by his first client, a grateful Elmer Thorpe, into his home. There was plenty of room. The store's counter was a fine breakfast bar. He had updated the old kitchen and one of the bathrooms with money from a fee for handling an estate a few years earlier. He had his own water well, deep and cold water, so he didn't have to drink the noxious stuff from Velda. And, of course, there was this porch, where he could get his bearings before going to work. His cell phone rang. He let it go to voicemail. *It's probably Eugene, reminding me we're having breakfast at the Greeks'.* The phone stopped, then rang again. This time he looked at the Caller ID. It was Anna Kaye Nordstrom. He put down his coffee and answered.

"Good morning, A.K.," he said. As far as he knew, he was the only one who called her that. To everyone else she was Anna. He'd started saying A.K. back when they were a couple. *That was a long time ago. Why did I start calling her A.K.? Can't remember.* "You know this is my navel-contemplating time."

"Good morning, lover." He loved her sugary Central Texas accent. "I know this is when you recharge from your high-pressure life up there in Velda, but I need to talk to you."

"Did you know that Elmer's Number 1 pump jack pumps twelve times a minute and the Number 2 only pumps half that?"

"Something to do with the hydraulic pressure I imagine."

"So, you're not just a pretty face."

"Lover, you have no idea."

"Oh, I have some idea." He paused and let himself picture her. "What's up in the last bastion of socialism in the free world?"

"Austin is fine, but I did want to talk to you about David Lewis."

"The Bionic Man?" He knew he had no right to, but Donnie resented that Lewis had taken his place in A.K.'s bed.

The blonde had tried to accept Velda and join Donnie there; she said he was the only man she really loved, but ultimately she was an Austin girl and couldn't give it up, and he was a grieving widower who couldn't give that up. They had parted on good terms and still hooked up on occasion when it was impossible for him to avoid Austin.

"Don't call him that. He's a war hero who lost his legs fighting for his country."

"He did a good job. The Iraqi Army was defeated before they got to the Texas Panhandle."

"This is serious. David shot someone. Last night. Here in his condo."

"Did I hear you right? David Lewis shot somebody? Who?"

"Don't you read the local paper?" she responded, exasperated. "He runs the KL papers. You have one there, remember? You represented the former editor."

"We get one at the office, but I don't read it. We use it to check legal notices and the accident reports, in case there's some ambulance I need to chase. How's Charlton Denning doing?"

104

"I don't have time for small talk," she retorted, "this is serious."

Donnie heard the genuine concern in her voice. "What is it?"

"Well, David flew in from Akron late last night. When he got to the condo that they have here, he heard voices coming from the bedroom. Apparently, the Lehrer family had been threatened and he thought his wife was in danger. He opened the door and this figure in the shadows leaped at him and he shot her."

"Shot *her*? Shot who?"

"Francoise Gaulle. The French woman who works for the company. The figure in the shadows was Francie. He says he doesn't remember, but he must have killed her!"

"What does that mean?"

"I'm not sure. David says he had a flashback, like to Iraq when he was wounded, some sort of blackout. He says he doesn't remember anything about the shooting, but when he came to…she was dead on the floor and he had his gun in his hand."

"What do the cops say?"

"I talked to June. She says the DA's office thinks it probably was an accident. It'll have to go to the grand jury, but they're not detaining him."

"How's he taking it?"

"He seems cool. But his wife, Cordelia, is a wreck. She's left. I guess she's gone home to Akron. They have a little boy. God, it's awful."

"It could have been an accident, I guess. Keep me posted."

"I'll do that, lover."

The phone rang again. This time it was Eugene. "Lawyer Cuinn, I have departed the ranch and will see you at the Greeks'." Eugene hung up. Eugene did not favor long phone conversations.

Donnie went into the kitchen to rinse out his coffee cup and turn off the coffee maker. He straightened his bed and touched his fingers to his lips and then to the picture of his dead wife on the nightstand. *Hasta la tarde,* Cecilia."

He circled the little Antelope City town square. The Antelope statue gleamed like alabaster in the morning sun, safe inside its iron fence. No graffiti for Donnie to have removed. *Maybe the high schoolers have moved on to something else to desecrate. I hope not. I rather enjoy hearing them rustling around the square at night, doing something dangerous.* The vacant shops, remnants of a long-ago oil boom, were still boarded up. No addict or desperate hitchhiker seemed to have broken into one, which would have required Donnie to call the sheriff's office. Ever since Boom Gordon retired, he hated calling the sheriff's office. The new sheriff didn't give Antelope City crime the respect Donnie thought it deserved. *The new jail's gone to his head.* The gas station was closed. Hybrids didn't run low on gas, and they just blew silently right on through the small town, hardly ever slowing to the forty-five-miles-per-hour speed limit. Sometimes a car from Ohio or even New Jersey would stop and look at the Antelope, read the historical marker and take a few pictures. The VFW post had cut its bingo games to every other Saturday night. The Korean vets were dying off and the Iraq and Afghan vets didn't come home to Antelope City, or even to Velda.

It was just how Donnie liked it.

When Donnie got to the Greeks', Eugene's bright green Escalade with the logo for the Pervoy Cattle Ranch and Guest Spa was parked in front. Donnie pulled in slowly, careful to leave enough room to avoid dinging the Escalade with his pickup's door. He didn't want Ginelle Pervoy getting on her husband's case about that. George Poppoppolus, the older Greek brother, was taking breakfast orders behind the counter. Donnie nodded at him, but George didn't return the gesture. Nobody in Velda but George and Donnie remembered exactly why they hated each other. The girl had moved away. She couldn't abide Donnie's unwillingness to commit and she couldn't put up with George's neediness. So naturally, they each blamed the other one when she decamped for the Gulf Coast. Donnie was willing to shake hands and forget the past, but he was damned if he would apologize when he hadn't done anything wrong.

Eugene was sitting at his regular table in the corner. He sported a neatly trimmed beard, a recent haircut, a crisp white shirt with pearl buttons and pressed jeans. His scuffed boots were the only part of his appearance Ginelle hadn't been able to alter. "Sit down, Matlock."

"Nobody remembers who that was, Eugene."

"Sheriff Andy, that's who it was. Still the best show on TV." Eugene watched old reruns in his spare time. "Here's your breakfast taco." He shoved a taco, still wrapped in foil and steaming, across the table.

"Thanks." George would either ignore Donnie and refuse to serve him, or give him a cold taco left over from the day before. "Fucking Taco Nazi," Donnie muttered, unwrapping the taco and reaching for the bottle of salsa.

"Most people would stop coming in here." Eugene poured half a bowl of sugar into his coffee and stirred it until it made a muddy mess. "You just do it to annoy George, don't you?"

Donnie nodded, his mouth full of the freshly made tortilla. The eggs and chorizo were perfect. "It's also a damn fine taco."

"I hope you two don't ever make up. It lends a little suspense to my mornings."

"I'm happy to oblige." Donnie finished the taco, wiped his hands, and drank the black coffee Eugene had ordered for him. "What brings you to town?" he asked.

"Oh, Ginelle needs a new tent pole. The last one got broke in that windstorm the other night."

"There was a windstorm?"

"Nothing you would notice. Sixty miles or so. But it blew away the tent and broke the center pole. Nearly lost a dozen dudes from Houston, but most of them were too heavy to blow away."

Donnie nodded again. "I have noticed that the Pervoy Cattle Ranch and Guest Spa seems to attract people of the portly persuasion."

"They're the ones with the money. We've had to put in beds the size above king-size and find some extra strong horses for their little field trips. Anyway, soon as we're done here, I've got to run out to the discount store and see if I can find a tent pole."

"An urgent matter, this tent pole."

"According to Ginelle, it's very urgent. We got a group of dudes going out to the Intersection. I got to set up the tent before they get there so they eat and drink in Old West comfort."

"Ah yes, the Intersection. I went out there once."

"Were you lost?"

"As a matter of fact, I was. I had to follow the Amarillo tour bus back to the main road."

"Liar. There ain't no main road out there."

The Intersection was where a famous scene in a Scotty Pewter movie was shot. Scotty played an outcast and when he got to the intersection of two farm to market roads not far from his home in the movie, he fell to his knees and kissed the dirt road. Since then, tourists came to the area just to see the Intersection, where they would have their picture taken re-enacting Scotty's Oscar-winning dirt-kissing scene.

Donnie tossed some bills on the table. "I don't recall any picnic space at the Intersection. Where are you putting this tent?"

"In the Intersection of course. Where else would we put it?"

"Suppose a car comes by?"

"Hell, I guess they'd be as surprised as us, probably. Get out and have a beer with us and the dudes would thank us for the extra color."

"What a business." Donnie looked at his phone. "I need to be going."

"I didn't hear no ambulance."

Donnie smiled. "Me either. But I need to go get my marching orders from Lil' Faye, see what she has lined up for me today. I think I may have a dead rancher's widow to take to lunch."

"You do treat your clients well. How many of those widow ladies are you squiring around, or do you know?"

"I promised their husbands I'd watch after them. That's what I'm doing."

Donnie's practice included most of the Velda County ranching families. Word got around that he would make sure the widows, usually widows not widowers, were protected—it went with having Donnie Cuinn handle your estate. He taught seventy-year-old women how to balance their checkbooks. He went with them to the bank when they opened a safety deposit box. He defended them from needy relatives with sob stories. Once, he persuaded a grieving mother not to turn everything over to a son living in a beach house in Rockport with his third wife. He did those things, but just as important, he visited them at their new houses in town, took them to lunch at the Velda

Country Club, sat in on meetings with their brokers and answered questions. His long-suffering secretary Faye, now retired and living with her twin sister, Maye, in a retirement home in Amarillo, had given her successor, her niece Lil' Fay, the list of go-to house cleaners, maids, nurses, plumbers, handymen, yardmen, exterminators, electricians, painters, stone masons, firewood hackers and carpet cleaners—anything a rich woman might need in her daily life. Faye instructed her niece, "One complaint, and take that name off the list. Check the prices and the bills before you send it next door to get paid." Next door was Woody Woodson, the CPA to whom Donnie entrusted the finances of his widows. Woody was slow, but he never made a mistake.

Donnie checked his calendar. *Aw shit.* Lunch today was with Widow Janice Stonemaker. She came from a ranching family and married into another. Between her family's ranch and her dead husband's, the Stonemaker holdings made up one of the larger mid-sized ranches in the county. It had one drawback. No oil. Donnie would have to explain once again to Janice Stonemaker that it was geology, not the perfidy of the oil companies, which prevented her from being as rich as the rest of her bridge club. *The oil and gas lease on the ranch runs out in two more years. If Exxon hasn't done anything by then we'll look for another company that will,* he'd tell her. She wasn't going to be happy.

He parked his truck in the reserved space behind the Hasbro Building and thanked God one more time that he had sold it.

He wasn't cut out to be a landlord. Now he could do the complaining about the creaky elevator and the leaky windows. It didn't do any good, but complaints were better to give than to receive, and besides, he enjoyed complaining.

Wiley was already there, standing at Lil' Faye's desk, talking. "Let Lil' Faye get back to work, Wiley," Donnie said. "I thought you had that Singer deposition today."

His heavy-set junior partner winked at Lil' Faye and said, "That's what we're talking about, Donnie."

"Not the basketball game?" High school basketball was the sport of choice in Velda.

Donnie shook his head and said to Lil' Faye, "What do I have today besides Mrs. Stonemaker?"

The skinny young woman, dressed in a low-cut blouse and form-fitting pants that outraged her aunt when she visited the office, handed him his schedule. She had left a folder on his desk that contained letters and pleadings to sign along with a stack of case files. She brought him a cup of steaming coffee. Faye had taught her well. He opened the top file and tried to get ready for a meeting with the lawyer from San Angelo who was in town to try to settle a claim for defective bull semen that the Pervoys had made against his client. Donnie wanted to settle, because otherwise he would have to spend two days in court trying the damn thing. That would mean rescheduling a conference with the Langees who wanted to revise their wills now that their eldest son had entered the federal penitentiary and country club in Wichita Falls. He would also have to miss the monthly board meeting of the Major Hansard Velda Foundation, so it wasn't all bad.

ccccc

A week later, Anna Kaye Nordstrom called him again. This time he was in a meeting in the conference room. "She says it's an emergency," Lil' Faye whispered. He excused himself and motioned for Lil' Faye to close the door to his office.

"A.K., what's wrong?"

"It's David Lewis, Donnie. An Austin police detective wants him to come in and answer some questions."

"I thought everybody agreed it was accidental. What happened?"

"I called around, finally got June. She knew about it. All she would tell me was that the Austin Police had received some additional information they needed to investigate."

"I wonder what...? Where is Lewis?"

"He's still in town. They asked him to come in right away. He made an appointment for tomorrow morning."

"He needs to lawyer up."

"That's the thing, Donnie. He wants you."

Surprised, Donnie plopped down in his chair. "He wants to retain me?"

110

"Yes. He asked me to call you. He said you're who he wants."

"That supports an insanity plea right there."

"He's serious, Donnie. He insists he wants you."

"Why me?"

"He knows you from that gay editor thing with Charlton Denning and trusts you."

"That was a whole different matter than a shooting."

"I…may have also mentioned that you'd slept with the District Attorney."

He laughed. "He ought to check with June about how that turned out."

"No really, I think it has something to do with you understanding his history."

"His legs you mean."

"Yes. He believes you get it. Not everybody does. He thinks you will understand what really happened."

"This isn't a good idea," he protested. "Convince him to get Seth Robbins. He needs the real deal for this. He killed a woman."

"There's no use arguing about it, Donnie. He said you name the fee. He's sending the Lear to Velda to pick you up. It will be there at three o'clock this afternoon."

Donnie paused, thinking about the logistics. *One day's work and a ride in a Lear jet. And the fee, of course.* "I guess I can go to the interview with the police. But if that turns bad, he needs to get Seth. Three o'clock you say?"

"Yes. We're waiting to take off."

"We?"

"I'm coming up on the plane. We can discuss things on the way back. And David gave me something to give to you."

"What?"

"I don't know. It's a flash drive. He said to give it to you."

"I'll bring my ordinary client engagement letter. I don't want to see any flash drive until I'm sure it's protected by attorney-client privilege." He paused, thinking about the blonde woman's curiosity. "Don't you open it either."

"Oh, Donnie, just a peek?" she laughed. "Just joking."

FIFTEEN

The ride to Austin on the Lear went smoothly. Anna briefed Donnie about Cordelia Lehrer-Lewis and Francoise Gaulle's high profile lives in Austin.

"Drayton was a good friend," Donnie said. "I never thought he would sell *This Texas*."

"You can't imagine how ill he was. He had several offers, but I think he saw something appropriate in a blind man selling to an amputee."

Donnie fingered the flash drive. He resisted the temptation to look at it. *This man killed someone. Did he have something to hide?* They sat silently for a minute, getting ready for the descent into Austin. "How is June? I haven't seen her since Papa's funeral. I didn't have a clue she was planning to run for District Attorney." His affair with June Fennel had been brief. They parted friends and he doubted that their two weekends together would give him much leverage in a homicide case.

Anna smiled. "You two were so cute together, both pretending you were interested in the other one's work. Anybody could see it wasn't going to last long."

"Unlike you and David Lewis, huh?" He hated the idea of the two of them together. *Irrational.*

"Oh, Donnie. With David and me it's comfort sex. That's all it is."

"Who's comforting who?" he asked, bitterly.

She didn't answer. "I love you, Donnie Ray, even when you talk mean. I always have."

"That's quite a way to show it. Comfort sex with him."

She laughed. "You know you'll never love another woman after poor Cecilia. And don't talk that way about your client."

"He's not my client until he signs an engagement letter."

Anna drove them in from the airport and parked her little Fiat in the *Reserved for Penthouse One* space next to a black Lexus. She waved the concierge over. "This is Mr. Cuinn. He is Mr. Lewis' attorney. Please put him on the admit list."

"Of course, Ms. Nordstrom. Is Mr. Lewis all right?"

"He's fine."

"A terrible thing."

"Come on, Donnie." They stepped into the elevator. She nervously bit her lips. "I hope to God he's fine," she said. They were met at the apartment door by a man in a black suit, shirt, and tie. His jacket bulged with what looked like a gun.

"Hello, John," she said. "This is Mr. Cuinn."

He nodded. "Are you the lawyer? He's waiting for you in the study."

"Security," she explained to Donnie. "Protection from the Filipino Mafia."

"What?"

"That's who David thought was attacking his wife. The Filipino Mafia."

"Whatever you say." Donnie had never heard of the Filipino Mafia, but it didn't seem like the time to mention that. The drapes in the room were open and the late afternoon Texas sun lit the place like a movie set. David Lewis sat in a chair at a desk talking on his cell phone. He motioned for them to sit down.

"Whatever you say, Chief. We all want the best for her. How's little Tony? Tell him I'll call him before his bedtime."

He hung up and turned to face them. For a man who had shot a business associate in front of his wife, he looked remarkably calm. He and Donnie shook hands and he kissed Anna on the cheek. He started to say, "That was…"

Donnie interrupted. "Before you say anything, let's be sure we understand that from now on I'm your lawyer. Is that what you want?"

"Of course," he said, impatiently. "That's why you flew down here, isn't it?"

Donnie laid the engagement letter in front of them. "This makes it clear, so anything we talk about is covered by attorney-client privilege."

David picked up the letter with distaste. "And now we enter the world run by lawyers. You wrote in a fee, I'm sure."

Donnie was pissed. "I don't plan on being your lawyer past tomorrow's meeting. It's my regular hourly rate. If it doesn't suit you, I can get the next commercial flight home. But we can't discuss your case until you've engaged me."

"Oh, for God's sake, boys," Anna said, "Don't start all that. Sign the fucking paper, David. And you," she said to Donnie, "Be nice to your client."

"There's one for you too, A.K. I'm engaging you as a consultant on this matter," Donnie said.

He put the signed letters in his bag. "Now, you were saying, David?"

David turned to Anna. "Babe, I need to be able to do business from here. Can you get a couple of the boys from *KL Online* to get me set up? I may be stuck here for a while."

"Certainly, David. I'll call Peter Hays."

David turned to Donnie. "I can run things from here. You remember Charlton Denning?"

"Sure do."

"He's taking over the magazine for the time being."

"How will your father-in-law like that?"

"He'll never know. That was him on the phone. He wanted to talk about Cory."

"Your wife? How is she?"

"The Chief says she made it to Switzerland and has been checked into a clinic there, near Lucerne. She is well...devastated."

"That's understandable. She witnessed a shooting. In her bedroom."

"There was blood everywhere," Anna added.

"Yeah, there was," David said. "The Chief had her flown over. She'll be able to have some privacy and get the treatment she needs."

Donnie thought for a second. "I'm not sure how that will look. I mean if tomorrow doesn't go well."

"You mean if they indict me? I don't care how it looks. If it's best for Cory, that's how it's going to be."

"Did she talk to the police?"

"She was in no state to talk to anyone. When they came, she was in her bathroom, in hysterics. I told them what happened."

The security man brought in a tray of coffee. Donnie watched him leave. "Shut the door, A.K., will you?" When the three were alone, he said to David, "Are you ready to tell me what happened?"

"There's not much I can tell you that you don't already know."

"Why were you in Austin?" Donnie asked.

"The Chief dismissed the Filipino staff. All of them. He said Dakila, he's the Filipino who provides the staff, demanded a million dollars or he would harm the family. The Chief got rid of him but he was afraid that Dakila's associates, who he called the 'Filipino Mafia,' would take revenge on the family. He told me to come get Cory and bring her back to Akron where she would be safe."

Donnie glanced at Anna. "Are you recording all this?"

She held up her phone and nodded.

"What happened after you got here?"

"I was in bed in my bedroom…"

"You sleep apart?"

"Yes. We have ever since the baby came."

"I see."

"All of that's on the flash drive."

"We'll get to the flash drive. Go on. You were in bed?"

"I heard noises. I got in my chair. I thought about the Filipinos. I got my gun out of my nightstand…"

"You're licensed to carry a concealed weapon?"

"Yes. In Ohio, Texas, Illinois, anywhere I travel often."

"And then?"

"All I remember is opening the door and somebody jumping out at me. I don't remember firing the gun, although I know I must have. The next thing I remember is the gun in my hand and Francie on the floor. Cory was screaming, 'You shot Francie,' over and over. I called downstairs and said there had been an accident, to get EMS. Then the room was full of people and the police came. Cory was in the bathroom sobbing."

"Let's go back. You don't recall the shooting itself? Before the shooting, when you opened the door, what did you see?"

David answered slowly. "Do you ever have nightmares?"

Donnie nodded. "I do." *Of finding Cecelia dead on the side of the road in Mexico, her father and brothers beside her, all riddled with bullet holes from the cartel's ambush. Yes, I have nightmares.*

"Then maybe you will understand. I have a recurring one, from Iraq. We were in Fallujah, supporting the Marines, who were going house to house, cleaning out the jihadists. They emptied one block, but some Hajis slipped back in. We were ordered to finish the job. I was on point. We had to go house to house, and at one house the front door had been blown off. I was standing in front of a big wooden door at the back of the house when it flew open and this Haji screamed and threw himself at me..." He paused and wiped his face. He was perspiring heavily. "That was the first man I killed in Iraq. That's my nightmare."

Donnie waited while Anna poured David a glass of ice water.

He went on. "When you ask me what I remember about killing Francie, what I keep seeing is that day in Fallujah and that Haji. I don't see Francie at all. It's all blurred and part of the nightmare."

They sat silently for a few minutes.

"Does that help at all?" David asked.

"You didn't mean to kill Francoise Gaulle. That's what it means to me," Donnie said. He reached into his case and took out the flash drive. "Now tell me what's on here."

"I kept a journal," David explained. "Not a diary really, but when something happened I wanted to remember, I wrote it down. It's all there."

"What's all there?" Donnie asked, a little nervous.

"My life with the Lehrers. Up to now. Including the other night. The shooting. It's all there."

"Is this the only copy?"

"It is. I never saved it to my computer's memory. Cory warned me that her father's spies were everywhere. I was careful."

꯭꯭꯭꯭꯭

He left his client in Anna's care and walked to the hotel where she'd booked him a room. It was halfway between David's penthouse and the Travis County Courthouse. Donnie didn't remember a hotel being there, but he found it. He'd made his way past the crowds waiting to get into clubs or bars that had sprung up all around Second Street. Once there had been warehouses in the area…and a spaghetti house…and somewhere over there, a basement cigar bar. He was tempted to go in search of a martini and a cigar, but he had work to do.

The room had a view to the north. He could see the capitol with Lady Liberty atop the dome, blithely ignoring the hive of legislators below her, busily doing what they called "the people's work." They only met every other year. The people had that going for them. Beyond the capitol, the University Tower was lit orange. Somebody had won something. He remembered the feeling—the team won, the Tower was lit and the party at Scholz's was on. How reckless, how alive, how young. He sighed. He turned on his laptop and inserted the flash drive.

The screen went blank, he selected the drive, put in the password David had written down for him, and waited. After a few seconds the journal appeared. The first sentence read: *I had never been in the Ritz Carlton before Cory took me there, the winter she came looking for me in Cleveland.*

It was two in the morning before Donnie finished the journal. *What the hell had David Lewis gotten himself involved in?*

He went to bed pretty sure that the Austin Police Department had something to question David about that he was not going to like.

SIXTEEN

Anna drove them in David's Lexus to police headquarters, a nondescript modernist building that faced the interstate. Bullet holes where a drive-by shooter had strafed the building and blown out the front glass doors were still visible, somewhat belying Austin's claim to be the safest city in Texas. Donnie checked his notes. "Who is this Lieutenant Chambers?"

Anna answered, "After I talked to him, I checked the APD organization chart. Chambers is the head of the Homicide Unit."

"Uh, oh," David said from the backseat. "This doesn't sound like a formality to me."

"It probably isn't," Donnie replied. "Remember, look at me before you answer any question. Any question at all, okay?"

"You're the boss."

Anna dropped them at the curb and they made their way inside the cavernous police headquarters, where they waited for Lieutenant Chambers. He came through double doors with a *Warning: Authorized Visitors Only* sign in bright letters. Chambers was a tall black man, with an athletic build and a closely shaved head. He pulled his suit jacket on as he came toward them. The neon lights reflected off his service revolver before the jacket concealed it. "Mr. Lewis? Come this way." Donnie stepped forward and Chambers said, "You are?"

"Don Cuinn. Mr. Lewis' attorney."

"I don't think we've met. Are you local?"

"No, I'm not." He handed Chambers his card.

"Have you signed in?"

Donnie grimaced. "I'm afraid not."

Chambers sighed. "Over there," he said, pointing to a uniformed policeman sitting behind a counter. "Show him your bar card and he'll give you your pass." He took David's arm. "In the meantime, you come with me, Mr. Lewis."

"Can you wait until I get this done?"

"No." He turned and led David through the doors.

"How will I find you?"

"Ask around," Chambers said. The door closed behind them.

Fifteen minutes later, an obliging detective showed him to the interrogation room. It was larger and better lit than Donnie had expected. David sat at a table across from Chambers, who was leafing through a file folder. He closed the file and said, "You have a well-schooled client. He hasn't said a word. I read him his rights and told him this session was being videoed and recorded." He pointed at a card on the table between the two men:

MIRANDA WARNING

1. YOU HAVE THE RIGHT TO REMAIN SILENT.

2. ANYTHING YOU SAY CAN AND WILL BE USED AGAINST YOU IN A COURT OF LAW.

3. YOU HAVE THE RIGHT TO TALK TO A LAWYER AND HAVE HIM PRESENT WITH YOU WHILE YOU ARE BEING QUESTIONED.

4. IF YOU CANNOT AFFORD TO HIRE A LAWYER, ONE WILL BE APPOINTED TO REPRESENT YOU BEFORE ANY QUESTIONING IF YOU WISH.

5. YOU CAN DECIDE AT ANY TIME TO EXERCISE THESE RIGHTS AND NOT ANSWER ANY QUESTIONS OR MAKE ANY STATEMENTS.

WAIVER

DO YOU UNDERSTAND EACH OF THESE RIGHTS I HAVE EXPLAINED TO YOU? HAVING THESE RIGHTS IN MIND, DO YOU WISH TO TALK TO US NOW?

ENGLISH
(FRONT)

Donnie sat down next to David. "Well then, for your record, I am Don R. Cuinn, attorney for David Lewis." He smiled and flashed his new I.D. badge at the camera mounted on the wall.

Chambers did not smile. "Mr. Lewis, now that counsel is here, I'd like to ask you some questions about the events leading up to the shooting of Francoise Gaulle."

Donnie spoke up. "I'd like the record of this interview to show that Mr. Lewis has come here voluntarily. He thought it had been established that the shooting of Ms. Gaulle was accidental. You've Mirandized him. Does that mean that you consider Mr. Lewis a suspect in a criminal matter?"

Chambers gave Donnie a steely gaze. "We think he might have information that would help a grand jury decide whether a crime has been committed."

"And yet you read him his rights."

"I did. Read whatever you want into that."

"Let me ask you this then. Is he free to leave?"

"He is not in custody."

"So, he's free to leave."

"Anyone not in custody is free to leave. Now can we begin, or is he going to leave?"

Donnie nodded. "My client wants to help in any way he can."

"That's good to know." He opened the folder. "Mr. Lewis, you told Officer Garcia on the night of the shooting that you had flown from Akron, Ohio to Austin to take your wife home because your family was being threatened."

David glanced at Donnie, who nodded. "That's right."

"What was the nature of that threat?"

"My father-in-law told me that a Filipino named Raul Dakila who worked for the family had tried to extort money from him. He said Dakila and his family had been deported, but he was afraid the man's Filipino friends would try to take revenge on the family. He sent me to Austin to bring my wife to Akron, where the family could be protected at the family estate."

"Did he say it was the 'Filipino Mafia' that he was afraid of?"

"He may have. I'm not sure."

"But he was worried enough about your wife's safety that he sent you to Texas on a private airplane to get her, is that right?"

"Yes."

"What happened after you got to Austin?"

"I took a ride-share to our condo downtown."

"Did you go there directly or did you stop on the way?"

David hesitated. "I believe I had the driver stop at a burger shop. I hadn't eaten all day."

Chambers made some notes and checked off the question with a red pen. "Then what happened?"

"We drove to the condo; I got out and went upstairs."

"Did you speak to the concierge?"

David said impatiently, "Probably. I usually do."

"What time would that have been?"

"I'm not sure. About ten or eleven at night I imagine."

"Then you went upstairs?"

"Yes."

"Was your wife there?"

"Yes."

"Did you speak to her?"

"No. It was late. I was tired. She was sleeping. I decided to wait until morning to wake her. I knew she'd be upset, worried about our son. And the rest of the family, of course."

"Did you go in the bedroom?"

"Her bedroom? No, not then."

"You sleep in separate bedrooms?"

David looked at Donnie, who nodded again. "Yes. I have these prostheses. They're not easy to take on and off. They can be noisy. And she tells me I snore."

"That's why you sleep apart?"

"Yes."

Chambers made more notes and turned more pages in the file. Donnie could see photos of the bedroom and of Francoise Gaulle's body. Finally,

Chambers looked up and said, "I'm wondering, if you didn't go into your wife's bedroom, how did you know she was there?"

David hesitated. "How did I? I did know it, but how?" His face brightened. "The key. Her door key was on the table by the front door, where she always leaves it when she comes in. I saw, so I knew she was there. The apartment was dark. I assumed she was asleep and I decided to wait until morning to tell her what was going on."

"You decided to wait until morning even though this 'Filipino Mafia' was after your family?"

"He's told you that already, Lieutenant," Donnie interjected.

Chambers looked at Donnie as if seeing him for the first time. "Yes, he did." He looked back at David. "Let's move on, then. You went to bed?"

"Yes."

"You took off your prostheses and climbed into bed?"

"I have a bar by the end of the bed. I lift myself in."

"Does that ruffle the sheets a lot?"

David hesitated. "I'm a neat guy."

Chambers smiled. "A very neat guy. You went to sleep, heard voices and thought, 'It's the Filipino' Mafia.' Is that right?"

"Yes."

"You got in your wheelchair, retrieved your gun, and rolled to the bedroom door?"

"Yes."

"What did the voices sound like?"

"What do you mean?"

"Did it sound like a Filipino threatening your wife?"

"I don't know. I suppose it must have."

"It didn't sound like Francoise Gaulle and your wife?"

"I don't know. It's all a blur."

Chambers wrote down carefully as he repeated, "A blur." He turned to a red divider in the folder and examined a page. He looked up at David. "We would like to get a statement from your wife, Mr. Lewis. Where can we reach her?"

"She's in a clinic, being treated for shock. She's in no condition to talk to the police."

"Where is this clinic?"

"In Europe."

Chambers paused and looked at David. "Your wife is out of the country?"

"Her family wanted to get her the best care in the world and to protect her from all the media publicity about what happened. Her father knew of this clinic and he suggested she go there. I agreed."

Chambers said, "I see." He turned pages in his folder. "Mr. Lewis, do you know Francoise Gaulle's brother, Claude Gaulle?"

"Claude? Yes, I met him when he came to Akron."

"In fact, Claude Gaulle knew your wife in Paris, before you were married. Is that right?"

"Yes."

"He knew your wife and the deceased well?"

David shook his head. "I suppose he did. He was Francie's brother and Francie worked for my wife."

"Tell me, Mr. Lewis, did you know that Francoise Gaulle and your wife were lovers in Paris?"

David's head shot up. "What? That's a damned lie!"

"Her brother says different. And he says they were still lovers when you shot Francoise Gaulle. Did you learn about their affair before you came to Austin? Or was it when you opened the door and saw them in bed together?"

Donnie put his hand on David's shoulder. "Don't say any more." He turned to Chambers. "This interview is over. Come on, David."

Once they were back in the car and on their way home, Anna looked in the rearview mirror at David's grim face. "What's wrong? What happened in there?"

Donnie turned to David and said, "Don't say a word. Not until we're back at the condo."

Anna navigated the traffic on Sixth Street. A cyclist turned in front of her, waving his arm for her to yield. She sat on her horn and yelled, "You're going to get killed doing that, you motherfucker!"

The cyclist gave her the finger and sped across the intersection, causing cars on both sides to come to sudden stops. Brakes squealed, horns honked and bumpers bumped. Ordinarily, Donnie would have said something about Austin and cyclists' rights but he was lost in thought about Chambers' last question.

Anna pulled into David's reserved parking place. She turned to them and said grimly, "Will one of you please tell me what happened?"

"Upstairs," Donnie said.

"You know what?" David said from the backseat. "I'm hungry. I'm hungry for some barbecue. Let's go to Curtis'."

Donnie leaned back. David wasn't ready to talk about what just happened, and that was all right with Donnie. In fact, some Curtis Matl brisket sounded good to him, too. "Take us there, A.K." he said.

Instead, she cut off the engine and opened her door. "We can walk. Matl's has moved downtown."

"Downtown? Curtis Matl? How can that be?"

She led the way out of the building. The sidewalk was crowded with office workers, most in jeans or khakis and polo shirts, almost all chatting on their phones and dodging oncoming pedestrians. "He sold the old place on the creek. Curtis says the money was just too good. And that bank buildings don't usually flood."

"Curtis' is in a bank building?" He tried to picture that. "The real question is, how's the brisket?"

"As good as ever. It doesn't care."

The line at Curtis Matl's stretched out the door and down the sidewalk. "Where's Pruitt?" Pruitt Matl was Curtis' brother. They had fought and sued over the family recipes and finally opened competing barbecue joints. "Still over there on South Lamar, watching Curtis expand. Curtis has trailers all over town. One is next door to his brother's place. They say Pruitt's business has shriveled away to nothing."

On the other hand, prosperity agreed with Curtis. He was straddling a bar stool in the passageway to the food counter. He looked a hundred pounds heavier to Donnie. His beefy forearms, neck and face were mahogany, stained from all his years over the wood-fired pit. Even more startling was to hear Curtis talk. In all the time Donnie had eaten at Curtis', he had only heard him say a half dozen words, and two of them were "All gone" to a customer who had offended him. Now he was laughing and joking with the customers, shaking hands and pushing them genially forward in line.

"What the hell happened, A.K.?" Donnie asked.

"The new Curtis? His investors sent him to charm school. Money talks, and now so does Curtis."

Donnie watched Curtis grab David by the arm. "Come in, come in, David Lewis. So good to see you. I've been thinking about your troubles. You're our hero, man. Don't you ever forget that." He climbed down off his stool with a grunt and shoved the others in line to one side. "Make way. This man is a genuine war hero! Let David Lewis through!"

He led the protesting David to the head of the line. "Get that new brisket. Cut this man some brisket!"

When Donnie and Anna finally reached the table where Curtis had ensconced David, he was surrounded by well-wishers, taking selfies and asking for autographs. "You didn't tell me we have a media star on our hands," Donnie said to A.K.

"They loved his book. They can't wait for the movie to come out. And ever since the night, you know, the Internet has gone viral with stories about the bionic war hero." She smiled modestly and whispered to Donnie, "No shit, I do a wonderful job. These pictures will go viral, too."

I hope the grand jury follows social media, Donnie thought.

⸌⸌⸌⸌⸌

Anna dropped them back at the condo and Donnie and David went into the study and closed the door behind them. "At least we know where the 'new information' came from. Is it true?"

"That little prick, Claude," David said.

"Yes. So. What Claude says, is it true?"

"No. They were not lovers." He sat down and stared out the window. "I would have known, wouldn't I? I always liked Francie. We jogged together. If something was going on, I would have suspected, wouldn't I?"

"Unless you were blinded by love."

"You've read the journal. You know everything."

Donnie thought, *something's been bothering me.*

"Remember, your meeting with Francoise, when she told you that Cory didn't want sex in your marriage?"

"Yes?"

"Why did Cory do that?"

"I thought about it a lot. I think it was just what Francie said. It was a business arrangement all along. Cory passionately wanted an heir so she could take over the business. She was even more passionate to screw her sisters out of their share." He shook his head and grinned a little. "And she was passionate with me for as long as she had to be. Not a day longer."

"That's a lot of passion. And you never suspected Francie and Cory might be lovers?"

"It never entered my mind. Not once."

"If you did know, and shot your wife's lover in a fit of passion…"

"How many times do I have to say it? They weren't lovers."

"Let me finish. As I was saying, if you shot the French woman in a fit of passion, that could go to mitigate the punishment. You might be able to make a plea deal with the DA."

"I'm not making any plea deal."

"I understand. I'm just giving you the options. It used to be the law in Texas that sudden passion was a defense to murder. If a husband caught his wife in bed with another man and shot the guy in a fit of passion, some people called it The Unwritten Law. The legislature changed that. Now sudden passion just applies to how much punishment the killer gets, not to whether he is guilty or not."

David shook his head in disgust. "No plea deal. Ever. They weren't lovers."

"It would be better if your wife were here to corroborate your story."

David stared at Donnie defiantly. "I'd never put Cory through that. She was so stricken by what happened that I don't know if she'll ever get over it."

"All right. I get that. But I'm afraid we haven't heard the last about her being in Europe."

Donnie took out his phone and checked the Internet. *A.K. was right.* Pictures of David at Curtis' were everywhere. "Sometimes we don't know ourselves at all."

David leaned back in his chair and stared at the ceiling. "Do you think it's possible I found them together and shot her and don't remember?"

"Do you?"

He sat back up, leaned over his desk, and looked Donnie in the eye. "If I don't remember, I guess it could have happened."

"Don't you think you would remember if you saw your wife and her French friend having sex?"

David smiled wryly. "You'd think. But honest to God, all I remember is the door busting open and somebody jumping at me. After that, everything is blank. Nothing. Just the Iraq nightmare."

"So, you don't remember if you saw them in bed together. Something, any shape came at you. What's the first thing you remember after that?"

"Her body, lying there. Cory screaming. I called the concierge. I told him there'd been an accident, to call 911 and the police."

"Nothing in between?"

Donnie asked Anna to join them. "I think you're going to be indicted, David. You should get a big-time criminal lawyer to take it from here."

David stood up and dropped his pants. The T22s gleamed. "Help me take these off, babe."

She brought his wheelchair. He sat down in it and she knelt beside him. She helped him remove the prostheses. The stumps of his legs were red and sore-looking. Donnie turned away. He didn't like to see the two of them like that. "We need to decide who to call."

David rubbed his legs. "Nope. You're my guy. You understand me. And I think you believe that it happened like I told you. You do, right?"

Donnie nodded. *I do.*

"Then I'm afraid you're on for the duration."

Donnie rolled his eyes. "All right then. We need to discuss my fee."

They agreed on a high flat fee plus costs. It was more than Donnie had ever charged and he sensed that David would have agreed to almost any number he named. He emailed the details to his office in Velda, and in a few minutes the document appeared, ready for David's printer. They signed the new retainer agreement.

Donnie turned to Anna. "A.K, find out from June when she's going to the grand jury. Find out who's assigned to the case and ask her to arrange a meeting to discuss David's surrender and bail."

"You mean if I'm indicted, right?"

"Right. *If* you're indicted."

Anna hurried from the room, her phone in her hand. David smiled. "This June, the District Attorney? She's the one you slept with?"

Donnie frowned. "Unfortunately, the women I've known often leave on bad terms."

They reviewed some of the questions Donnie had from reading David's journal. Anna returned a few minutes later. "Well, June said to tell you hello. She said she was surprised that with all his resources, Mr. Lewis was playing small ball. She said she had expected a higher profile defense."

"That's me. Small Ball Cuinn." He looked at David. "There's still time to change pitchers."

"It does sound like you charmed the hell out of her, Cuinn. No, I'll stick with you. I want to see your slider."

"It'll be right on the outside corner."

Anna waved her hands. "If I may interrupt ESPN, she also said she was handling the matter herself."

"Really?" Donnie replied. "Is it an election year?"

"Next year. But that's the same thing, isn't it? Anyway, the grand jury will hear testimony this week and if all goes as she expects it to, she would be willing to discuss things with you this weekend."

"Okay, then. David, you are to sit tight. Do not go out. I don't want any revelry on the deck of the Titanic showing up on social media. And of course, don't leave Austin."

David nodded.

"A.K., keep the posts positive, nothing that might bite us at trial. I'll call my office and clear my calendar. What else?"

For the first time, David looked worried. "This is happening, isn't it? How the hell would I survive in prison?"

"You're not going to prison. We're going to win this thing."

"Go get 'em, cowboy!" David said.

SEVENTEEN

Donnie had a couple of days before the grand jury did whatever it was going to do. He knew he needed help and decided on a long shot. Two telephone calls later, he sat in the cramped University of Texas Law School office of Professor Frederick Stayman. The walls were covered with bookcases overflowing with law books and periodicals. The desk of the most noted authority on Texas criminal law was cluttered with scribbled notes, sheets of manuscript, open law journals and a dark computer screen.

Professor Stayman, or, "Prof. Freddy," as everyone called him when not in his presence, scurried in, carrying an armful of law books. He was old, bent over, short and thin with a wasp of unruly hair around his big ears. He wore heavy black-framed glasses. He dropped the books on a table, hurriedly took off his jacket and put on a frayed burnt orange sweater. He reached out for Donnie's hand. "Sorry to keep you waiting. An idiot law student tried to stop me after class with a question about something we covered last week." He dropped into his wooden office chair and sighed. "Now, then. You weren't a student of mine?"

"No, sir."

"But you are a lawyer?"

"Yes, sir. My practice is in the Panhandle, in Velda. But I have this case in Austin and I need some help."

"Velda? Is that where Jake Rosen practices? I was at Harvard with Jake."

"That's right. I took over the practice when Jake retired."

"Retired? Jake? Lucky man." He put his hands on his desk and looked down at Donnie's card. "And you? Where did you go to law school, Mr. Cuinn?"

Donnie smiled. "In Beaumont. I'm a proud graduate of the Jeff Davis School of Law."

"Jeff Davis. I taught some courses down there and they buy a lot of my books. I got rather fond of all those policemen and landmen, spending years in night classes to become lawyers. A practical place. Not an ivory tower, like here."

"I got through in a couple of years and went to work for Jake. He taught me a lot."

Prof. Freddy sighed. "Poor Jeff Davis. I believe they had to take down his statue. Political correctness."

"That's right. And re-name the school. I got a new diploma. It says I went to the Texas Gulf Coast School of Law."

Prof. Freddy's eyes twinkled. "Not quite the same ring to it." He leaned back in his chair. "How can I help you?"

"I've gotten myself involved in a murder case. The defendant is a well-known person. I want to retain you on his behalf to advise me on the case."

"I don't go to court."

"I understand that, Professor, but I need someone I can trust to help with the defense and, if necessary, to handle the appeal."

"I don't take *pro bono* cases, you know. And I don't take cases that don't interest me. I don't need to."

"My budget is big enough. As to the case, you may have read about it. It involves the shooting in a downtown condo of a French woman by a war hero. David Lewis, the shooter, is my client."

"The Bionic Man?"

"That's him."

"I didn't know he had been indicted."

"I expect he will be soon. The DA has taken a personal interest in the matter."

"Fender?"

"Yes. She's handling it herself."

Prof. Freddy motioned at the door. "Close the blinds on that door." The professor's struggles with alcohol were legendary among Texas lawyers.

"Prof. Freddy is on leave again," someone would say when the old man went away to dry out. As soon as Donnie closed the blinds, the leading expert on Texas criminal law took a bottle of whiskey from a desk drawer and, without offering any to Donnie, poured himself a half-glass of bourbon and drank half of it. He then retrieved a package of Camels and an old chrome cigarette lighter from the pocket of his sweater, shook out a cigarette and put it in his mouth. He steadied one shaking hand with the other and pushed down on the thumb piece of the cigarette lighter. It sparked, and the flame shot up. Prof. Freddy lit his cigarette and inhaled deeply. He exhaled a plume of smoke into the air above him and sighed.

Donnie watched with interest. The only other lighter like that Donnie had ever seen had been his former law partner Jake Rosen's. "They allow you to smoke in here?" He was too diplomatic to mention drinking.

Prof. Freddy smiled. "'Allow' is the wrong term. They don't see it and so they don't know it. Otherwise, I might defect to the Texas Gulf Coast School of Law." He shuffled through a desk drawer and took out an old glass ashtray. "June Fender was in the last class when I could call on a woman to recite the *Calhoun* case. Did they cover that case at Jeff Davis?"

Donnie nodded. "Elements of forcible rape?"

"Yes. Force, lack of consent, penetration."

Penetration, however slight, is sufficient to complete the offense.

"Every year, I would entertain the class by calling on the best-looking woman student to present *Calhoun.* Then we would engage in a Socratic discussion of 'penetration.' What did the term mean? Full intercourse to coitus, naturally, but what lesser act constituted penetration? Penetrate five inches? Less than that? One inch? I would lead the poor woman back until it was a mere brushing of the penis to the woman's silk panties. But what about thick cotton ones? And so on. It always got laughs. Ms. Fender was prepared for me. If she was embarrassed, she didn't let the class know it. Before we were done, she had the class on her side. The dean suggested I give up my annual ritual. A woman in law school wasn't a novelty anymore."

Prof. Freddy snuffed out his cigarette and turned on a fan that sat on the table behind his desk. He watched calmly as papers flew in all directions.

"I believed then that there was no place for women in the legal profession. I was a misogynist. But I was in error. Now half the students in this place are women. Not only that, but they are the smart ones; I have to have my fun with gay men discussing anal sex. My heart isn't in it." He took out his long yellow legal pad. "Tell me about your case."

Donnie told Prof. Freddy all he knew. When he finished, he said, "I need to decide on a defense. An accident? These blackouts? Or something else?"

Prof. Freddy lit another Camel. "Why don't we wait and see what the charge is? Who knows? Fender may settle for unlawfully discharging a firearm."

Donnie smiled. "Not likely."

"No, of course not. What you need to focus on first is seeing that the client is released on bail."

"Yes. Imprisonment would be hard for a double amputee."

"I assume he won't be charged with capital murder. He didn't kill a peace officer or fireman, there was no kidnapping, sexual assault or arson. No murder for hire, and he didn't shoot more than one person." Prof. Freddy smiled.

"No," Donnie replied. "None of that."

"Then I'll just say that your client is fortunate to be in Travis County."

"I never heard that before."

"Oh, yes. The accused in Travis County have a strong chance of obtaining bail. Within forty-eight hours of his arrest, he must be taken before a judge. The judge must inform him of the charges against him and advise him of his rights. Your client will enter his plea of not guilty and the judge will then set a reasonable bond."

"Sounds pretty routine."

"All individuals, except those charged with capital murder, have a right to be released on bail if they can provide sufficient collateral, are not a flight risk, have ties to the community and are not a danger to the public. That's true throughout the state. But in this county, defendants are interviewed and categorized based on their likelihood to be re-arrested or miss a court date during the pretrial period, taking into account their ties to the community, which include current employment, housing and family information. Travis

County uses standards that are effective predictors of pretrial risk. Defendants are classified as being low-, moderate- or high-risk."

Donnie thought a minute. "I need to convince June that David Lewis is low-risk. Which he is."

"It will be a notorious case. She may worry about public criticism if she seems too lenient. But perhaps you can work out an agreement."

Prof. Freddy gave Donnie his consulting agreement. Donnie wrote him a check for his retainer, whereupon Prof. Freddy gave him a notebook of draft motions.

Donnie stood up to leave. He offered to pull up the blinds.

"Leave them," Prof. Freddy said and poured himself some more bourbon. "I'd say your defense is weak. He claims he didn't know they were lovers, so there was no reason for him to intend to kill, and he blacked out. That could be difficult to prove. Look at temporary insanity, or better yet, plead it out. Fenton would probably settle for manslaughter."

"David's determined not to serve jail time."

Prof. Freddy grunted. "Closer to the day of judgment, he may feel differently."

Donnie returned to the rental car Anna had arranged and looked up at the UT Law Building. Its massive stone design reminded him of pictures he had seen of monumental Stalinist architecture. Additional wings had been attached awkwardly as the Law School doubled in size. He wondered what it would be like to go to class in there, walking the halls with the state's future political and legal leaders. He was almost glad for his time at Jeff Davis. Not exactly proud, but glad. It gave him what he needed then. It took him in when he was without any purpose or meaning in his life. Jeff Davis didn't end the grief or the guilt. Those were still with him. But it put him alongside people from all parts of society and provided them all with the possibility to escape the unhappy place fate had dumped them.

He started the car and drove up Red River to the I-35 overpass into east Austin. He had some free time and he had personal business that needed his attention.

He made his way slowly up Manor Road. New restaurants had appeared since he was here for Papa's funeral. In addition to the comfort food of black-owned Cooledge's and the herb bed next to Sidey's, both of which had been there forever, there was now an upscale butcher shop and café, promising all locally grown fare. Food trailers were everywhere, one selling homemade pasta and old style Italian food, another hawking breakfast tacos and burritos, still another promising fresh-squeezed lemonade. There was even a gelato trailer. It made him wish he was hungry.

He headed toward Navasota Street and parked in front of the Texas State Cemetery. He walked through the sand colored stone entrance and made his way past the stream that trickled down over boulders. The circular Meditation Area was empty. He was alone. The Texas flags lining the walk hung limply against their poles in the still Austin air. He glanced at the rows of white crosses that marked the resting places of Confederate veterans and turned the opposite way, toward the graves of Lena and Ralph Rothschild, the couple he considered his parents. He touched their simple headstones and, as he always did, said *Thank you, Lena. Thank you, Papa.*

Lena had been the first to be buried there, given a place because legislators remembered how many poor students she had furnished refuge for in her small hotel west of the UT campus. Papa, Professor Ralph Rothschild, a poet, had been taken to the cemetery in a grand procession led by his second wife, Minerva Wisconsin, the rich oft-married *doyenne* of Austin society. Now the only relatives he had left were his mother, Dorrie Louise, and his half-sisters. His mother had left her six-year-old son with the Rothschilds when she married the The Son-of-a-Bitch. After she divorced The Son-of-a-Bitch, she took care of Papa, by then a widower. When he re-married, she went to live with her oldest daughter, Donnie's half-sister, in Museum, a small town fifty miles east of Austin. Donnie had just learned that she was in a nursing home there. He needed to visit her next, as soon as he finished some business concerning Papa's estate, of which he was the executor.

The business was to pick up a check at the Cartwright House, the retirement home where Papa was living when he died. It had taken nearly a year, but they had finally sold his apartment and the estate's share of the proceeds were ready to be paid out. Donnie could have had them send him a check, but he wanted the facility's manager to explain all the deductions to him. It was the last thing of value of Papa's estate and he needed to be sure it was right. He parked in front of the building and looked across the street where the Primate Preserve had been. The developers had been busy. The preserve was gone. The trail that he and Papa had walked so often was closed by a construction barrier. A large crane stood next to a partially completed five-story building. He sighed. Papa's quixotic fight against the development of the Hieronymus Parcel had ended predictably. The developers had won.

The literature Donnie picked up at the Cartwright House claimed the mixed used development would provide expensive condos with lake frontage; a boutique hotel; specialty shops selling expensive gadgets no one needs,; an eco-friendly coffee shop; a sushi restaurant; a wine bar; and a *brasserie,* offering *steak-frite* and *croque-monsieur.* There would be *al fresco* dining, a mile of walking trails, a dog park and a playground, *where young mothers can watch their children network with the best of New Austin,* he supposed. There would be everything except what Papa wanted, a quiet green space in the middle of the city and a memorial to the poor animals that gave their lives to scientific research in the Primate Preserve.

After useless haggling about the details of Papa's settlement, Donnie pocketed the check and headed for Museum, Texas. The arteries across Austin were clogged. Construction delays on MoPac, according to his radio, an accident on the 183 fly-over where a motorcycle had jumped the wall and crashed fifty feet to the access road below. The condition of the rider was unknown. *Well, I can make a pretty good guess.* He exited abruptly at Anderson Lane and crawled along the familiar street, grumbling at the changes. What had been a busy shopping mall with a large department store was now a discount grocery store. Condos were under construction in the old parking lot. The beer and pizza movie house had expanded and Donnie counted three coffee shops before he rejoined the highway east of I-35 and located the toll road to Museum.

When I was a grad student at UT, you would've had to pay me to go to Museum, and now you have to pay to go!

He soon saw why. Sprawling strip centers flanked both sides of the highway, and behind them the rooftops of new subdivisions stretched for miles. Each subdivision he passed had a massive stone entrance, a sales office and a billboard promising a clubhouse, a pool (or two) and excellent schools. Everything seemed to have grown exponentially since he was last here.

The toll road ended at Manor and the old divided highway looked more familiar, with the gas stations and junkyards he associated with that part of Central Texas. Here, the land was still being farmed, but probably not for long. "Suitable for Development" signs cropped up from time to time, especially around four-way stops. Museum itself, when he finally got there, hadn't yet fallen victim to the Austin sprawl. *It's on its way*, Donnie thought grimly. The wide highway had a hamburger joint and some gas stations for motorists driving the scenic route from Houston to Austin, but when he turned off the highway onto Pleasant Street, the old homes and well-tended yards were a step back into the last century.

The Mus-Tex Rest and Retirement Home occupied a half block next to a dry creek and just past the residential area. *This land must be in the flood plain*, he guessed. When the late spring flash floods came, they would fill the dry creek with raging waters.

He parked in the paved area, dreading what he might find inside. The building was a rectangular brick affair, with dark, screened windows. The outside had been designed for minimal maintenance. The flower beds were gravel and a few cactus plants were placed here and there. The lawn, such as it was, consisted of Bermuda grass and weeds. There was a lonely elm tree at one corner of the property, and by the sidewalk, a flagpole with an American flag.

He forced himself to get out of the car and walked slowly to the front entrance. He pushed the buzzer and heard a click as the door unlocked. A large woman sat at a desk; she was staring down at a clipboard.

"Excuse me," Donnie said after a few minutes.

"Be right with you, sir," she mumbled, still not looking up. She stared at the clipboard longer than was necessary, then made a large, dramatic check by an item. She sighed, put down the clipboard, and looked up at him. "Did you sign in?"

"Yes, ma'am," Donnie answered politely.

The large woman took a deep breath and looked at the flowers Donnie held in his hand. "If you're here to visit, meal time is in an hour and visitors in the room interferes with meal service."

"I'm here to see Mrs. Smith."

She gave him a blank look.

"Mrs. Dorrie Louise Smith?"

"Alright," she said, turning around in her swivel chair. "She's in Room 166B. Meal time is in an hour. Visitor meals have to be ordered in advance."

Donnie couldn't imagine the conditions under which he would eat here, but there probably were some. He walked down the wide hall, past open doors in which he could see residents in various stages of declining health. Televisions buzzed from most of the rooms. He passed the common area where some residents were engaged in kindergarten projects or just dozing in the sunlight that streamed through the back windows. His mama's room was halfway down the next hall. There, slouching against the door, talking on his cell phone, was The Son-of-a-Bitch himself.

Grover Smith looked up. His squinty eyes, enveloped in his fat face, hadn't changed. This was just an older version of the man Donnie remembered—more wrinkles, more fat, but smaller. Grover pocketed his phone and smiled. A gold molar glistened with saliva when he spoke. "I believe that's Donnie Ray. Hello, boy," he said, extending a beefy paw.

Donnie ignored the hand. "What're you doing here, Grover?"

His mother's ex-husband smiled greasily, just like Donnie recalled. "I'm here to see after the woman I love, seeing as how her only son will not."

"You're divorced. Where's Betty Ann?"

Just then, his half-sister came out of Room 166. "Oh, Donnie Ray, you're here. You won't believe what I've been through." She linked her arm with Grover's. "Thank God Daddy is here, what with you living up north."

"I came as soon as you called. Is Mama alright?"

"No, Donnie Ray, she is not. Like I told that woman in your office, she is completely out of her head. She's depressed. She cries all the time. She's un…re…sponsive, isn't that what the doctor said, Daddy?"

Grover kissed her on the top of the head. "That's what he said, baby girl. But don't worry, your daddy's here."

"When did all this happen?"

"It's been coming on. The doctor has tried everything, but nothing seemed to help, so he said we should bring her here until he can decide what to do next."

"I want to see her."

"They're getting her dressed. They'll tell us. Of course, they had to take care of her roommate first."

"Roommate?"

"The woman in 166B. Of course, she has the window. She's deaf as a doorknob so she has that television on so loud. And complain, complain."

"Can't we get Mama a private room?" Donnie asked.

She smiled at Grover. "Like Daddy said, it's just not worth the money. Medicare won't pay for a private room and she doesn't know where she is anyway."

"I'll pay for the private room. This isn't up to him." Donnie couldn't bring himself to say Grover's name.

She ignored him. "Daddy's been such a help. Tell him about this morning, Daddy."

"It was just an old stray dog, baby girl."

"There are no little pit bulls, Daddy. You taught me that when we all lived up at Smithberg. Before Mama ran off to take care of that professor. Anyway," she turned to Donnie and went on, "I was on the way to the garage when I hear this growling sound. I did what Daddy always said. I froze. I stood perfectly still. It bared its teeth at me. I yelled for Daddy and he came out with his gun and shot it dead." She looked up admiringly at Grover. "My daddy saved my life."

"What are you doing here, really?" Donnie asked Grover.

Betty Ann said, "I'm going to go get a Coke. Do you boys want anything?"

Donnie shook his head no.

Grover said, "A Diet Pepsi, baby girl, for your daddy, if you please." He reached in his pocket. "Do you need some change?"

"Oh no, Daddy. But thank you." She turned and went toward the common area.

Donnie stared at Grover. "I asked you what you're doing here."

"Just doing what I can." He looked around helplessly. "I know this is not the best place. But Betty Ann couldn't pay someone to look after Dorrie Louise on her teacher's pay. I would have helped, but my money's all tied up in my frac sand project over in Burnet."

"I have no idea what you're talking about. Why didn't Betty Ann call me? I would have sent her money."

"I told her to just call you and let you see for yourself the state the woman is in. Then maybe you would hurry up and close the professor's estate. Your mama inherits from him, right? There'll be plenty of money then." He hesitated just a second. "Plenty to give your mama the best care in Texas."

Papa's money. Of course. "What do you have in mind? Remarry her? Get yourself or Betty Ann appointed her guardian?"

"Whatever is best for Dorrie Louise," he said sanctimoniously. "Like I said, I love that woman. Even if she did leave me to go take care of that pansy professor."

Donnie laughed. "The joke's on you, Grover. There is no money. Ralph Rothschild left everything to a primate preserve in Louisiana. Those of us who love her will have to come up with the money. How much will you kick in?"

The fat man's florid face drained pale. "Monkeys? He left everything to monkeys? Everything?"

Betty Ann returned. Grover ignored her when she offered him his Diet Pepsi. "I'm sorry, baby girl, but I'm needed up in Burnet. Frac sand business. I'll call you."

Betty Ann watched him leave. "Poor Daddy, he's so busy. I've been trying to get him to retire and move in with me and Mama. They would be so good for each other."

Donnie brushed passed her and went into Room 166. His mother was sitting up in bed. A plastic curtain separated her from whoever was in 166B. As Betty Ann had said, the television was blaring. He turned the sound down and the woman in 166B yelled. "Turn up the TV. I can't hear."

140

Donnie ignored her. He leaned over and kissed his mother. "It's me, Mama. I'm here."

His mother's eyes were glazed and her speech was slurred, but she smiled. "Oh, Donnie Ray. I didn't want to leave you. You understood, didn't you? You were happy with Lena and Papa, weren't you?"

"Of course, I understood, Mama," he lied. "That was a long time ago. I love you, Mama. Now we just need to get you well." *That's not a lie. I want my cheerful, funny little mother back!*

"I'd like that," she said drowsily.

He finally got in touch with the doctor, who said Mrs. Smith was depressed but physically strong. He had prescribed increased doses of tranquilizers to help with the depression but they had not helped. There was not much more they could do in Museum. *Psychiatric care perhaps?*

He called the best lay therapist he knew, Ginelle Pervoy. "Ginelle," he said when he got the blowzy West Texan on the phone, "is there room at the Pervoy Guest Ranch and Spa for my mama? She needs to dry out."

"Oh, Donnie Cuinn. You never told me your mother was an alcoholic. It would explain some things, though."

"No, not booze. They've pumped her so full of tranquilizers she doesn't know which way is up. My hope is that after she gets that crap out of her system, she'll respond to the Pervoy spa treatment."

"You bring her right up here and I will personally see that she gets just that."

EIGHTEEN

He had just enough time to drive to Velda and get Dorrie Louise safe in Ginelle's care when Anna called. "It's happened."

"Manslaughter?"

"No. Murder. June will meet with you in the morning to agree on surrender and discuss bail."

"Send the KL plane and tell her I'll be there."

⟨⟨⟨⟨⟨

When Donnie got back to Austin he found David busy at work in his study, showing no concern about the indictment. The story had not yet become public. "I guess now the fun starts," David said. He looked at Donnie "You look awful. Is the pressure already getting to you?"

Donnie collapsed on the nearest chair. "It isn't that. I just looked evil in the eye and rescued my incoherent mother."

"You need a drink." He pointed at the tray and Donnie poured himself a stiff drink. "You rescued your mother, you say?"

"From her ex-husband. I had to lie to him." He sipped the single malt and let out a deep breath of satisfaction. "Good stuff. I told him my mother was broke and he skedaddled. Actually, she's pretty well off, but she wouldn't have been for long if Grover Smith had hung around."

They sat silently for a few minutes.

"I re-read your journal," Donnie said. "You don't say anything about the dreams."

David hesitated then said, "They're pretty painful to think about,

142

much less write down. The army shrink said I should write them down. I just never did."

Donnie sat up. "But you did tell the shrink about them?"

"I did. Major Siddiki. When I was in rehab at Brooke."

"Is he still in the army?"

"Damned if I know. Why?"

"I'll track him down. I need to interview him."

"He kept trying to get me to talk about Iraq, and after I told him about my mother, he wanted me to talk about that all the time. I hated that."

"Why?"

David held out his glass and Donnie refilled both their glasses. "I guess," David said slowly, "that it wasn't anybody's business. I felt guilty about my mother and the way she died. That was my fault. Her accident and the Iraq thing are all jumbled together in my nightmares. The shrink said if I talked about it I could get over the guilt." He held the glass up and examined the amber whiskey in the light of his desk lamp. "The thing is, I don't want to get over it. I have no right to get over it."

"That's amazing," Donnie said.

"Why do you say that?"

"Because I feel exactly the same way about Cecelia's death. Cecelia, my wife. I should have been there when the cartel ambushed her family and murdered them all. I was supposed to be with them…" He stopped. He was saying more than he wanted to but it seemed important to tell David. "…but I took a later flight. Something came up and I took a later flight. So, I wasn't in the car with her when she was murdered. Something came up and it was so unimportant I can't even remember what it was."

David laughed. "Jesus. You're as messed up as I am."

"The thing is, I understand what you've gone through. I totally understand. I have nightmares too."

ccccc

The next day, Anna drove Donnie to the Blackwell-Thurman Justice Center to meet with District Attorney June Fenton. Anna let him out onto the crowded sidewalk and he looked at the long security line that stretched outside the entrance. He was already late. He scrolled in his cell to June's number and was surprised when she answered.

"You're late, counselor." The familiar voice was matter-of-fact and a little husky. It fit June Fenton perfectly. "Where are you?"

"I'm here," Donnie replied. "Outside the building in the security line."

"Jesus," June said. "Nobody told you to get an attorney pass?"

"Obviously not. How do I get one?"

"The same way you do anywhere. Have your office get the form from the sheriff's office. Maybe you'll pass the background check." She paused. "Or maybe not. Are you carrying?"

Donnie laughed. "We don't carry weapons into the Velda County courthouse."

"I'll send Craig out to get you. This time only!" She hung up.

In a few minutes, a young man in chinos and an open-collar un-tucked dress shirt came down the line, calling his name. He led Donnie to the DA's office, which hadn't changed since he was there last, except for the name on the door.

June Fenton, small, tanned and with a platinum streak strategically placed in her dark hair, was at her office door. She stood on tiptoes and kissed him on the cheek; he hugged her. She said, "That's for old times' sake. After this, you're just another scumbag defense lawyer to me."

He laughed. "You look good, June." He looked around the government-issue decorated office. "Love what you've done with the place."

"Oh, wait until you see our fifty-million-dollar office across the street."

They sat down in front of her desk—the old oak chairs creaked. "I heard about the boondoggle. When do you take possession?"

"Lord knows. It'll probably be my successor who gets the pleasure."

"Why? Do you miss private practice? I thought you had a sweet deal being Minerva Properties' general counsel."

She smiled. "Oh, the real estate business wasn't for me. I decided I'd rather prosecute developers than defend them."

"Good luck with that." They paused, waiting for the other one to get down to business. Finally, Donnie said, "Prof. Freddy sends his regards."

June pursed her lips. "How is the old drunk? Is he consulting for the defense?"

Donnie replied, "He is."

"So I imagine you'll show up at the arraignment with a fistful of Freddy motions. We're used to that here. I have a crack staff of Austin's finest ready to spring into action."

"You're frightening me now."

"Shall we get this show on the road?" She stood and moved behind her desk. She called out, "Sheila, come in please." A neatly dressed young woman came in. She handed June a document in a blue cover, stapled at the top.

"Sheila, this is Don Cuinn, who represents David Lewis."

Sheila nodded at him and he smiled at her.

June handed him the document and said, "This is the indictment that the grand jury for the 969th District Court handed down yesterday. It charges your client with murder. Take a moment to look at it before we proceed."

Donnie thumbed through the indictment. "You're overreaching, June, uh, I mean Madam District Attorney."

June glanced at Sheila, sighed, and said, "Ms. Fenton will be just fine, Mr. Cuinn. As to the charge, you'll have plenty of time to argue that. I'll just say that the grand jury found probable cause to indict your client for the murder of Francoise Gaulle."

"That's really a stretch. This was an accidental shooting."

"As I said, you'll have plenty of time to argue that. Now, will your client surrender voluntarily?"

"Of course." He put the indictment in his briefcase. "Can we discuss bail?"

"There isn't much to discuss. This is a murder case."

"Come on. What about Travis County's famous risk-assessment system? He qualifies under that for personal bond."

"The assessment system is to help poor people who can't afford bail, not to let murderers walk the street."

"Do I need to remind you he's a double amputee? He's not a flight risk. He's an amputee. How far could he get?"

"He's rich. He has access to a private jet. He could be on his way to Brunei while we're talking, for all I know."

"He's in his apartment, in a wheelchair, minding his business. Travis County doesn't want this guy in its jail. How will they take care of him?"

"They'll manage. They've had disabled people before."

"I promise you this. I'll be in court every day pointing out some inhumane, unreasonable condition. He is innocent until proven, right?"

June sighed. "What do you suggest?"

"He'll post a reasonable cash bond and will accept home confinement until the trial is over." He saw her glance at Sheila and added, "If you want, we'll pay for off-duty cops to stand guard."

She sighed. "Where'd you get that idea? Some TV procedural?"

He grinned. "I think it was *The Good Wife.*"

She stood up. The meeting was about over. She extended her hand. "Okay. We'll do the *Good Wife* thing plus a million-dollar cash bond."

"A million?"

"Take it or leave it, counselor."

He took it.

The arraignment was the next day, limiting the time David Lewis spent in the booking facility and the Travis County jail to a few hours.

When they arrived at the Justice Center, Anna pushed David in his wheelchair through the crowd of reporters and television cameras.

Donnie fended questions. "Nothing at this time, except that David Lewis is innocent. He's looking forward to the trial at which he can clear his name."

They had discussed whether David should walk into the courthouse or be pushed. They even considered hiring a nurse in a white uniform to push him. They agreed a wheelchair had the best chance of favorable air time.

After David was booked, fingerprinted and photographed, they were escorted by deputies to the eighth floor and into the courtroom past curious onlookers, hoping to get a seat.

"Look this way, David," one shouted, taking a selfie. The courtroom was already packed and the bailiff had brought in deputies to maintain order. The bailiff turned away three teenage girls for inappropriate attire, pointing to the sign on the door forbidding shorts, tank tops, low-cut blouses, pajamas and t-shirts with obscene language or graphics. The girls threw kisses in David's direction. "We love you, David!"

June sat with a single assistant at the prosecutor's table. She nodded and turned to speak to one of the lawyers who had come to watch the show.

Donnie, Wiley and David settled in at the defendant's table. Wiley would have resigned if Donnie hadn't let him be in on the biggest case the firm had ever had. Anna charmed a man into giving her his seat immediately behind them.

The judge did not keep them waiting long. Donnie looked at him closely. He had heard of Judge Nzube Okeke. The seven-foot tall Nigerian had been an All-American forward on the University of Texas basketball team, followed by ten years with the San Antonio Spurs, where he led them to three NBA championships. He'd gone to Harvard Law where he was editor of the *Harvard Law Review*. He returned to Austin to practice and after five years, he left the most prominent firm in the capital city to run for district judge. Smart money said he would be a federal court of appeals judge in a few years. Now Judge Okeke stared down at Donnie from the bench. "Welcome to my courtroom, uh …is it pronounced Swinn or Quinn?"

Before he could answer, June broke in. "Excuse me, Your Honor. Defense counsel is Mr. Don R. Cuinn, pronounced *Quinn*. Mr. Cuinn is a prominent member of the bar in Velda, Texas."

The judge smiled. "Velda? Where is Velda, Mr. Cuinn? I'm not familiar."

"In the Texas Panhandle, Your Honor."

"Welcome, then. You'll quickly learn how we do things in my court, professionally and with dispatch."

"I'm sure I will, Your Honor."

"Now then, is the defendant present?"

"He is, Your Honor." Donnie motioned to David, who raised himself out of his wheelchair and walked around the table on his T22s to face the judge.

The judge looked at David. "Mr. Lewis, you have been furnished a copy of the indictment returned against you. Have you read it?"

"He has, Your Honor."

"Let's have Mr. Lewis answer from now on, Mr. Cuinn."

"Of course, Your Honor."

David looked up at the judge. "I have read it."

"Very well. Do you waive your right to have the indictment read in open court?"

David looked at Donnie, who nodded. "I do, Your Honor."

"Do you have an attorney?"

"Mr. Cuinn is my attorney."

"I am required to inform you that you have the option to remain silent, you have the right to have your attorney present during any questioning by police officers or attorneys representing the state; you have the right to an examining trial to determine if there is probable cause for your arrest. Do you understand all of that?"

"I do."

"David Aaron Lewis, how do you plead to the charges against you?"

David stood at attention. "Not guilty."

A buzz circulated through the courtroom. Judge Okeke looked around the room with a steely stare and the noise ended immediately. "It seems we have an agreement on bail?"

June stood. "We do, Your Honor. Mr. Lewis will be released on house confinement after posting a one-million-dollar cash bond, if that meets with the court's approval."

"The terms of the house confinement include a deputy at his residence? That's a little unusual."

"It is. However, because of the defendant's physical impairment, the state believes that confinement with surveillance, at the defendant's expense, is the best solution."

"You agree, Mr. Cuinn?"

"Yes, Judge. Mr. Lewis is prepared to post bond immediately."

"Very well then. So ordered. Motions due in the ordinary time?"

"Yes, Your Honor," June and Donnie said, almost in unison.

The judge made a note and said, "Defendant is remanded to the sheriff's custody pending bail. Ms. Fenton, Mr. Cuinn, in my office in half an hour to discuss scheduling."

After posting cash bond with funds arranged by his Chicago bank, David was wheeled out a back door of the Justice Center accompanied by a retired county deputy, one of a team of four agreed to by Donnie and June. Donnie saw the party safely through the crowd and off into the waiting car. He repeated his client's innocence for the cameras and then made his way to Judge Okeke's chambers.

June was waiting for him. "Before we go in there, now's the time to discuss a plea."

"What do you have in mind?"

"I don't have anything in mind. If your client is willing to plead to manslaughter, I'd consider it."

"Involuntary, probation, no jail time?"

"Of course not. He's going to prison. Whether it's for ten years or for life is what he needs to decide."

"I'll ask him, of course, but I doubt he'll even consider it."

June opened the door to the Judge's chambers. "You're his lawyer. It's your job to convince him."

The judge waited for them in his office along with his clerk, who sat at the side of the room ready to take notes. The former professional athlete had shed his robe and wore a burnt orange t-shirt that stretched tight across his chest muscles and his huge biceps. He looked up at them "What are we doing here, people?"

Donnie looked at June who said, "We're discussing a plea, Judge."

"To manslaughter? How long?" the judge asked.

Donnie answered, "We aren't close, Judge. I told Ms. Fenton my client is probably going to refuse any plea that involves time behind bars."

"He shot this woman, right?"

"Yes, sir, he did, but he suffers from blackouts under stress caused by his experiences in Iraq."

The judge looked at June. "We've heard that before, right Ms. District Attorney?"

"Yes, Judge." She looked at Donnie. "It's often argued. It never succeeds."

"Even if it's true?" Donnie asked.

"It's hardly ever true," the judge stated.

"There's always a first time," Donnie responded.

Judge Okeke glared at Donnie. "I don't think your heart is in this, Mr. Cuinn."

"Judge, my client is a double amputee. His life would be hell at Huntsville."

"He should have thought about that before he shot her." He looked at his clerk. "Find us some dates." He turned to the lawyers, but his anger seemed to be directed at Donnie. "I've already seen the social media from your client's arrival this morning. There will be no circus in my courtroom, do you understand me?"

"Of course, Judge," Donnie managed.

"No goddamned circus where I'm the ringmaster and you two are snarling cats, and all the clowns and trapeze artists are making a mess. Am I clear? There's a gag order in place from this moment forward, get it?"

They both nodded.

"Good. Clear your calendars because I'm going to get this over with. No continuances, no delays." He waved his hand in dismissal. The meeting was over. They stood up to leave and the judge said, "Does he really box and run marathons?"

"He does, Judge."

"Amazing. What a shame."

NINETEEN

Colonel Priam Siddiqui had retired from the Army and was practicing psychiatry in San Antonio. It did not take long for Anna to track him down and make an appointment for Donnie to meet and discuss the David Lewis case. "He didn't sound very busy," she said. "Actually, he sounded eager."

Donnie drove down from Austin. There was only one delay, an overturned truck near New Braunfels. He navigated the access road detour and then pushed his rental car to the limit so he was only a few minutes late when he got off the interstate. He passed the San Antonio Arsenal, repurposed as the headquarters of Texas' biggest grocery chain, and drove slowly through the King William Historic District, looking for the address the doctor had given him. He drove past large homes fronting the San Antonio River, down St. Mary's Street with its carefully restored homes that might have been featured in *Architectural Digest*, then past simpler brick and frame houses with bright colors and blooming flowers around the doorways. Doctor Siddiqui's office was off of St. Mary's Street in a narrow three-story frame bungalow.

The doctor met him at the door. He was short and heavy with dusty East Asian features. His dark hair was slicked down and his dress shirt bulged out at the waist. He wore a Fitbit on one arm and two wristwatches on the other.

He ushered Donnie into his office, a plain space with DIY bookcases slightly atilt and filled with thick, bound books. On one wall was his diploma in psychiatry from the Perelman School of Medicine at the University of Pennsylvania and his certification from the American Board of Psychiatry.

151

Donnie sat down on a patient chair, carefully avoiding the stereotypical couch. The doctor sat across from him, leafing through his notes. Donnie had sent him David's medical records and when he got to the doctor's office, Doctor Siddiki, "Call me Doctor Sid," he had said, was prepared to discuss David's blackouts. "They certainly could be a symptom of post-traumatic stress disorder. I see military veterans regularly with PTSD. In fact," he said a little smugly, "I'm something of an expert. I've written on the subject." He handed Donnie a monograph.

"And testified?"

"Oh, yes," the doctor answered.

"Mr. Lewis says he blacked out and doesn't remember shooting the dead woman. Is that believable?"

"It certainly could have been an aftermath of what he went through in Iraq, particularly when compounded by the experience he had involving the death of his mother."

"Her automobile accident with the train?"

"Yes. I saw him several times before he was discharged. He told me he had been troubled with nightmares about that and feelings of guilt. He complained of nightmares when I saw him. He relived an experience he had in Iraq."

"From nightmares to blackouts? You've seen that in your practice?"

"Not specifically. But even so, I'm sure such cases are in the literature."

They talked about the technical aspects of PTSD and the doctor agreed to testify for the defense. Donnie called Anna and told her to arrange a time for Dr. Sid to see David.

⟨⟨⟨⟨⟨

Donnie returned to Velda to clear his calendar for the upcoming trial. The morning after he returned, he met Eugene Pervoy for breakfast. Eugene finished his breakfast taco and wiped his mouth with a handful of the thin paper napkins the Greeks provided their customers. "I heard the jet come in last night. You flew right over our house. I said to Ginelle, 'Here comes Donnie.'"

Donnie pushed his empty plate away. "I'm sorry if it disturbed your rest."

"Oh, hell no. Ginelle was blabbering about something and for a little bit there, I couldn't hear a word she said."

"I suspect she'll repeat it for you."

"That's already happened. That's why I'm in town, having breakfast with you."

"Buying a tent post?"

"No. Taking this to the bank." He lifted a bank bag from beside him.

"I'm glad you're prospering."

Eugene held his coffee cup for the waiter to refill. "Everything—I mean the oil, the dude ranch, the online grape jelly and crap Ginelle sells—everything except the cattle business, is making money. She says I spend her profits on my cattle business and I ought to quit it."

"Really? Quit the cattle?"

"I put the *kibosh* on that. You can't have a ranch without cattle. I'm sorry, but you just cannot. You know what she said?"

Donnie smiled. "You're going to tell me."

Eugene ignored him, getting angrier at the memory. "She said, 'You go on and play cowboy, but remember what puts money in the bank.' Then she handed me this bank bag."

Donnie picked up the check, written in pencil on a green sheet. "I need to get to the office. Tell Mama I'll be down to see her tonight."

"Come in time for supper. By the way, I really like your mama."

"She's a lot better, isn't she? You and Ginelle have been good for her."

"Ginelle's put her to work, greeting the dudes. And I heard her in the kitchen this morning explaining to the French cook how to make biscuits." Eugene stretched. "How long will you be here for?"

"Just a few days. I need to catch up on some Velda work then get back to Austin for the trial."

"How's it going? You know, the town's all divided."

"How so?"

"Well, half of Velda, I call them the Donnie-fors, think he'll get off despite having you for a lawyer; the other half, the Donnie-againsts, think you'll screw up so bad they'll haul him off to Huntsville for lethal injection."

Donnie laughed and shoved the check across the table. "Just for that, you pay for the tacos. You forget, I've got Anna Kaye Nordstrom on my side."

"If that woman's for you, who can be against you?"

Wiley was waiting for Donnie in his office. Lil' Faye brought Donnie a stack of papers he had to review and approve. There were dozens of phone calls to be returned. And there was the state's witness list. He had given Wiley the task of trying to interview the most important ones. "How was your trip to Akron?"

Wiley flopped into the chair across from Donnie. "Not too good. Sheriff Wilson confirmed that Kingston Lehrer had told him the Filipino Mafia was after him and his family. He says he went along to humor the old man, but he doesn't think David Lewis really believed there was a real threat."

"Did David tell him that?"

"More of an eye-roll thing."

Donnie frowned. "So, June will argue that David didn't go to Austin to protect his wife, and that he lied when he thought she was being threatened. Did you talk to the family members while you were in Akron?"

"I tried, but the old man was the only one who would talk to me and he's out of it. He kept quoting Shakespeare. At least I think it was Shakespeare."

"No chance for family members to rally around the innocent brother-in-law then?"

"I'd say not. I can keep trying."

"Don't bother. They probably would just as soon see him convicted."

"Wow." Wiley went on, "Nobody else on the witness list will talk to me. The Frenchman, Francoise's brother, Claude, refused to take my call. He's camped out down in Austin 'in mourning' the message on the machine said. Fucking French."

Donnie laughed. "Have you ever met one?"

"No, but I hate them. Stole our recipe for frying potatoes. *French* fries. Disgusting."

Donnie started on the paper pile. "That doesn't seem to keep you from eating them though." He handed Wiley his meeting notes with Doctor Sid. "So far he hasn't come up with any blackout sufferers for us."

ⅭⅭⅭⅭⅭ

Donnie moved the entire operation to Austin two weeks before the trial was to commence. Most of Donnie's motions had been denied. Prof. Freddy was not surprised. "I tried out some new ones I've been wanting to use on appeal—grand jury composition, jury panels, discrimination against the disabled—all are very interesting. We'll get to argue those all the way to the Supreme Court when the jury brings in a guilty verdict."

"You mean *if* the jury brings in guilty, right?" Donnie said, handing the professor another beer.

Prof. Freddy laughed at their running joke. They were in the guest house at the Lake Austin waterfront estate that Anna had leased for David during his house arrest. Its owner was a tech billionaire who had sold his company and said the house reminded him too much of his pre-sale wife and children. He was busy building a new home for his new wife on a vineyard he had bought outside of Fburg. The ten-acre estate David was leasing came complete with a gym, jogging trails, an indoor-outdoor pool, a spa, a screening room, a stable with a pony for Tony during his visits, a helicopter pad, eight bedrooms and twelve baths, and a guest house that had been converted into a war room for the duration of the trial. David liked it. "It's almost like not being in Austin at all."

As the trial approached, a jury consultant named Sam Sams joined the deliberations. Sam, Prof. Freddy and Donnie sat outside the war room watching their client and Anna trot around the jogging trail.

"He's really an athlete," Sam said.

"Yes." Prof. Freddy said. "He and Miss Nordstrom seem to get along very well." He looked at Donnie. "Is that a problem?"

Donnie watched the pair disappear behind a clump of trees. "I don't think so. They're discreet. Our blogger with the telephoto lens hasn't seen them yet." As the trial date neared, social media was full of pictures of David. Some dated back to his boxing days in Cleburne, Texas, but most showed him with his T22s, in a half-marathon or in the boxing ring in San Antonio. As the trial neared, profiles of Francoise Gaulle, the French mystery woman and editor of *This Texas*, began to appear, with hints of a motive for her killing, maybe even a love triangle.

"Tell me the perfect juror," Sam blurted.

"I'm baffled," Donnie answered.

Prof. Freddy jumped in. "A war veteran whose wife dumped him."

⸢⸢⸢⸢⸢

They got the veteran. They also got six women, three of them professionals. There didn't seem to be any lesbians, although June fought hard to get one or two butch-looking women. A transgender was excused after declaring "their" hatred for all wars and all soldiers.

After he empaneled the jury, Judge Okeke told them they would be sequestered at the old Capitol Hotel near the courthouse. He told June and Donnie, "Opening arguments at 10 AM in the morning. I want to finish this trial in a week." He called them to the bench. "There's still time, Mr. Cuinn."

Donnie looked back at his client, sitting in his wheelchair, staring into space. "I'm afraid not, Judge," he said quietly.

"We tried, Your Honor." June had offered a reduced charge of manslaughter and a term on two to five years. David had flatly refused.

"Would you do that?" David had asked Donnie, and Donnie had no choice but to reply, "No. We're going to win this."

Saddened by the news, Prof. Freddy shook his head and asked for the rest of his fee in advance.

TWENTY

David wheeled himself through the crowd in the hallway outside Judge Okeke's courtroom. There had been a mad scramble for seats. Donnie and Wiley escorted David to the defense table. Behind them, Anna had arranged seats for the Parsons family. Will Parsons, the KL editor from Northern California, his wife and teenage daughters were there to act as David's surrogate family. When the jury was brought in, they saw the Parsons talking animatedly with David, who smiled a little grimly. They planned to repeat that scene every day of the trial.

The bailiff called "All Rise…"

David lifted himself out of his chair with his strong arms and shoulder muscles and held himself there.

The judge took his place and they all sat down. He whispered something to the bailiff, who repeated the whisper to Donnie, "Your client may remain seated if he prefers." Donnie nodded his thanks to the judge.

Formalities out of the way, June Fenton rose to address the jury. "Good morning. My name is June Fenton. I am the Travis County District Attorney and I will be representing the State of Texas in this case. Mr. Don Cuinn, seated there," she pointed at Donnie, "represents the defendant, David Aaron Lewis, who is seated beside him." She looked at the jury with a serious expression. "In this indictment, the State of Texas charges that the defendant committed murder by intentionally and knowingly causing the death of the decedent, Francoise Gaulle." She read the indictment to the jury, speaking in a calm conversational tone. When she finished, she handed the indictment to the court reporter. She turned again to the jury and moved a step or two closer to them.

"This is a simple case, really. David Lewis shot Francoise Gaulle, a vibrant, intelligent woman, the editor of *This Texas* magazine. In her short time in Austin, Francoise quickly became an influential member of the artistic community of this city with a long life ahead of her. The defendant ended all that. There is no question that the defendant shot and killed Francoise. He admitted to Officer Garcia, the first officer on the scene that he shot her. The only issue is, did he know what he was doing at the time?"

She paused and turned halfway, staring at David. "David Lewis is a hero. He was decorated for his bravery. He paid a horrible price for his service through the loss of his legs. But just because David Lewis is a war hero, does not mean that he is above the law. David Lewis is a determined man, a competitive runner, a boxer. He has succeeded in the rough and tumble life of journalism.

"You will hear evidence that he is also a violent man, with a hair-trigger temper. What would drive him to murder? He is also a proud man. He married a beautiful woman, a woman who betrayed him. At some point, even before their marriage, his wife Cordelia and Francoise Gaulle became lovers." She took a single step in David's direction, "He is a very proud man, so proud that he could not abide his wife's betrayal and so he killed her lover when he discovered them together in his wife's bedroom."

There was a buzz in the courtroom. Two reporters dashed out to report what the DA said. The judge rapped his gavel twice and signaled to the bailiff to quiet the courtroom. June walked back to the counsel table and waited for the buzz to die down. David stared at the district attorney. His face betrayed no emotion. She went on, "The state will prove that he took revenge on Francoise; that he knew exactly what he was doing when he fired the gun. Mr. Cuinn will tell you that the defendant was suffering from a form of post-traumatic stress disorder that left him unaware of what he was doing; that he shot and killed Francoise while he was in such a complete blackout that he has no memory of doing it.

"But we only have the defendant's word for that. It's something any murderer can claim. How do we know if he is lying or telling the truth?" She leaned against the railing of the jury box and spoke very slowly and clearly. She aimed most of her remarks at a young woman in the front row.

Donnie thought back to Sam's warning: *The accountant, a CPA, with her own firm, single, a career woman, she's going to be sympathetic to the prosecution.* Donnie turned his attention back to June.

"You will tell us. It is your job as David Lewis' peers to determine the facts. Listen carefully to the evidence both sides present and decide who is lying and who is not." She stepped back and smiled. "When you do that, you will find David Lewis guilty of knowingly and intentionally murdering Francoise Gaulle."

She sat down and the courtroom was silent.

"Mr. Cuinn," the judge said.

Donnie waited a long count of twenty, waiting until all eyes were on him. Then at last, he rose and stood in front of the jury. "Thank you, Your Honor. Ladies and gentlemen of the jury, my name is Don Cuinn. I represent David Lewis, who is sitting there." He pointed at David in his wheelchair. "I'm a lawyer in Velda, Texas." He paused a half-count, then smiled. "I suspect many of you don't know where that is. In fact, when I was introduced to Judge Okeke here, he didn't know, either." He looked at the judge, who showed no expression. "I was so in awe, meeting the famous Nzube Okeke I could hardly talk. I had followed his career. What a step-back jump shot he had! Anyway, I told him it was in the Texas Panhandle, halfway between Dallas and Denver."

There were a couple of smiles from the jurors. "So, what is a small town lawyer from the Panhandle doing down here in the capital city of Texas, in front of the most famous district judge in Texas, in the most publicized trial of the decade? Why did David Lewis choose me?" He waited another half-beat. "He chose me because I'm his friend, because he's my hero, because I know that David Lewis is not guilty of murder and because I will do everything in my power to prove that to you."

He stepped to the defense table and took a sip of water. He put his hand on David's shoulder. "All I ask now is for you to withhold judgment until you hear all the evidence, all the witnesses, from both the State and the defense. I probably won't agree much with Ms. Fenton during this trial, but I do agree when she says this is a simple case. Did David Lewis black out or not? Did he shoot the decedent on purpose or not? Was Cordelia Lewis unfaithful to her husband or not? And even if she *was* unfaithful, did David Lewis *believe* she was unfaithful?"

He paused and then went on. "The defense will show you how David Lewis was wounded in combat, how he overcame his wounds, but was never able to overcome the nightmare of Iraq; how along with thousands of fellow heroes he relives the horror of combat; how sudden stress can cause the memories to resurface and cause the mind to respond the only way it knows to preserve a person's sanity. He blacks out and when he awakens has no memory at all of what happened. His army doctor will describe David Lewis' treatment for post-traumatic stress disorder and why he continues to experience it. His brother will testify about the tragedy of their mother's accidental death and how even then, years before Iraq, David was already suffering nightmares."

He took another sip of water and then said, "In the English-speaking world where the common law applies, in the United States, where our Constitution governs and in Travis County, Texas, where the American system of justice prevails, all persons are presumed to be innocent, and no person may be convicted of an offense unless each element of the offense is proved beyond a reasonable doubt. The fact that a person has been arrested or indicted is immaterial." Donnie looked directly at their middle-aged veteran juror and said, "David Lewis killed Francoise Gaulle. He did not murder her." Donnie returned to his seat.

"Call your first witness, Counsel," the judge said to June.

"The state calls Detective Ralph Garcia."

Garcia testified that when he arrived at the condo he found Francoise Gaulle dead on the bedroom floor, dressed in running shorts and a navy blue tee. He identified photos of the scene.

"Where was the defendant, Detective?"

"He was in his wheelchair."

"Did he say anything?"

"Yes. He handed me the gun, a Smith and Wesson 4006, and said, 'I shot her.'"

June held up an evidence bag holding a handgun. "Is this the gun?"

"Yes."

"What happened next?"

"I asked him what happened; he said he didn't know. He said he must have blacked out. I asked him why he shot her and he said it was all a blur."

"Did he say anything else?"

"No. He just sat there, like he was off somewhere, in a daze."

"Was he in custody or under arrest at the time he told you he shot Miss Gaulle?"

"No, ma'am."

"In fact, the defendant was not arrested until sometime later, is that correct?"

"I believe so."

"And he voluntarily said that he shot Francoise Gaulle."

"Yes, he did."

June glanced at her notes then asked, "Did you see Cordelia Lewis?"

"She was in the bathroom. I tried to get a statement from her, but she was hysterical."

June turned to Donnie. "Pass the witness."

Donnie said, "Detective, I believe your testimony was that David Lewis '...just sat there, like he was off somewhere, in a daze'. Is that correct?"

"Yes."

"Detective Garcia, you've been a policeman for ten years. Have you investigated many shootings resulting in death during that time?"

"Quite a few, yes, sir."

"Any where the person firing the weapon was present at the scene?"

"Yes, sir."

"Do you recall any of those where the person who fired the weapon 'just sat there, like he was off somewhere, in a daze?'"

The officer looked at the DA, then said, "I don't recall any."

Donnie smiled and said in a friendly tone, "Well, if it had happened before, you'd remember it, wouldn't you?"

The officer shrugged. "Probably."

Next, June called Lieutenant Phillip Chambers. He described his meeting with David at police headquarters.

"Tell the jury, Lieutenant, what did the defendant say was his reason for coming to Austin that night?"

"He said his father-in-law was afraid that the Filipino Mafia were going to harm the family and that he wanted the defendant to come to Austin and bring his wife back to Akron."

"He used the words 'Filipino Mafia'?"

"Yes. He also said that when he heard noise coming from his wife's bedroom, he thought it was the Filipinos."

June looked at the jury as if to confide and said, "It seems that the Filipino Mafia is at the heart of this case, doesn't it, Lieutenant?"

Donnie was on his feet. "Your Honor ..."

"Yes, Mr. Cuinn, I agree. Just ask a question, Ms. Fenton. No speeches."

June answered quickly, "Of course, Judge. Tell us, Lieutenant, what is the Filipino Mafia?"

The imposing black policeman shook his head. "I have never heard of it. It's not listed in the FBI records of transnational criminal organizations operating in this country."

"What else did the defendant tell you about that night?"

"He said that he stopped on the way from the airport for a burger. Then he went up and went to sleep in his bedroom and that he and his wife slept in separate bedrooms."

"Did those actions sound like a man who was fearful for his wife's safety?"

Donnie jumped to his feet. "Your Honor..."

"I'll withdraw the question, Judge," June quickly replied.

"During that interview, did you ask the defendant if his wife and Francoise were lovers when they lived in Paris?"

"I did."

"What did he say?"

"He denied it."

"What else did you also ask him?"

"I asked him if he learned about their affair before he came to Austin or when he got to the apartment that night and saw them together."

"What did he say?"

"It was at that point his lawyer ended the interview."

"That would be Mr. Cuinn over there who ended the interview?"

"That's right."

Donnie rose. It was his turn to question Chambers. "First of all, Lieutenant, you said David Lewis denied that Cordelia Lewis and the deceased were having an affair. What exactly did he say?"

Chambers looked at his notes. "He said, 'What? That's a damned lie!'"

Donnie looked at the jury. He caught the eye of the veteran juror and said, "Well, that would have answered any question you had about that, wouldn't it?" Before Chambers answered Donnie went on, "Let's turn to why David Lewis came to Austin and the Filipino Mafia. Lieutenant, have you ever heard of the *Satanos?*"

"I believe that's a California street gang."

"A Filipino gang?"

"Filipino-American I believe."

"How about the *Demonios*? Or the *Diablos*?"

"Same answer."

"So, would you agree that there are Filipino criminal gangs?"

"Those are street gangs, mostly in Southern California. They're not a *Cosa Nostra* type of operation."

"Do any of these gangs refer to themselves as the 'Filipino Mafia'?"

"I've never heard of it."

"You don't know if they do or not, so it's possible they do?"

June stood. "Asked and answered, Your Honor, and he's asking the witness to speculate."

"Yes, Mr. Cuinn," the judge said. "I suppose just about anything is possible. The witness never heard of it. Move on."

"That's all I have, Your Honor."

The judge said, "In that case, we'll adjourn until 10 AM tomorrow."

The cameras, along with David's impromptu fan club thronged the street outside the Justice Center. Donnie pushed his way to their waiting car. He muttered, "No comment," and "Can't comment" to the microphones and smartphones pushed toward his face. He climbed into the backseat next to Prof. Freddy, who had decided to watch the proceedings from the back of the courtroom.

The television cameras and dozens of phone cameras caught the moment when David took off his jacket and swung himself athletically into the passenger seat of the car.

When they were finally away from the courthouse, David turned in the front seat and said, "I didn't know we were best friends, Don."

"None closer," Donnie replied.

It took them forty-five minutes to get back to the lake property. David and Anna went for a run. Donnie poured Prof. Freddy a drink, opened a Shiner Bock for himself, and the two began preparing Donnie for his cross examination of the next day's witnesses.

First, they reviewed the transcript of the day's testimony. "Remember what I told you," Prof. Freddy said. "Stay in your chair and let her go. Limit yourself to one or two objections unless she really goes crazy. You don't want the jury to see you as nervous and interrupting all the time."

"Better they see me as a country rube who doesn't know what he's doing?"

Prof. Freddy flashed a knowing grin. "Then David's new lawyer and I can appeal on the grounds of your incompetence."

"Sure, fire reversal, huh?"

They were discussing the Akron sheriff's testimony when David and Anna returned. She got them bottles of water and David sat on a stool, stretching his racing blades in front of him.

"I feel contaminated, sitting there all day listening to that damn district attorney."

Prof. Freddy finished his drink and poured himself another. "I know it's personal to you, but it's a job to her."

"She's not sure you're guilty," Anna said. She wiped the sweat from her arms with a large terrycloth towel. She leaned over and dried her legs. Donnie was distracted. She looked up at him and smiled. She had caught him looking. *Too many shared memories.* "I'm going to shower. You should, too," she said to David. He nodded and stood up and they went off together.

"That should relieve some of his tension," Prof. Freddy said with a smile.

"Back to work," Donnie said. The look he had exchanged with A.K. reminded him once again why he was jealous of David.

〈〈〈〈〈

The next morning, the crowd outside the courtroom was even larger. The case had made the national news, complete with photographs of Cordelia and Francoise framing a shot of David in his wheelchair. There were aerial shots of The Heath. A long shot of David running on the lakeside Austin estate had brought a crowd to the front gate. They tried to swarm the car as they left for court.

The six o'clock news would show the shot of David being wheeled into the courthouse next to the zoomed-in shot of his previous day's run.

June resumed, "The State calls Roger Wilson."

The lanky sheriff wore a brown suit and yellow tie instead of his police uniform; he smiled and nodded to David as he walked to the witness stand.

After some preliminary questions June asked, "Sheriff Wilson, do you recall events at the Lehrer estate in Akron last February 28?"

"Yes, I do."

"Why were you there?"

He looked at his notepad, then answered. "I had stationed two of my deputies at the Lehrer property, The Heath, to provide protection to the Lehrer family. I was there to check on them."

"Why did the family need protection?"

"At Mr. Lehrer's request, my office had escorted a group of Filipino workers from the estate to the airport in Cleveland and made sure they boarded flights out of the country."

"Was that a usual sort of thing for the sheriff's office to do?"

Wilson smiled. "No. But the workers had been discharged by Mr. Lehrer. He's a prominent citizen and I agreed to see that they left the country."

"Who was present when you arrived at the Lehrer estate?"

The sheriff looked at David and said, "Mr. Lehrer was there and also David Lewis was there."

"Sheriff, during that time, was the Filipino Mafia discussed between you and the defendant?"

"Not discussed exactly."

"What do you mean?"

"We were alone. Mr. Lehrer had gone off to check on something. He was very agitated. Anyway, after he left, I said to David, 'Your father-in-law believes you all need protection from the Filipino Mafia'."

"What did he say?"

"He didn't say anything. He just rolled his eyes and shook his head."

"What did you interpret that to mean?"

"I took it to mean, *Humor the old man.*"

"And that's what you did? Humor him?"

"Yes."

"Sheriff, what is the Filipino Mafia?"

"If it exists, I never heard of it."

"Your witness, Mr. Cuinn," June said.

"Hello, Sheriff Wilson," Donnie said. "We appreciate you coming all the way from Akron to testify in this case."

The sheriff chuckled. "You're welcome. I always wanted to see Texas."

"Tell me, Sheriff, how well do you know David Lewis?"

Wilson nodded to David, who smiled and returned the greeting. "I met him when he moved to Akron several years ago. We've been involved in civic affairs, youth camps, the half-marathon, things like that. I know him pretty well."

"During all that time, have you ever heard David say anything disrespectful about his father-in-law or in any way act disrespectful toward him?"

"No, not that I ever heard."

"Did you ever see him roll his eyes, referring to Mr. Lehrer?"

"No."

"Or ask you by words or gestures to humor Mr. Lehrer?"

"No."

"So, when he made the gesture you saw, is it just as likely that he meant something like, *Isn't this weird?* or, *Isn't this scary?*"

"I didn't take it that way."

"But you did take the threat seriously enough that you spent taxpayers' money escorting all those Filipinos out on the country, didn't you?"

The sheriff paused. "As I said, Mr. Lehrer is a prominent citizen."

"But you must have believed there was some basis for his concern? If this was an old man's paranoia, you wouldn't have taken all the actions you took, would you?"

"I thought his fears were exaggerated, but I wanted him to feel we were responding to his concerns."

"Remembering the extraordinary effort your office took, did you believe that although Mr. Lehrer may have exaggerated it, the threat to the family was real?"

The sheriff paused then replied carefully. "I had to assume there was danger at some level and make sure the family was safe."

"Sheriff, you say you know Mr. Lewis pretty well. Do you know his wife, Cordelia?"

"Not as well, but yes, I know her."

"Did you ever have any indication that there was a problem in the Lewis marriage?"

"No. They seemed very much in love."

"And Francoise Gaulle. Did you know her?"

"I met her, that's all."

"Was she a lesbian, do you know?"

The sheriff smiled. "I have no idea."

Donnie thanked the witness and turned to June. On redirect she asked, "Did the defendant say he thought the family was in danger?"

"No. He didn't say anything."

"He just rolled his eyes?"

"Yes, ma'am."

《《《《《

During the lunch break, Donnie met with Sam, the jury consultant, who said, "Our veteran has stopped taking notes. He just stares at David. He's sizing him up. Tell David to meet his gaze."

"What about the woman CPA?"

"She's writing like crazy. She looks around at the other jurors. She nods when the DA makes a point. She's building her case. She's trouble."

"Fuck."

《《《《《

"The State calls Claude Gaulle."

The thin Frenchman was dressed in a black suit, a black shirt and a black tie. He brushed back his bleached hair with a shake of his head and then turned his aquiline gaze at David Lewis with a detectable sneer.

"Thank you for being here, Mr. Gaulle," June said. "Tell the jury your name, your occupation, and where you live."

"My name is Claude Gaulle. I am a *couture* designer. I live in Paris... France."

"That was a long way for you to come."

"I would go to Mars to face the murderer of my sister."

"Was Francoise your sister?"

"Yes, she was."

"Mr. Gaulle, when did you meet the defendant's wife, Cordelia Lehrer?"

"In Paris, ten years ago."

"How did you meet?"

"I met her through Francoise. She and Francoise were lovers."

June looked at the jury and let the statement sink in. Donnie rose to his feet. "Objection, Your Honor. That's the witness' opinion."

The judge said wearily, "Ask the witness what he saw, not what he believes, Ms. Fenton."

"Of course, Your Honor." She smiled at Donnie as if to say, *You're not going to like this.* "How do you know that, Mr. Gaulle?"

"How do I know? I saw them in bed together. I saw them kiss. My sister told me..."

"Objection." Donnie was on his feet again.

The judge broke in, "The jury will disregard that last comment."

That's my two objections for the day, Donnie thought.

June resumed her questions. "Did there come a time when Cordelia and Francoise left France and moved to the United States?"

"Yes. They moved to Cordelia's home in Akron, Ohio."

"Did you visit them there?"

"Yes."

"What was the occasion for your visit?"

He sniffed. "I visited to assist Cordelia with her wedding dress."

"And what wedding was this?"

"Cordelia's wedding to…him." He pointed a long slender finger, its tip polished deep black, at David.

"Let the record show the witness is pointing at the defendant." David sat stoically. June went on. "What did you observe about your sister's relationship with Cordelia Lehrer when you were in Akron?"

"They were still lovers. *Certainement.*"

June looked at Donnie and smiled. "For Mr. Cuinn's benefit, what did you observe?"

"I observed them kissing. I saw them in bed together. I heard them talk as lovers do."

"And yet Cordelia Lehrer married David Lewis."

"*Oui,* she did."

"Why?"

"For her, it was a business arrangement, I believe."

Donnie couldn't help himself. He was on his feet again. "Objection."

"I withdraw the question, Your Honor. Mr. Gaulle, how well did you know the defendant when you were in Akron?"

"I met him several times."

"Tell us about the first time you met him."

"I was playing a game, flirting with Cordelia, to see how he would react."

"How did he react?"

"He was very jealous. I was afraid he was going to assault me, *mon Dieu.*"

"So, the defendant was very jealous when you flirted with his fiancée." Seeing Donnie rise to object, she said, "Withdrawn. Thank you, Mr. Gaulle. Your witness, Mr. Cuinn."

Donnie waited, pretending to read through his notes. Then he said, "I am sorry for the death of your sister, *Monsieur* Gaulle."

Claude sniffed haughtily.

"I'd like to take you back to that first meeting in Akron. You testified that you pretended to flirt with Cordelia to make David Lewis jealous. Is that correct?"

"Yes. It was a little game."

"Whose idea was it to play that little game?"

"I don't understand."

"Well, did you discuss playing a little game to make David Lewis jealous with anyone else?"

"No," Claude said. "I didn't discuss it. I just did it." He smiled at the jury. *"Oui. Je suis français* after all."

Donnie smiled also. "Yes. You *are* French. And I believe you testified that your game worked and that he became jealous?"

"Yes, he did."

"How did David act toward your sister?"

"He never showed any jealousy toward her. He was such a *naif.* I don't think he had any idea they were lovers before the wedding."

"I ask you, *Monsieur*, are you a homosexual?"

Claude raised his eyebrows and looked at June. She shrugged. Then Claude said, "Yes, I am. Is that a crime in Texas?"

Donnie laughed. "Certainly not in Travis County."

There were some chuckles from the audience. The judge rapped his gavel lightly and said, "Proceed, Mr. Cuinn."

"Monsieur, as a gay man, did you find this *naif*, David Lewis, attractive when you met him?"

Claude turned and looked at David as if examining him. "No, not really. He's not my type."

"Really? After your little game, did you not proposition David Lewis?"

"I do not know the word."

Donnie smiled and looked down at his notes. "I believe the word in French is *partenaire*. Did you ask David Lewis to be your *partenaire*? That is, to have a homosexual relationship with you?"

"Did I ask him that? Of course not."

"And didn't he refuse that offer?"

"No. That did not happen."

"And aren't you still resentful that he turned you down?"

June stood. "Your Honor, the witness has said that he did not ask him. He's arguing with the witness."

"Yes, the objection is sustained. Anything else, Mr. Cuinn?"

"Just a couple more questions, Judge. *Monsieur*, you have had many *partenaires*, have you not?"

Claude raised his head disdainfully. "I have many friends."

"So is it fair to say, *Monsieur*, that you are not accustomed to being rejected by men you find attractive?"

"As I said, I have many friends."

"Do you hate David Lewis?"

June stood up to object but the judge waved her down. Claude said, "I despise him. He killed my sister."

"Do you hate him enough to lie about whether his wife and your sister were lovers?"

"I am not lying about that."

"About something else then?"

June rose. "I object, Your Honor."

"I withdraw the question," Donnie said. "I have nothing more for *Monsieur* Gaulle."

Donnie huddled with Sam after the court recessed. "How did our guy react to my cross?" He was referring to the veteran, their key juror.

"Well," the consultant said, "when the sheriff was testifying, he never took his eyes off David."

"And Claude?"

"I'd say he hates the Frenchman."

They returned to the courtroom.

June's next witness was a housekeeper at the condo. She testified that Francoise often spent the night in Cordelia's apartment, except when the *señor* was there. She admitted to Donnie that she did not know if they shared a bed.

June's final witness was a psychiatrist, Dr. Patrice Graves. She was a tall blonde woman who had been sitting in the back of the courtroom during the trial. She was pleasant-looking and neatly dressed. The contrast with Doctor Sid was not favorable. Donnie knew that. *What's done is done,* he thought.

June qualified her as an expert on traumatic stress disorders. She had written on the subject in scholarly journals and had been retained by the Veteran's Administration to design treatment protocols for returning veterans with Post-Traumatic Stress Disorder.

"Doctor," June asked, "what is PTSD?"

The doctor turned to address the jury in a familiar, comfortable way.

"Post-traumatic stress disorder," she said, "is an anxiety disorder. It is a result of experiencing or witnessing a terribly frightening, life-threatening event. PTSD sufferers re-experience the traumatic event in some way. They tend to avoid places, people or other things that remind them of the event, and are hyper-sensitive to normal life experiences."

She paused, took a sip of water, then turned again to the jury, using the same conversational tone. "Although this condition has likely existed since human beings have endured trauma, PTSD has only been a formal diagnosis since 1980. However, it was called by different names as early as the American Civil War, when combat veterans were referred to as suffering from soldier's heart. In World War I, it was called combat fatigue. PTSD has also been called shell shock."

"Dr. Graves," she asked, "what are the symptoms of PTSD?"

"The main symptoms are re-experiencing the traumatic event, flashbacks and nightmares, and feelings of distress or intense physical reactions when reminded of the event, such as sweating, pounding heart, or nausea."

"Thank you, Doctor Graves. Do all soldiers who experience trauma in combat suffer from PTSD?"

She answered, "Thank God, no. Many more have stress from the trauma, but it is short-lived and they're responsive to treatment. In the military, it is referred to as 'combat stress.'"

"Doctor, in your experience, if a person suffers severe trauma in combat, for example the loss of both legs, but is treated and fitted with prostheses, then adapts well enough to the prostheses to run marathons and engage in prize fighting, has a successful career in the newspaper business and writes a best-selling book, is that person more likely to have suffered from PTSD or from combat stress?"

"Combat stress. Also, I would say it is highly unlikely that such a person suffers from PTSD."

"Doctor, what are blackouts?"

"A blackout is a period of unconsciousness or lack of awareness when you are unable to recall what happened or what you did."

"What causes blackouts?"

"Blackouts may occur as a result of brain damage, drug side effects, excessive alcohol consumption, or disorders affecting brain function, such as epilepsy. Blackouts can also be due to a recent traumatic event, in which case you may forget everything that happened right before or right after the event. That is called anterograde amnesia."

"Are blackouts associated with combat stress?"

"No, they are not. I might add, blackouts are rarely a symptom of PTSD, either."

"Thank you, Doctor. Your witness."

Donnie smiled at the witness. "Hello, Doctor Graves. My name is Don Cuinn. I represent Mr. Lewis here."

"Hello."

"Doctor, you seem very at ease here. Have you testified in court a lot?"

She smiled. "It depends on what you mean by a lot."

"You tell me, Doctor. How many times have you testified on behalf of the government in cases involving PTSD?"

"I couldn't say exactly."

Donnie looked down at the pad in front of him. There were some doodles on it. "We don't need exact numbers. Approximately. Two dozen times?"

"I'm sure."

"At least twenty-four times then? Maybe more?"

"Is that a question?"

"Well, I thought so, but never mind. Let me ask you this: in any of those cases were you ever a witness on behalf of the armed services member or veteran involved in the case?"

This time she answered more carefully. "Probably not."

"Probably not? Surely you would recall if you ever testified for a soldier or sailor or a veteran. Did you or did you not?"

She raised her head haughtily. "I did not."

"And in those two dozen or more cases, did you ever conclude that the claimant or defendant in fact had PTSD?"

She shrugged. "I don't believe I did."

Donnie held up a monograph. "Do you recognize this?"

"It looks like a paper I prepared for the *American Journal of Psychiatry*."

Donnie nodded. "It is. I read your paper. Is it fair to say you are very skeptical about many of the claims of PTSD?"

She said, "I do believe that the symptoms in many of the cases are exaggerated."

"Why would someone do that?"

She shrugged. "To establish a claim for compensation. Or," she turned and looked at David, "as a defense when they are accused of a crime."

Donnie thought, *Why the hell did I ask her that?* He recovered and went on. "Doctor, do you know David Lewis?"

"I've never met the defendant."

"So, you have never treated him or examined him, is that correct?"

She laughed. "I said I've never met him."

"Would you think that a doctor who has met him and treated him would be in a better position than you to diagnose his medical condition?"

She folded her hands and met Donnie's gaze. "That would depend on the doctor."

"I agree with you about that, Doctor."

TWENTY-ONE

The next morning, Don sat alone in the courtroom, waiting for court to begin. The prosecution had rested and it was now time for Donnie to present the witnesses in support of David Lewis. He had come ahead so he could walk in without the clamor of the crowd and the harassment of news cameras. He needed quiet time to compose himself. Prof. Freddy and Wiley had critiqued the situation the previous evening, and he reflected back on it.

"Fenton has made her case," Prof. Freddy said. "You need to talk to your client again. If he pleads to manslaughter, you can argue at the punishment phase that he was enraged and in a sudden fit of passion."

"That's right, boss," Wiley chimed in. "Nobody is buying the blackout story."

"How many murder cases have you defended, Wiley?" Donnie asked.

Wiley didn't reply but Donnie knew what he was thinking, 'As many as you, boss.'

Prof. Freddy smiled. He enjoyed dustups. "His wife and the Mademoiselle from Armentières were lovers. You believe that, don't you?"

"I don't. But even if they were lovers, David didn't know about it, so he had no motive. If he blacked out, then he couldn't have intent or knowledge. Therefore, he's not guilty of murder. Now I need to get to work on making the jury believe that."

Prof. Freddy picked up the whiskey bottle and shuffled out of the room. "You do that. I'll go work on the appeal."

Donnie was busy reviewing his notes when people began to enter the courtroom. David was wheeled in, a blanket over his lap, as usual.

Donnie smiled at the Parsons family. They filed in and sat in their usual places. Anna had warned him they were getting tired of their paid vacation in Austin and she told him she had promised the teenage daughters a trip to the Domain shopping center after today's session.

Donnie looked around the crowded room. There were no empty seats. The courtroom was not large, nor made for spectators. It barely paid lip service to the defendant's Sixth Amendment right to a public trial. He thought about the courtroom in the Velda courthouse, with its rows of benches and the balcony where lawyers gathered and watched notorious cases, whispering to each other until the judge sent the bailiff up to tell them to shut up or leave. The public was not screened there. You did not have to stand in line for hours to observe the dispensing of justice. By comparison, this place seemed more like Orwell's *Room 101*.

Judge Okeke made his entrance. All rose. The room was still, only the occasional rustling of paper. The court reporter looked at Donnie expectantly. *Showtime!*

"The defense calls Timothy Lewis."

David's brother gave his name and his address as Vandenberg Air Force Base, California and admitted he had just recently been promoted to major general in the United States Air Force. Donnie had insisted Tim wear his dress uniform and all his braid.

"General Lewis," Donnie began. He had gone over the brother's testimony carefully with him. "How would you describe your brother's emotional health?"

Tim paused and looked at David who was staring down at his hands. "I'd say it is very fragile."

"For how long has his emotional health seemed fragile to you?"

"Since my wedding day, fifteen years ago."

"That was before he served in Iraq?"

"Yes."

"Tell the jury what happened on your wedding day."

"Our mother was killed in an automobile accident."

"Go on."

"My wife and I had left on our honeymoon. I got a call from the Cleburne police that my mother and a neighbor had been fatally hit by a train at a crossing on the way home from our wedding reception. Of course, we turned around and returned to Cleburne."

"What did you find there?"

"David was a wreck. He wouldn't come out of his room. I had to drag him to the funeral. He and Mom were close, but this was beyond that."

"What do you mean?"

"He said it was all his fault, that if he had driven Mom home like he was supposed to, the accident wouldn't have happened."

June interrupted him. "Objection. Hearsay, Your Honor."

"It goes to the defendant's state of mind, Judge."

"I'll allow it," the judge said, "go on, General."

"He could hardly function, he wouldn't eat; he was having nightmares that woke the whole house up. My wife and I stayed the week. He finally calmed down and we felt it was safe to leave him."

"What happened next?"

"David finished college. He should have been looking for work. Instead, he just hung around town, drinking and getting into trouble. Finally, when I had to bail him out of jail for fighting in a bar, I suggested he should join the army."

"Join the army? Why?"

"I thought he needed a hard job with the kind of discipline he would get in the army. He needed to put the accident behind him. I hoped that an army tour would allow him to get on with his life."

"Did it? Was he able to get on with his life?"

Tim looked at David. "Not in the way I had hoped," he lamented.

"What happened?"

"David was in a street battle in Iraq. He lost both legs."

"How often did you see your brother after he was injured?"

"Not often. He stayed with us for a few days after he left the hospital. He woke us up with nightmares. He was moody and withdrawn. But then he got his prostheses and started boxing and learning to run in them and we didn't see him often."

"Why?"

"He said he was busy. He got a job in Cleveland on a newspaper. He seemed to be doing well. And then of course he got married."

"What happened at his wedding?"

"We quarreled. He blamed me for talking him into joining the army and for the loss of his legs."

"How do you feel now about your brother?"

He looked at David, who still refused to meet his eyes. "I'm proud of how he has overcome his tragedy. He runs the Lehrer newspapers. He wrote a book. He's done very well. I'm very proud of him and I love him very much."

Donnie turned to June. "Your witness."

She began at once, "General, have you ever been there when the defendant experienced a blackout?"

Tim thought a minute. "Only once."

Donnie could tell that June was surprised. So was he. *Tim's improvising.*

June continued, "The defendant experienced a blackout in your presence? When was that?"

"At his wedding, when we quarreled, I think he did."

"You think he did? What did he do?"

"He went blank. He didn't answer me. I think now that was because we were talking about his injuries, he just blacked out."

"You said, you think that now. Did you think it at the time?"

"I didn't know what to think."

"Did you send for medical help, call EMS?"

"No. It lasted a short time and then he snapped to. That was the last time we spoke."

"He could have just been angry, couldn't he?"

"I think it was more than that."

"You *think*, but you don't know, do you?"

Tim shook his head. "I believe he blacked out."

"You're a good brother, General. That's all I have, Your Honor."

Tim looked to the judge. "May I say one more thing, Your Honor?"

The judge looked at both counsel then said, "Go ahead, General."

"I want to say that I love my brother, and I am truly sorry for whatever I did that led to his injury." He looked at David. "I'm so sorry."

"You may step down, General," the judge said.

Tim walked erectly across the room. He leaned down and hugged David, who whispered, "That's all I ever wanted to hear, Timmy."

Donnie's next witness was David's platoon leader who testified about the patrol on which David was injured. He also read into evidence the citation David received:

The President of the United States
Takes Pleasure in Presenting
The Distinguished Service Cross
To DAVID AARON LEWIS, Corporal, *U.S. Army*
For Services as Set Forth in the Following Citation:

For extraordinary heroism in action while serving with Mortar Platoon, 2nd Battalion, 47th Infantry Regiment, 1st Stryker Brigade Combat Team, 15th Infantry Division, Multi-National Corps-Iraq. Corporal Lewis distinguished himself while engaged in combat operations against armed insurgents in Baghdad, Iraq. While his platoon was patrolling Baghdad's Huriyah neighborhood, they were ambushed with an array of explosively formed projectiles, small arms fire, and rocket propelled grenades. After being burned, wounded, and knocked temporarily unconscious, Corporal Lewis began to engage the enemy with his M4 carbine. Under heavy enemy fire, he recovered his immobilized platoon leader from the smoldering Stryker vehicle, then returned to the vehicle to man the .50-caliber M2 machine gun despite the threat of exploding ordnance and enemy fire. By establishing fire superiority against the enemy, Corporal Lewis freed other soldiers who had been pinned, which allowed them to administer first aid to his wounded and burned comrades, during which time he was severely wounded himself, resulting in the loss of both his legs to the knees. His valorous actions and bravery, which saved his platoon leader's life and forced the enemy to flee, are in keeping with the finest traditions of the military service, reflecting great credit upon himself, his command, and the United States Army.

June had no questions for the platoon leader and Donnie called his next witness, Doctor Priam Siddiqui. Doctor Sid gave the same general description of PTSD that the prosecution's expert witness had given. He described the times as a psychiatrist in the military he had treated David during David's recovery and rehabilitation.

Donnie asked, "Doctor, what is your professional opinion of David Lewis' medical condition?"

"I saw him for several months before his discharge. He complained of flashbacks and bad memories and nightmares. He had negative feelings of guilt and shame, centering on the death of his mother, for which he felt responsible. I diagnosed him as having post-traumatic stress disorder, aggravated by a pre-military traumatic experience, arising from the sudden death of his mother."

"What treatment did you prescribe?"

"Cognitive Behavioral Therapy. The goal is to help the patient understand how to replace negative or fearful thoughts about his trauma with more accurate and less depressing thoughts and ways to cope with feelings such as anger, fear and guilt. I also prescribed anti-depressant medication."

"How did he respond to the therapy?"

"Moderately well."

"At that time, what was David's prognosis?"

"In some cases, with therapy and medication, a person can be rid of the symptoms altogether. In other cases, the symptoms may be less frequent or less intense. I put David in the latter category. The symptoms might reappear, but they should be manageable. I encouraged him to continue therapy and to continue his medication. There was no reason he could not perform everyday activities, succeed at his profession or enter into a meaningful relationship."

Donnie went on. "Now, Doctor, when did you see David Lewis last?"

"I examined him on two occasions in preparation for my testimony."

"What did you observe?"

"He was in distress, obviously as a result of the events."

"The events?"

"The shooting. He said that he had experienced the symptoms I noted before, but discontinued therapy and medication. He said the symptoms were less frequent, but more severe, and that he had blackouts."

"To what do you attribute these blackouts?"

"Severe stress causing him to relive the traumatic experiences he suffered. His defense to those experiences was to black it out completely."

"In his statement to the police, David Lewis said that before the shooting, he blacked out and remembered nothing after reliving a wartime experience. Would that be consistent with his condition at the time you examined him?"

"Yes, it would."

"Doctor, did you hear Dr. Graves' testimony, where she suggested David might be suffering from combat stress?"

Doctor Sid smiled. "Yes, I heard her."

"Doctor, what is combat stress?"

Dr. Sid shook his head. "It's a military term."

"What do you mean by that?"

"When a soldier experiences traumatic stress during an engagement, he may be sent to the rear for a short time, until he's deemed fit to return to duty. He's said to have 'combat stress.' After a short time, he is sent back to his unit. He is not treated by a physician or given medication. Instead, he is counseled by a superior, what I call a 'pep talk' and urged to go back to his unit where his buddies are counting on him. It's a farce, really. Many of the men I have treated, those who have PTSD but have been told they only had 'combat stress,' are justifiably angry when they learn they have PTSD."

"In your opinion, did David Lewis experience combat stress?"

"Certainly not."

Donnie turned to June and nodded. "Pass the witness."

The swarthy plump doctor wiped his forehead with a large handkerchief. He looked up at the judge. "Hot in here, isn't it?"

"Maybe more down there than up here," the judge said with a smile. The jury smiled also.

June began her cross examination. "Doctor Siddiqui, how many cases of post-traumatic stress disorder have you seen in your practice, both in the military and in private practice?"

The doctor pursued his lips. "I'm not sure. Hundreds certainly."

"Hundreds. And in how many of those cases did the patient experience blackouts?"

He hesitated. "I don't recall all of the symptoms of all those I saw."

"Besides the defendant, do you recall any you might share with us?"

"As I said, I don't recall."

Her assistant handed her a monograph. She held it up. "You also have written about PTSD, haven't you? Do you recognize this monograph?"

She handed it to the clerk for identification and the clerk handed it to the doctor. "Yes. I wrote it."

"What is its title?"

"Symptoms and Treatment of Post-Traumatic Stress Disorder."

"If you would, Doctor, look through your monograph and point out any place in it where you mention blackouts as a symptom of PTSD."

The sweat was back on his forehead. "I don't think there are any. But that doesn't mean…"

June stopped him. "That's all, Doctor. You've answered my question."

Donnie stood. "Let him explain his answer, Your Honor."

The judge nodded.

"I was going to say that I was talking about primary symptoms in this paper. I was not discussing secondary symptoms that appear later when the syndrome is prolonged and untreated."

"Thank you for that explanation," June said, looking at the jury with a shrug. "One last question. If a person tells you he has one of these secondary symptoms such as blackouts, how do you know if he's telling you the truth?"

Doctor Sid replied. "I'm a trained therapist. I believe I would know if the symptom was imaginary…which I might add, can be debilitating in itself."

"I'm sure. But what if it was contrived, say as a defense in a criminal case. Would you always be able to tell?"

"I hope so."

"Well, hope springs eternal. That's all I have, Your Honor."

Judge Okeke looked expectantly at Donnie, as if to say, *is that all?* Donnie disappointed him. "The defense calls David Lewis, Your Honor."

A rustle sounded through the courtroom. David removed the blanket, pushed himself out of his wheelchair, steadied himself, and walked to the witness stand. The jurors watched him closely. He stood erect while he was sworn in, then moved easily up the one step and into the witness chair. He turned to Donnie and waited.

He gave his full name and Akron address, then Donnie said, "I see you are walking today, David. How?"

David smiled and raised the cuff on his pants leg nearest the jury box. "These are my T22s, my prostheses. I can walk in them, but they're not comfortable if I'm going to be sitting a long time, like in a courtroom." He smiled at the jury. "This is the first day I've worn them at the trial."

Donnie took him quickly through his childhood, college, his courtship and marriage and his present employment. "Now," he said, "I'd like to turn to your experiences in the military. "Why did you enlist?"

"I was a mess. My mother's car had been run into by a train and she was killed. My brother thought a tour in the army would help me get through all those bad memories."

"Did you serve overseas?"

"Yes."

"We've heard about your citation for bravery in Iraq. What other combat experiences did you have there?"

"The one that haunts me most was in Fallujah. We had to go house to house, I was standing in front of the door of one house. Suddenly, the door flew open and this enemy soldier screamed and threw himself at me."

"What happened?"

"That was the first man I killed in Iraq. That's been my nightmare."

"Tell the jury about that."

"I dream about the door flying open and the man screaming. It's so real, it seems like I'm back in Iraq."

"How long did the dreams continue?"

"They never really stopped. They've become less frequent, but when I have them, they're more intense. And then sometimes, when under stress, I'll have these flashbacks while awake—I relive the experience and then black out."

"How long do your blackouts last?"

"Not long, as best as I can tell."

"What do you recall about what takes place during a blackout?"

"Nothing at all. Some times I've moved, and I don't remember doing it, but I'm in a different room, things like that."

"How many times have you had these blackouts?"

David thought a minute. "Once or twice a year. Something I thought about or read or saw on TV would bring back the scene in Iraq and I would black out."

"What treatment have you had for these problems?"

"None since I was discharged. The medication made me feel loopy." He smiled at the jury. "And I don't like going to shrinks. I found that extreme exercise and really challenging work keeps them under control. Together, of course, with a happy home life."

"What kind of extreme exercise?"

"Mainly running and weight training. I have sports T22s that work really well. I run every day. I've run in marathons and half-marathons. I ran in the 10-K here in Austin."

"Tell us about the challenging work?"

"I'm the managing editor for the KL Media newspapers. There are fifty of them. My job requires a lot of travel and long hours."

"And the happy home life?"

"I have a beautiful wife and a young son."

"Tell the jury about your wife."

"Cordelia is a wonderful wife and mother. We met in college. She is a jour-
nalist and she is also an art historian. She worked in Paris. She is the publisher
of *This Texas*. She's a loving and caring mother to our son. I love her very much."

"You heard the deceased's brother testify that your wife and the deceased had a sexual relationship. Is that true?"

"No. It's a lie. I understand why Claude hates me. But his testimony
about Cordelia and Francoise was not true."

"When did you first hear such an accusation?"

"The very first time I heard such a thing even mentioned was when
Lieutenant Chambers brought it up in our interview."

"So, before the shooting, you had never heard such an accusation?"

"No. Never."

"Do you and your wife love each other?"

"Yes. Very much."

"Now I want you to walk us through the events on the day Francoise
Gaulle was shot. What was the first thing that happened that day?"

"I got a call from my father-in-law asking me to come to his house
right away and to bring my son with me."

"Who is your father-in-law?"

"Kingston Lehrer. He is the owner of KL Media."

"What happened next?"

"When Tony and I got to his house, the Chief, I mean Mr. Lehrer,
told me that the head of the household staff, Raul Dakila, had tried to extort
money from him. Dakila was responsible for all the domestic staff at the estate—housekeepers, gardeners, drivers. He said they were his family, nephews
and nieces, grandchildren, and so forth. There were about twenty of them, all
Filipino. Mr. Lehrer refused to be extorted and Dakila threatened our family.
Mr. Lehrer called Sheriff Wilson, who escorted the entire staff to the airport
and saw that they left the country."

"What happened next?"

"My father-in-law told me to go get Cory…Cordelia and bring her
home. I flew to Austin in a company plane to fly her to Akron, where she and
the rest of the family would be safe."

"Safe from whom?"

"Safe from Mr. Dakila and his associates who might want to harm us."

"When did you first hear the term 'Filipino Mafia'?"

"When Mr. Lehrer used it to describe the people who might want to harm the family."

"Sheriff Wilson testified that when Mr. Lehrer used the words 'Filipino Mafia,' you rolled your eyes. Did that happen?"

"I don't recall. It may have. If I did that, I think what I was indicating was, something like *Wow, what a strange day.* I didn't mean I didn't take the Chief's concern seriously, because I did. He received threats all the time." He looked at the jury and smiled. "Some readers don't like his papers' political positions. Whenever the Chief was threatened personally, he just shrugged it off. It never seemed to bother him. This was different. I could see that he was really worried."

"What happened next?"

"Like I said, I flew to Austin. I took a ride-share to our condo downtown. I hadn't eaten all day, so I asked the driver to stop at a burger shop. We drove to the condo, I got out, and went upstairs. It was about ten or eleven at night. I saw my wife's door key on the table by the front door, where she always leaves it when she comes in. I saw it so I knew she was there. The apartment was dark, so I thought she must already be asleep. I decided not to wake her and to wait until morning to tell her what was going on. I knew she'd be upset, worried about our son. And the rest of the family, of course. I went to my bedroom."

"You have separate bedrooms?"

David looked at the jury. "Yes. Taking my T22s on and off can be noisy. And she tells me I snore." A couple of the jurors smiled. "I took off my prostheses and lay down on top of the covers."

"And then what happened?"

"I guess I fell asleep. I don't know for how long. But voices coming from Cory's bedroom woke me up. My first thought was that the Filipinos were in the apartment."

"What did you do next?"

"I remember thinking I didn't have time to put on my T22s so I hoisted myself into my wheelchair. I started to Cory's room, then I remembered to get my gun out of the nightstand."

"Did the voices continue?"

"Yes. I got to the bedroom door as fast as I could. I was at the door and it flew open."

"Think carefully now, David. What happened next?"

David shook his head. He looked directly at the jurors, waited, and then said, "The door flew open. I saw a shadowy figure. The next thing I remember is being in my wheelchair, holding the gun, and Francie dead on the floor."

"Did you shoot her?"

"I know I did, but I don't remember doing it. I completely blacked out."

"Where was your wife when you came out of the blackout?"

"She was screaming. She was covered with blood. She went into the bathroom. I could hear her crying. After I called for help, I tried to calm her down but she was in hysterics."

"Where is she now?"

"She is being treated for nervous exhaustion and shock. I just wish she was well enough to be here and deny the lies about her and Francie."

June started her cross-examination immediately, not giving the ending of David's testimony much time to sink in.

"Mr. Lewis, do you consider yourself a violent man?"

David thought a minute. "I've been in violent situations, like in the war, but no, I don't."

"And yet there's been violence surrounding your life since an early age, hasn't there?"

Donnie jumped to his feet. "Your Honor, what kind of question is that?"

"I'll rephrase, Judge." Her assistant handed her some documents. "You were in a Golden Gloves program when you were in high school, is that correct?"

"In Cleburne, Texas, yes."

"Isn't it the case that you were suspended from high school for fighting and one of the conditions of your reinstatement was that you sign up with the Golden Gloves?"

David hesitated, then answered. "I believe that's right."

"Did you consider prize fighting in high school *extreme* exercise?"

"I guess so."

"Let's move on to your college days. Do you recall a fight in the hall outside the offices of the college newspaper?"

"I believe I do. The jerk didn't like something I wrote."

"Did you knock him out, and were you then placed on probation?"

"Yes to both questions."

"So you were violent long before you served in Iraq?"

Donnie said, "Argumentative, Your Honor."

June nodded. "Withdrawn."

"Let's turn now to the months after your mother was killed. I believe you testified that, 'you were a mess.' What did you mean by that?"

"I was guilt-ridden and angry at the world."

"Do you act out when you feel guilty and angry?"

"I don't know what you mean by 'act out.'"

June took another document from her assistant. "Were you arrested for driving while intoxicated?"

"Yes, but not convicted."

"Were you arrested for brawling in a bar?"

"Yes, but not convicted."

"Isn't the reason you were not convicted was that your brother made a deal with the district attorney not to prosecute you if you enlisted in the United States Army?"

"He may have."

"After your discharge from the army, you went to work for a newspaper in Cleveland, correct?"

"Yes, I did."

"During that time, were you arrested for brawling in a strip bar?"

"Yes. I spent the night in the drunk tank."

"Yes, you did. Now you testified that you have a beautiful wife and that you are in love with her?"

"That's right."

"Are you a jealous husband?

"No, not really."

"Before you married, didn't you warn Francoise Gaulle's brother to stop flirting with your fiancée?"

"No. That was a joke."

"And after you married, didn't you get in an argument and almost come to blows with a man in the Upside Down Bar on Sixth Street here in Austin?"

David answered belligerently, "He was making passes at my wife. She was annoyed and I told him to cut it out."

"So, you were very protective of your wife, right?"

"Like most men would be, I imagine."

"Your Honor," June said, "I am going to jump to another subject. Would this be a good time to recess?"

"Mr. Cuinn?"

Donnie stood. *I don't really want to give the jury all night to reflect on what just happened.* "We're ready to keep going, Your Honor."

The Judge looked at the jury. "You've had a long day. Get a good night's sleep, don't talk about the case, and we'll see you in the morning."

Fuck.

After the jury filed out, the judge called them to the bench. "I want to finish this up and have it in the jury's hands by this time tomorrow. And Mr. Cuinn, tell your media person to turn it down a notch. The gag rule applies to her too." Donnie tried to explain, but the judge cut him off. "I know, I know. And you two get together on a schedule for the penalty phase." He looked meaningfully at Donnie. "Just in case your boy goes down. Now let's get at those jury instructions."

⟨⟨⟨⟨⟨

It was gloomy back at the lakeside compound. David was angry. "I pushed a kid down in kindergarten, too."

"All that violence stuff hurt us," Donnie admitted, "I should have prepared you better."

David shrugged. "Now you tell me. Oh, what the hell. It is what it is. What's tomorrow?"

"Your wife is a lesbian, yada, yada, yada."

David turned to Anna and asked, "I think I need my manhood reinforced. How about you and me hit the hot tub?"

Anna looked at Donnie.

Donnie nodded. "Sure. Go ahead. Come back later and we'll go over your answers again." He watched them leave and said to Wiley, "Sometimes I hope we lose."

Wiley looked shocked. "Christ, boss."

"Just joking. But David Lewis can be a pain in the ass, can't he?"

❝❝❝❝❝

The next morning, the last day of the trial, the jury filed in, somber faced. David quickly walked to the witness chair, almost jauntily. He settled in, took a drink of water, and looked at June, expectantly.

She began, "Mr. Lewis, were your wife Cordelia and the deceased Francoise Gaulle lovers?"

"No, they were not."

"So when Claude Gaulle testified, under oath, that he saw your wife and Francoise kissing and in bed together, he was lying?"

"Yes, he was lying."

"Let me ask you this then: Were your wife and Francoise close friends for a long time?"

"Yes, they were."

"They were close friends before you moved to Akron?"

"Yes. I believe they met in Paris."

"Did they spend a lot of time together?"

"Yes. She was Cordelia's personal assistant, and then the editor of *This Texas*."

"You and your wife slept in separate bedrooms?"

"I explained that."

"Your wife owns a penthouse here. Do you spend much of the time apart?"

"She was here getting the magazine we bought on course."

"Working closely with Francoise Gaulle?"

190

"Francoise was the editor, so yes, of course."

"The two of them lived in the same condominium complex?"

"Yes. Francoise had her own apartment."

"Did you know that the two of them went to parties and receptions together and were perceived as a couple by Austin society?"

"Your Honor, move to strike." Donnie was angry.

"Yes. The jury will disregard the last question," Judge Okeke said.

"Mr. Lewis, did you come to Austin intending to kill Francoise Gaulle?"

"No."

"Did you surprise your wife and Francoise Gaulle making love?"

"No."

"Were you so angry when you found them together that you shot Francoise?"

"No."

"Isn't this entire blackout story a fabrication?"

"No."

"Before the shooting, did you ever complain to anyone that you were having blackouts?"

"Not that I recall."

"Why not?"

"I was ashamed."

"I see. Ashamed of being perceived as weak?"

"I don't know."

"You're a proud man, aren't you?"

"I guess."

"A proud man forced to use artificial limbs, a proud man with a quick temper and a history of violence…that's David Lewis, isn't it…?"

"Your Honor, I object." Donnie shouted in the middle of June's question.

The judge replied, "Yes, you don't have to answer that, Mr. Lewis. Save your speeches for your closing argument, Ms. Fenton."

"One last thing, Mr. Lewis. There is one person alive besides you who knows what went on that night, and that's your wife, isn't that true?"

"She was there."

"Yes she was. Where exactly is she?"

David hesitated and looked over at Donnie, who rose. "Your Honor?"

The judge shook his head. "No, Mr. Cuinn. You brought it up. His wife's whereabouts is a fair area of questioning. Answer the question, Mr. Lewis."

David answered, "She's under a doctor's care, in a clinic."

"A clinic in Akron? Or in Cleveland maybe?"

"No. In Europe."

"Why did you decide to send your wife to a clinic in Europe, Mr. Lewis?"

"I didn't decide. Her father made the decision. I was stuck here in Austin, so I agreed."

"So, unfortunately, the only witness who can corroborate what you say happened in your marriage and what happened on that night, is in a clinic, somewhere in Europe?"

"What's unfortunate is that she's very ill."

"That's all I have, Your Honor," June said.

⸺⸺⸺

Judge Okeke gave his instructions to the jury immediately after lunch. The two sides had argued over its content and the judge had looked at some of Donnie's suggestions with amusement. "These have Prof. Freddy's fingerprints all over them." He tossed one back to Donnie. "Denied. Tell the professor he may finally get to argue that on appeal. And if he does, he'll lose."

It was time for final arguments. June made the first argument. She stood, thanked the jury, and then said, "I told you at the beginning of this trial that this was a simple case. The defendant shot Francoise Gaulle. He was found with the gun and he does not deny shooting her. His only defense is that he doesn't remember, that he blacked out.

"The State has proved that he did not come to Austin to protect his wife from the so-called 'Filipino Mafia' as he claims. The witnesses all agree there is no Filipino Mafia. No. He came to Austin for some different reason. When he got here, he didn't act like a man concerned about his wife's safety, did he? He was in no hurry to get to her side. He stopped for a burger. He

192

chatted with the concierge. He went upstairs and went to bed. He says he fell asleep and woke when he heard voices and he thought, *Oh gosh, it's the Filipino Mafia.* But there were only two people in his wife's bedroom, two women who, according to Claude Gaulle, were in a lesbian relationship. The only voices he could have heard were theirs. And the only person who can corroborate what he now says happened in that bedroom is in a clinic outside this country.

"The defendant has a history of violent acts, all the way back to high school; long before his time in Iraq. He is also a jealous man. He admits to brawling with a man who flirted with his wife. So, this violent jealous man takes his gun, goes to the bedroom where Cordelia and Francoise are making noises, and he shoots Francoise. Those are the facts. That much we know. The defendant says he blacked out. But the only person who can corroborate what he says is now in a clinic outside this country.

"The defendant now says he often had blackouts, but he never told his doctor about them or sought treatment for them. Remember what Dr. Graves told you. Did he really black out, or is this the convenient story of a violent and jealous man who *intentionally and knowingly* killed his wife's lover? That is the only question you have to decide."

After June finished, Donnie rose to make his closing argument. He reviewed David Lewis' life story, focusing on his injuries and the traumatic events in his life. He reviewed Dr. Sid's testimony. He repeated David's account of his blackouts, the reason he flew to Austin that day, the sounds from Cordelia's bedroom, the door suddenly flying open, the shadowy figure, David's inability to remember anything about the shooting.

"The judge has instructed you on the law in this case. He has told you that to convict David Lewis of the murder of Francoise Gaulle, you must find beyond a reasonable doubt that David Lewis acted *intentionally and knowingly.* He instructed you that intentionally means that this man," he pointed at David, "had a conscious objective or desire to murder the deceased. He also told you that knowingly means that this man," and he again pointed at David, "was aware that his conduct was reasonably certain to result in her death. Intentionally and knowingly. I ask you remember those two words as you deliberate.

"At the beginning of this trial, I asked you to keep an open mind until you heard all the evidence. The judge has also told you that if you do not find *from the evidence* that David Lewis acted intentionally and knowingly, or if you have a reasonable doubt whether he acted intentionally and knowingly, you *must* find the defendant not guilty.

"Ask yourself this: Is there any believable evidence in this case that his wife and Francoise Gaulle were having an affair? Is there any believable evidence that David Lewis even suspected such a thing? David denies it, and the only person to claim there was an affair is her brother Claude, who admitted that he hates David and would go to Mars to testify against him. Claude also admitted that before the wedding, David had no suspicion of this so-called affair. David was a *naif,* he said, a naive bridegroom in love with his wife. The Akron sheriff had never heard any such rumor. There is no other evidence of an affair. If there was no affair, and if David did not even suspect an affair where none existed, then you can only conclude—from the evidence—that he did not intentionally kill Francoise Gaulle.

"The truthful evidence is that he came here for just the reason he said, to protect his wife, whom he loved very much, from threats against their family; that when he heard noises, he went to the bedroom door, and a figure sprang at him. For an instant he relived his Iraqi nightmare, and in that instant, he blacked out and shot Francoise Gaulle. He shot her without a conscious objective to shoot or kill her and without being aware of what he was doing.

"Ms. Fenton has tried to make much of Cordelia Lewis' absence from this trial. David testified that she was hysterical and under doctors' care. Ms. Fenton does not dispute that. Cordelia Lewis is not here. What she *might* have said if she were here is not evidence. The poor woman has suffered a terrible shock and deserves to be left alone. I ask you to consider the evidence, just the evidence, and find David Lewis did not intentionally and knowingly kill Francoise Gaulle and is therefore not guilty of murder."

June rose and addressed the jury again. "You'll be pleased to know this is the last time you will hear from the lawyers in this case." She smiled and the woman CPA in the front row of the jury box returned her smile. "It is my job to make the final argument in this case."

She then proceeded to review all the State's evidence in the case. "So, that's the story. You have now heard the evidence and Mr. Cuinn's justification for his client's actions. She paused a second before going on. "Let's examine that. Why do *you* think the defendant came to Austin? Mr. Cuinn says it was to save his wife from the Filipino Mafia. But does that ring true to you? He was in no hurry to rush to his wife's side. He had a burger first. He was hungry. He says he didn't even go to her bedroom. She was in mortal danger, but this army veteran took a nap first. Is that credible? Consider this. He and his wife sleep apart. They spend most of their time apart. He is a jealous man. He brawls with a man talking to his wife in an Austin bar. What was in his mind when he made this surprise visit to Austin? Because it was a surprise visit. He didn't call to warn her that her life might be in danger. Why? Did he wonder what was going on when Cordelia was down here in Austin, far from the prying eyes of her family and neighbors in Akron? Was he concerned about his marriage? If he suspected Cordelia Lewis was unfaithful, then what better way to find out than to come in the night, when he wasn't expected, and surprise her?

"When his father-in-law became agitated about the Filipino Mafia, it gave the defendant the opportunity he might have been waiting for, an excuse to surprise his wife and see if his fears were justified. So, when he got to Austin, he spent enough time getting a burger and chatting with the concierge so the hour would be later—then he went to the apartment, where his worst fears were confirmed. He heard noises, but they weren't someone threatening his wife, were they? No, they were sounds of love-making. He took his gun, opened the door to confront the couple, and to his amazement, it wasn't some man that Cordelia had taken up with in Austin. No. His wife was in bed with another woman. And that woman was Françoise Gaulle. In that instant, with that revelation, the defendant did not black out. Instead, in a jealous rage, he fired his gun and killed his wife's lesbian lover. He killed her in front of his wife, traumatizing her. In that moment, this jealous, violent man intended to kill her. He killed her knowingly. The classic definition of murder.

"Killing another person in the heat of passion is not a defense to the charge of murder. If you find the defendant guilty, there will be a time later, in the punishment phase of the trial for you to decide if sudden passion ought to mitigate his punishment. Not now. Your job is to decide if he intentionally and knowingly killed Francoise Gaulle. I submit the evidence is overwhelming that he did.

"The defendant is a hero. But even heroes are not allowed to commit murder in Texas and go free. All the State asks is that you do your duty and consider the evidence. If you do that, I am confident you will return with a verdict of guilty."

ссссс

Afterwards, Donnie and June met in the hall. He looked at June. "I'm beat. How do you do this every day?"

"I don't. That's why there's a Criminal Division."

"The cameras are everywhere. You'll get national publicity on this case."

"Yes."

"Win or lose."

She walked to the water fountain and got two cups of water. She offered him one. "There's no lose in this case, Donnie. It's as open and shut as it gets. Your guy should have taken the deal."

"I believe him. All I need is for someone on the jury to believe him and fight for him."

"Which juror? The veteran?"

"Stranger things have happened."

"Has Prof. Freddy got his bill of exceptions ready with a mistrial motion?"

"All of that. *Just in case.* By the way, he says you are responsible for converting him from misogyny to homophobia."

"I must apologize to the gay community."

She smiled and her dark eyes sparkled the way he remembered. "I'll tell you what, Donnie Ray Cuinn, I'll bet you the biggest steak at *Leechums.* Loser buys."

He grinned. "It's a bet. But if I win," and he leaned over and whispered in her ear.

She laughed. It was good to hear her laugh again after all the arguing in court, "That'll never happen. But what if I win?"

He whispered in her ear again.

"What a charmer," she said.

The bailiff stuck his head out the door. "They've quit for the night. They'll be back at nine in the morning."

Donnie looked at June. "It's in their hands now. What's say we go have dinner? That wouldn't violate the prosecutor's code of ethics, would it?"

"Who cares?" She looked around. "Tell your people and I'll tell mine. I'll meet you in the garage, first floor."

❝❝❝❝❝

They headed down Guadalupe Street toward the river. "Where to?" she asked him.

He thought a second. "Go out on South First and I'll show you the house where I was born."

"House? You were born at home?"

"Yeah. Not like you Highland Parksters."

She steered her Lexus sedan through the four lanes of buses, cars and bikes converging on the First Street Bridge. They all seemed to be headed toward the egg-shaped Long Center. "It's Pops Night at the Symphony," June said.

"I liked the old building better," Donnie said. The old Palmer Auditorium had been repurposed as a performing arts center, using recycled materials and sporting a distinctive roof and a ring-beam around an outside terrace.

"Jesus, Donnie. That was fifteen years ago. Give it up. Did you ever even go to Palmer Auditorium?"

He grinned. "No." He nodded at the Long Center. "That one either." They crept through the traffic. "Just once I'd like to come back to Austin and see that things hadn't changed."

To his surprise, the small-frame house still stood at the corner of South First Street and Myrtle, the latter a street that a developer named after his child. June parked in a fire lane in front of the house. Condos and shops were under construction only a half block away. She ignored the *Residents Parking Only* sign at the corner. "I can park wherever I please," she said proudly. "I am the district attorney."

Donnie stared at the house. "I was born in there, but I only lived there a few weeks. I used to walk over here to look at the old man sitting on the porch."

"Who was he?"

"My grandfather. I wanted to see what a man looked like who would kick his daughter and her little baby out of the house."

"My God."

"My mother got pregnant. She was sixteen. My father went off to Nam and she never saw him again. But his name was Cuinn, with the funny spelling. Her father, my grandfather, wouldn't have a bastard living in his house, so he kicked us out."

June reached over and stroked his cheek. "What did she do?"

"She ended up at Lena's. Lena had a hotel and café in the west campus area. Mama went to work there. Lena and Papa sort of adopted me. Then when I was six, Mama found Grover Smith. He married her. Grover didn't want me, but Lena did, so that's where I grew up, at the Haven Hotel. Lena and Papa gave me everything."

"It worked out for the best, then."

"Try telling that to a six-year-old kid whose mother deserted him for a bastard like Grover."

"Let's go get a drink. I need one." She started the car.

"You know the shittiest part?"

June glanced at him. "What?"

"Her father took her back. Once she got married and abandoned me, they reconciled. She cared for him when he got sick. She nursed the old man."

"He was her father, Donnie. He was your grandfather."

"No. He wasn't." He looked around. "Hey, let's go to Murche's. Isn't it around here? I could use one of their martinis."

"You wouldn't like it, Donnie."

"Don't tell me. Not Murche's?"

"I'm afraid so. New York money, New York chef, new menu, new furniture, new bar, new hotel wing."

"What happened to the peacocks?"

"Oh, they're still there, but they look frightened."

"Probably combat stress. They'll get over it."

She reached over and kissed him then pulled back and looked at him. "What is it about you, Donnie? All this resentment about change? Everything changes. You know that. It's the world."

"God, I do know that, June. Look at me, soon turning forty. I've changed. Everything changes. I've thought about it. What is it?" He turned in the car seat and faced her. "I fantasize. I sit on my back porch and drink my coffee and watch the sunrise and I fantasize about what things would have been like if I had done things differently."

He laughed. "I know it's just a fantasy, but I play out all these alternative realities where Cecilia is still alive or Mama didn't leave me or Lena's still alive and I didn't go off drinking with my so-called best friend that day. I feel bad for a while, then I shake myself like a wet dog and put my coffee cup down and get on with my life. All this change intrudes on my memories. Does that make sense?"

"Maybe a little."

"Lena's hotel is gone. I grew up there, but it's gone. It screws with my memories and I hate that."

"I've missed you, Donnie," June said. She turned the car around. "I know a place."

They sat in a quiet corner of a noisy deck outside a seafood restaurant on South Congress. She had parked in a *No Parking Zone* directly outside the restaurant and put her official placard in the windshield. He had a dirty martini and she nursed a glass of water with lime. "I cannot be too careful," she said, reminding him of the former DA who was caught driving while drunk. "I could ask you to spend the night at my place tonight," she said. "Save you the long trip out to your client's palatial estate."

"Yes, you could," Donnie said, pushing his empty glass aside and calling for the check. "You could, but you won't, right?"

"No, I won't. That would be a bad idea."

"A bad idea," he agreed.

"We had a good couple of weeks, didn't we, back in the day?" she asked.

He smiled at the memory. *Very good.* "Twelve and a half days, to be exact."

"But who's counting, right? We knew it couldn't be anything more than it was, didn't we?"

"Did we?"

"Anna's my best friend," June said.

"She's mine, too."

"No. She's more than that. At least you're more than that to her. Why can't you see that?"

"I tried. I really tried. But…"

"You should try harder." She stood up and kissed him on the cheek. "Good luck to you, Donnie Ray."

TWENTY-TWO

Everyone on Team Cuinn was prepared for a guilty verdict. Prof. Freddy was in court, ready to handle the appeal. Wiley would handle the punishment phase of the trial. Donnie said his part in the trial was over. He didn't want to force David to say, 'I saw them together,' or, 'I killed her in a fit of rage,' so maybe they could get the minimum sentence of two years. *Maybe.*

If the jury found his client guilty, Donnie's only job would be to convince the judge to let David remain free on bail through the punishment phase. Then he could go back to Velda and relive the trial and the mistakes he had made that sent this innocent client to prison. David remained serene. He even asked Donnie to help him with the statement he would make after he was freed.

No one was more surprised than the defense when the jury returned after a day and a half with a "not guilty" verdict—of all charges. Judge Okeke was impassive when he thanked the jury and told David he was a free man. The judge gathered up his papers and swept out of the courtroom.

June looked at Donnie and shrugged. "Juries," she said with a shake of her head.

Donnie spoke briefly to the cameras outside the Justice Center. He paid tribute to the fairness of the jury and thanked them for not rushing to judgment.

With no notes at all, David immediately began reciting the statement he and Donnie had prepared.

"First, thanks to my wonderful counsel, Don Cuinn, and of course to the jury. This was a terrible accident and I want to tell the family of Francoise Gaulle how sorry I am. I will be announcing in a few days that the KL Media Group is establishing a foundation dedicated to helping all the veterans who suffer from post-traumatic stress disorder. You are not forgotten. Thank you."

He was so sure of an acquittal that he memorized it. Donnie was amazed.

Down the street, Ball Busting Burnham, Houston's prime personal injury lawyer, announced that his client Claude Gaulle was suing David Lewis for the wrongful death of his sister and expected to establish in the civil suit once and for all that David Lewis was a murderer. "Damages," he expected, "would run to the hundreds of millions."

《《《《《

Donnie, Wiley, Anna, David, Prof. Freddy, the secretaries and clerks, the Parsons family, the drivers and even the off-duty security detail, gathered on the patio of David's rented estate to celebrate. Donnie and David hugged again, joking with the others for their lack of faith. Lil' Faye called with congratulations and told Donnie that three high profile homicide defendants in Houston and Galveston wanted him to defend them.

"Tell them I'm not taking any more criminal cases," Donnie said. "I'm leaving the field undefeated. Besides, my widows need me."

He was talking to his mother when Sam Sams tapped him on the shoulder. "I have a report," the jury consultant whispered. Donnie followed him into the house. When they were alone, he looked at Donnie and said, "The jury agreed not to talk to anyone, but our veteran decided to tell us what happened."

"What did he say?"

"A lot. He said none of them had any doubt that David shot Francoise because he found her and his wife in bed together."

"The blackouts?"

"Nobody bought that."

"Then why did they acquit him?"

The consultant shook his head. "Sudden passion."

Donnie sank into the nearest chair. "They went for the Unwritten Law? Seriously?"

"That's what he said."

Donnie wiped his brow. "You're telling me that our jury decided to ignore what the judge told them and apply the Unwritten Law? The one that supposedly says that a man can kill his wife's lover if he finds them in the act? I did not see that coming."

"Well, the reason it took them so long, was they were arguing whether the Unwritten Law applied here."

"What the hell are you talking about?" Donnie said. "Whether the law that *isn't* a law applied how?"

"Whether it applied *here*. To killing a wife's *female* lover."

"I need a drink," Donnie said.

"Our guy, the veteran we worked so hard to get, said he believed it only applied when a man found his wife with another *man*. But the woman juror, you know the CPA we thought was the prosecution's juror, turns out to be a feminist. She said the Unwritten Law applies just as much to a same-sex affair as it does to cheating with someone of the opposite sex. She said that if you are going to free a man who kills his wife's male lover, you had to do the same thing if he kills her female lover. She said it was a basic matter of women's rights and that she would never compromise on her feminist principles."

"A woman was killed!"

"Our guy said he argued original intent…"

"Original intent? Of the Unwritten Law?"

"Our guy finally gave in. He said he wasn't going to send a war hero to prison just because he made an honest mistake about how the Unwritten Law works."

"Oh, that's good. That makes sense." He thought a minute then said, "Prof. Freddy told me that sometimes you have to give the jury a reason to acquit and then get out of the way. Maybe he was thinking of the Unwritten Law. What should I tell David?"

"My advice? Don't tell anybody anything. The jury did its job. Nobody wants to know how the sausage is made."

⟨⟨⟨⟨⟨

Donnie Ray Cuinn woke the next morning to the naked body of Anna Kaye Nordstrom cuddled against him. "Well this is nice. Just like old times. Where is everybody?"

"They're all gone. The movers will be here in the morning to pick up the files and computers. We have the place to ourselves until then."

"David's gone too?"

"Wiley went with him to get his bond money back. After that, David Lewis is on his way back to Akron." She pressed closer. "I've missed this."

"Me too," he said, turning over and kissing her.

⟨⟨⟨⟨⟨

Later, they sat in the kitchen drinking coffee. He looked affectionately at Anna, the white bathrobe draped loosely over her naked body.

"There's something I need to tell you," she said.

He put his coffee mug on the counter. "Oh? What's that?"

"I had a conversation with David during the trial that I should have told you about."

"You're not going off with him, are you? I mean, Akron? He has a wife."

She laughed and pulled the robe closer. "No, nothing like that. It's about the case."

Donnie steadied himself on the barstool. "What about the case?"

"David told me something."

Donnie tried to put his coffee cup down carefully, but it banged on the counter anyway. "What?"

"I should have told you, but he made me promise not to."

"Are you going to tell me or not?" Donnie pressed.

"Don't hate me, Donnie."

"I could never hate you, A.K., but I swear I'll never speak to you again if you don't tell me what he said."

"All right, then. David said whatever the jury did, he would never go to prison. He had a helicopter on call. If the jury came in with a guilty verdict, he was going to run. Or fly. He had the helicopter standing by to take him to San Marcos. There would be a jet waiting to fly him to some country without an extradition treaty. He was going to leave you holding the bag. He wanted me to go with him."

"What did you tell him?"

"I told him, 'hell no!' It made him angrier than I had ever seen him."

"What did he do?"

"He said something that I hate to tell you. I think he lied to both of us."

Donnie sighed. "Oh, for God's sake."

"He said, 'You know, I never had a blackout.'"

"The blackouts were invented?"

"I think so. He blurted it out and then caught himself."

Donnie rubbed his forehead. He was getting a bad headache. *Whiskey and the truth will do that.* "Why me? Why did he hire me?"

"He told me that if he could convince you the shooting was an accident, then the two of you could convince the jury. He didn't think a big-name defense lawyer would *play* as well."

"I guess I did my part, but it didn't really matter."

"What do you mean?"

He took her hand. "Prof. Freddy had the appeal ready. Even he didn't think David would run and forfeit a million-dollar bail bond."

"You got him off, Donnie. You did this. Not David. It was you."

"Sure, I did. Remind me to tell you about the Unwritten Law sometime."

She took the cups to the sink and rinsed them. He stood behind her and pressed his body against hers. He kissed her neck and said, "I think we could use some Pervoy Spa time together. What do you say? Come to Velda and we can sit around the fire pit with Eugene, Ginelle and my mama. We can drink whiskey and tell tales on each other."

She leaned back against him. "Your mother never liked me."

"How could she not like you? Everybody loves Anna Kaye Nordstrom. Will you come?"

"I could never turn you down, Donnie Ray. But just for a few days. There's this bill coming up in the legislature…"

PART THREE
VILE THINGS PRECIOUS

TWENTY-THREE

David sat in Kingston Lehrer's high back chair at the end of the long dining table in the baronial dining room of the manor house. Douglas and Ginny sat on his left, Tom and Reggie on his right. David's lawyer sat at the other end of the table. Kingston Lehrer's funeral had been four days earlier and the evidence of the long day was gone, except for a single music stand in the corner. Lehrer's body had been laid to rest in the crypt beside his wife in the family chapel.

Ginny broke the silence, "Where's my mother's picture, David? It's missing from its place."

"It's crated. I'm taking it to Cory tomorrow. She asked for it. You don't mind, do you?"

"You might have asked us. Still, I can see why she would want it, off by herself at that place in Switzerland. She even missed Daddy's funeral."

David nodded. "She's moved into an apartment near the clinic. She's in and out of the clinic now, but she seems better."

"That's enough family pleasantries," Douglas said. "Why are we here?"

The lawyer placed a stack of documents before the two couples. As he did so, David watched Tony riding up the trail to the stable. "Pedro," he called.

"Sir?" The Filipino answered from the doorway.

"Tell Tony it's time for dinner."

"Yes, of course." He leaned over and whispered in David's ear. "Miss Jan is waiting in the family dining room."

David nodded. Jan's presence in the house was no secret, but Pedro was discreet. David answered him so the others could hear. "Tell Jan that she and Tony should start without me. I'll be along when we're done here."

Douglas pushed the documents away. "You have everything you need here, don't you? The Chief's place at the table, your *friend* from Chicago. Even the Filipinos are back."

David didn't bother to remind Douglas that besides sharing his bed, Jan was in charge of KL Media and making the company a *shitload* of money. Tom already knew that, whether Douglas had absorbed it or not. Instead, David said, "I always liked Pedro. He has lots of nieces and nephews and I trust him. Not like Dakila."

Reggie spoke up. "Will you be sending us some help? We need a gardener and a maid."

"I'm afraid not, Reggie. You'll see when you look at those documents that you won't be living at The Heath much longer."

Douglas' face lit up. "We're selling? It's finally happened? I thought after Austin the plans might have to change."

David smiled. "No. *We're* not selling. *Your* wives are selling."

Tom started thumbing through the documents. "You want to buy the girls' interests? How much are you offering?"

The lawyer broke in. "Technically speaking, Ginny and Reggie have no interests. Mr. Lehrer revised the trusts. Everything goes to his grandson."

Douglas sputtered. "When did he do that? He must have been insane. We'll contest. The trustee surely…"

David interrupted his red-faced brother-in-law. "He named me sole trustee. I am prepared to pay each daughter two million dollars a year for the next twenty years, a total of forty million dollars each. Cory has already accepted."

Now it was Tom's turn to sputter. "That's ridiculous. The company is worth close to a billion dollars. The online company, the media company, the cable television series. Even the newspapers alone are worth much more than that. Why, you got that much when you sold *This Texas*."

David had in fact received a good price for the Austin magazine when he cut his ties with Austin. The online business relocated to Mountain Home,

California. KL Media was in Akron. With any luck, he would never have to set foot in Austin again. "You don't seem to understand. This is not a negotiation. It's an offer I'm making as trustee to settle any and all claims the daughters may have against the estate. Take it or leave it."

Douglas snorted. "And if we leave it?"

David smiled. "There's also a termination letter in those papers, ending your's and Tom's association with the company and a severance check for your options and other accrued benefits. It isn't a small amount, but it won't support you for very long. Also, the houses where you are living belongs to the trust, so you will have to move out in ninety days."

"Move out?" Ginny gasped. "But why?"

"KL Real Estate Ventures is going to develop The Heath. Other than ten acres around this house, the property is going to be made into an exclusive subdivision. All three daughters' houses will be marketed as part of that project." He stood. "Take your time. Talk to your lawyers. Decide what you want to do. But as trustee, I'm warning you, if you refuse this offer, you'll never get another cent from the trust. Tony is the sole beneficiary of his grandfather's estate, just like the Chief wanted." He walked to the door.

Douglas spoke up. "Crime does pay, doesn't it? I always knew you were ruthless, insinuating your way into the old man's affections with your medals and artificial legs. You exiled your poor wife to Switzerland. You killed her lover. God knows what else you've done and gotten away with."

David turned and spoke deliberately. "Careful Douglas. I've been known to have blackouts."

TWENTY-FOUR

David stood beside Cory, looking out over the mist-covered lake. The Alps rose above the clouds.

The flight over had been a success. His lawyer had called en route. "You were right. I told them you would pay another five million dollars upfront and Douglas jumped at it."

"He couldn't resist the cash. At least Ginny will have her annuity. He can't get his hands on that. What about Tom?"

"He didn't want to take it, but he's not a fighter at heart, certainly not by himself. He and Reggie went along. Another piece of good news, we settled with Claude Gaulle. He's very sick and needs the money. It was a big disappointment to his lawyer."

David turned to Cory. Her hazel eyes were tired. Her hair and face were perfectly made-up, but there was little life or joy in her expression. The sadness might have made her even more beautiful, if that were possible. "You can see the Alps to the south and almost to the Black Forest, all from this window," she said.

David looked around. She was back in the clinic for more treatment. She had a private residence, her own pool, meals served in the residence and solitude. "How do they treat you?" he asked.

Her eyes brightened for a minute. "Like a Saudi princess."

The Sichbesser Practice was renowned for its custom care plans. Its team of doctors and psychiatrists provide the best care along with Swiss six-star standards of luxury, all with the strictest confidence.

"What do they tell you?"

She said, "For some reason, it seems I am depressed. They are revising my treatment plan. It'll take a while. All very individual. All very expensive."

"Don't worry about the expense."

"You can be sure I won't." She put out her cigarette and lit another one. "You have it all now, don't you? Francie and I underestimated you." David said nothing. "Has you being accused of murder affected the business?" she asked, but she did not seem interested in his answer.

"No. There's the notoriety of course, which I don't like. Another few years and people will quit talking about it."

The uncrated picture of Maude Lehrer leaned against the wall. "Thanks for lugging Mother over here."

David smiled. "We both had a good trip. She rode in the bed on the Gulf Stream. Do you remember that bed?"

She took a long drag on her cigarette. "Little Tony was conceived in that bed." She looked at mountains and said softly. "It is ironic."

"Is it?"

"Francie being dead. Ironic because it was all her idea. I loved her so much I would have promised her anything. I promised her the newspapers when Daddy died and we outsmarted my sisters and their idiot husbands. Together we would remake the Lehrer empire, just the two of us. But once we were in Akron, she saw immediately how impossible that was. So, she devised the plan."

David looked at her. "What plan?"

"The plan to find me a husband and use him to make an heir for Daddy and to take over the newspapers that way. We went through my college yearbooks and my scrapbooks, looking for the right person. You have no idea how many pictures we looked at or how many names we rejected. And then she found you. 'What about David Lewis?' she asked.

"'Who?' I asked.

"She pointed to your picture.

"'Oh, I remember him now. We had a little thing back in college. He might work.' And that was that. She researched you and found out you were a hero. She vetted you like you were a Supreme Court nominee. You were her candidate for the Husband of Cordelia project. You know the rest." She smiled faintly. "I think she got some kinky pleasure out of arranging a male sex partner for me. Even after the baby came, she wanted me to keep having sex with you, at least often enough to keep you under control. But I couldn't do that. I loved Francie so much, so we settled for the loveless marriage."

"I remember it well," David said. "And what did you and Francie plan for me after I had done my part?"

"The plan was to dump you, to pay you off and send you on your way. But *This Texas* changed everything. She loved that magazine. I think she loved it more than me."

"Francie? Surely not."

"Once we had *This Texas*, the papers didn't matter to her anymore. You were making a success out of the rest of the business. We believed we could all have everything that we wanted, Francie and me, you, even Daddy."

"He had little Tony."

"Yes." She lit still another cigarette. "How is Tony?"

"Getting bigger every day. He misses you."

"Does he? We hardly ever saw each other."

"He said to tell you he loves you."

She watched the cigarette smoke pluming above her. "When I am back in the apartment, maybe he can come visit."

"He'd like that."

They moved away from the window and sat quietly at opposite ends of the large leather sectional couch, facing the window. She said, "Our son is the sole heir. How did my sisters take that?"

"They're still in shock."

"Don't send them here if they get depressed." It was a flash of the old Cory.

He smiled. "Did I tell you when your father changed the trusts? When I got to the house that morning before the sheriff came, the library was full of witnesses. Father Joe. Three or four lawyers. His internal medicine doctor. Two doctors from Cleveland Clinic. He declared in front of all of them, 'I am disinheriting my daughters. All three of them. Ginny, Reggie and Cordelia. I am revising my will and the family trusts. Everything goes to my grandson, Kingston Anthony Lehrer-Lewis. I am appointing David Lewis the sole trustee to administer the estate until my grandson comes of age. Now ask me any questions, because you may have to testify about my sanity.' No questions. Everybody signed the documents, he gave them all a stiff brandy and sent them home."

"Daddy never did anything halfway, did he?"

"Never."

"Was that the same day he sent you to Austin?"

"Yes." He motioned to the *Gauloises* cigarette package. "Can I have one of those?"

She slid the package and a gold cigarette lighter down the coffee table. He lit the cigarette and inhaled deeply. "God, it's been a long time since I smoked a cigarette."

She watched him, waiting.

Finally, David said, "He showed me pictures. Pictures of you and Francie. Pictures he should never have seen."

"Fucking Dakila. But it was Daddy's own fault. All those spies. What did he expect?"

"I don't think he expected to be shown photographs of his favorite daughter having sex with another woman. In color. I know I didn't."

She smiled faintly. "An abomination before God."

"He asked me to go to Austin and get rid of the French woman and to send you out of the country. He said you could never come back and that you were never to contact little Tony. He said that you had forfeited all rights to be his daughter or to call yourself a mother."

"You didn't tell me all that."

"Well, we didn't have much time to talk. Your father recited Shakespeare."

"I imagine I know which part. 'How sharper than a serpent's tooth it is to have a thankless child!'"

"Of course."

She shivered and pulled her cashmere sweater tighter across her body. "Do you think it would have mattered if we had told the truth?"

"The truth? How would that have helped?"

"I don't know. Maybe if he had known, he might have forgiven me."

"Your fate was sealed the moment your father saw those pictures. Knowing that you shot Francie wouldn't have changed anything."

"Still…?"

"No. We did the right thing. I felt pretty sure I could get through a trial." He smiled. "After all, I'm a war hero with PTSD. But an heiress shooting her lesbian lover in a multi-million dollar penthouse in downtown Austin, with your double amputee husband sleeping in the other room? I don't think so."

"I was so angry. She was going to leave me, David. Leave me! Cordelia Lehrer? No one had ever left me. For some skank she met jogging. What about all our plans? She said they didn't matter anymore. 'I'm in love. Really in love this time', she told me. I couldn't believe it. I got your gun out of the nightstand. You didn't hear a thing."

"Until the gunshot."

She looked away and said softly, "Why did you do it? After the way Francie and I treated you? Why did you take the blame for me?"

He snuffed out his cigarette and made ready to leave. "Two reasons. First, I promised your father I would look out for you. I always keep my promises."

"And the second reason?"

He smiled wistfully. "God help me, Cory, but I've always loved you."

THE END